Sign up to my newsletter, and you will be notified when I release my next book!

Join my Patreon (patreon.com/jackbryce) to get early access to my work!

ISBN-13: 9798873104727

D1525479

FRONTIER SUMMONER 4
A SLICE OF LIFE FANTASY ADVENTURE

JACK BRYCE

*To belly button rings.*

# Frontier Summoner 4

# David's Character Sheet

Below is David's character sheet at the end of book 3.

Name: David Wilson

Class: Frontier Summoner

Level: 6

Health: 70/70

Mana: 35/35 (+10 from Hearth Treasures)
   Skills:

Summon Minor Spirit — Level 15 (3 mana)

Summon Domesticant — Level 11 (6 mana)

Summon Guardian — Level 11 (8 mana)

Summon Aquana's Avatar — Level 3 (10 mana)

Summon Storm Elemental — Level 1 (10 mana)

Bind Familiar — Level 2 (15 mana)

Identify Plants — Level 8 (1 mana)

Foraging — Level 9 (1 mana)

Trapping — Level 9 (1 mana)

Alchemy — Level 12 (1 mana)

Farming — Level 1 (1 mana)

Ranching — Level 1 (1 mana)

# Chapter 1

The morning sun shone down through the leafy forest canopy as Diane led the way along the winding trail, her foxlike ears pricked alertly atop of her head. Silence surrounded us, broken only by the calls of birds and the soft crunch of fallen leaves underfoot.

I walked a few paces behind, with Leigh following just after me. My rifle was slung over my shoulder, ready if needed, although I expected that — in combat — I would rely more and more on my summons. After all, I now knew how to call forth the avatar of Aquana, a water elemental, as well as a storm elemental and a guardian.

Between the three of them, I needed little else. But it was always wise to have a back-up.

But I was not sure if I would need my offensive capabilities on today's expedition. Yesterday, Diane had returned from an evening round of the homestead all excited and a little nervous.

She told us she had seen strange, large tracks in this area yesterday, and we were eager to investigate further. After all, we lived close to the Wilds, and dangerous beasts could creep in.

Now, sweeping my gaze side to side, I saw no immediate sign of the mysterious tracks. But Diane pressed on ahead confidently, trailing the unseen path of whatever had left its mark upon the forest floor.

Beside me, Leigh kept equal pace, her keen eyes

scanning the path ahead. An explorer's curiosity glimmered in her blue eyes. I could not help but smile, admiring her energetic stride.

Turning my focus back to our surroundings, I glanced upward. Was it my imagination, or had the very air seemed to grow heavier, laden with some unseen charge, as we ventured deeper beneath the bows of oak and pine?

Ahead, Diane paused, raising a hand to halt our approach. In a whisper, she called for us to draw near and indicated a disturbance in the leaf litter blanketing the path.

Kneeling, I could discern a large, clawed paw print pressed clearly into the loam. Three long talons had gouged the soft earth, beside a heavy central pad. My breath caught softly. These were no ordinary tracks.

"Some kind of monster passed through here," Diane murmured. "Maybe less than an hour ago. We should be cautious." Broken ferns and trampled undergrowth spoke of something bulky shouldering past. "But I never saw tracks like these before…"

I exchanged an intrigued glance with Leigh. Her blue eyes were alight with interest as she studied the unusual print. "I know these tracks," she declared in a hushed tone. "We've found ourselves a larroling!"

"A larroling?" I asked in a whisper, curiosity piqued by the unfamiliar name. "I don't think I've heard of those before. What exactly are they?"

Leigh's eyes shone as she explained eagerly. "They're these big, territorial critters that roam the forests. They're big, bipedal, and they got thick hides and these long tusks for fightin'. They're omnivores, but mostly eat plants and roots. But they can be right nasty if disturbed. I've always wanted to see one up close!"

Though I now had some grasp of what manner of beast we tracked, Leigh's enthusiasm still made me eager to pursue it further. With Diane's agreement, we pressed on, moving stealthily as we followed the meandering path of those distinctive prints through the dense forest.

We proceeded in tense silence, senses straining for any sign of movement ahead...

Hardly twenty feet up the path, a bulky, shaggy shape shuffled into view between the trees. I stared, awestruck. The creature was enormous, the beginning of its slab-like head level with my chest. Curved tusks protruded from its mouth.

The larroling stood taller than a bear on stocky, stump-like legs tipped with claws longer than my hand. Its coarse hide was a motley patchwork of brown and gray fur.

Beady eyes under a bony brow ridge surveyed the trail ahead intently. Snorting again, the larroling took several thudding steps forward, long pink snout quivering. It was sniffing for our scent!

My heart hammered in my chest. If the wind shifted, we would be revealed for certain! Diane and Leigh shrank back deeper into the shadows beside me. Nobody dared move a muscle, and our weapons were at the ready. When I made ready to call forth a summon, Leigh placed a hand on my arm.

"Don't," she whispered. "It won't attack if we don't."

After what felt like an eternity, the larroling

huffed in annoyance, lifting its blocky head and snuffling loudly. When our location remained hidden, it soon shuffled away down the path out of sight.

A full minute passed before any of us stirred or rose from our positions. Once the coast seemed clear, we extricated ourselves from the brush, gathering to confer excitedly.

"By Ilmanaria's grace, that was incredible luck!" Diane gasped, laughing giddily once she found her voice again. Her tail swished in elation.

I clasped Leigh's shoulder, my heart still racing with adrenaline. "That was amazing! What a majestic creature! Nice work spotting those tracks, Leigh."

Fortune had smiled upon us to observe the beast so closely unharmed. The larroling was, of course, a creature of Tannoris, and I was greatly intrigued by its mythical appearance.

As we turned to head back toward the homestead, Leigh spoke up thoughtfully. "You know, a creature that size could be dangerous roaming so near the cabin. Perhaps we should try to deal with it."

I pondered her words. Diane looked uncertain, likely wary of confronting the hulking larroling directly. But Leigh's daring spirit could not resist the challenge.

"In fact," Leigh continued excitedly, "I'd love to try binding it as a pet using my abilities as a Beastmaster! A larroling could be mightily useful out here. What do y'all think?"

"That's a great idea, Leigh!" I exclaimed. "We won't have to drive it away or kill it, and it could help us out in any Dungeon runs or other encounters."

Diane still appeared reluctant, but I knew Leigh's skills were up for the task of taming the beast if we could subdue it. "It's worth considering," I said. "But we'll have to plan this carefully."

Leigh nodded, grinning enthusiastically. "Just leave it to me! That critter will be eating out of my hand before long." Her confidence was contagious, and even Diane had to chuckle.

"Alright," I said. "What do you need?"

"A lure," Leigh hummed. "I can use my Class

abilities to craft it, but we'll need to find some ingredients."

I nodded at Diane. "Our Foraging skills might help with that..."

Resolved to capture and tame the larroling, Diane and I turned to Leigh. "What are we looking for?" Diane asked Leigh.

The blonde touched her plump bottom lip for a moment. "We will need faerie cap mushrooms, goldenseal, stoneshine lichen, and some spider silk..."

As a skilled Scout, Diane closed her eyes and concentrated deeply, using her intuitive connection with the forest to sense where useful plants might grow. I had a Foraging and Identify Plants skill, but Diane had a skill that also allowed her to specify which plants she was looking for and then locate them.

"This way," Diane said after a moment, eyes still

closed as she pointed confidently off the trail. Trusting her instincts, Leigh and I followed as she wove skillfully between the trees. I glanced around curiously, wondering where exactly she would take us.

Before long, Diane paused beside a gnarled oak tree. "Here," she declared, indicating a cluster of small azure mushrooms peeking from the thick carpet of leaves. "Faerie caps."

Leigh gave an excited clap of her hands. "Perfect! These have mystical properties that will help draw the larroling."

As Diane harvested the mushrooms with care, I stood guard, listening intently for any sign of the lumbering beast's approach. The forest remained tranquil, but we had to stay alert.

Carrying an armful of the iridescent fungi, Diane led us farther into a sunny glade dotted with wildflowers. "Now, we're looking for goldenseal," she explained, sniffing the air. "Its roots have a potent scent. I don't need to activate any skills to find them."

As a foxkin, her sense of smell was sharper than

that of ordinary people. For someone with a Scout Class, that was a boon...

At the glade's edge, she bent to gently dig up several goldenroot bulbs, their fragrance indeed spicy and distinct. Leigh nodded approvingly at Diane's finds so far. Just a few more vital ingredients remained.

Our search next led down into a shaded ravine split by a babbling stream. Moss-covered boulders lined its banks as we picked our way carefully between them, eyes scanning for any sign of danger.

"There," Leigh said suddenly, rushing over to a dense thicket. Delicately pinned between the barbs, wispy balls of spider silk shone in the dappled sunlight. "These will bind the lure's elements together nicely," she explained, collecting the filaments.

Her pack now brimming with faerie caps, goldenseal, and spider silk, Leigh paused to mentally catalog our haul so far. "One more should do it," she mused thoughtfully. "Stoneshine lichen — it grows on boulders."

Scanning the ravine, I quickly spotted a broad, flat stone encrusted with patches of glimmering chartreuse lichen. Drawing my hunting knife, I carefully scraped a sample off into Leigh's outstretched palm.

"Excellent!" Leigh said, holding up the shimmering lichen. She turned and gave Diane an approving pat on the back. "You located everything perfectly. Now let's get to crafting before our furry friend wanders too far off."

Finding a sunny clearing, Leigh knelt and removed her foraging pouch, laying out the ingredients with meticulous care while Diane and I watched in fascination. Taking up the faerie caps first, Leigh closed her eyes to focus.

As we observed, Leigh's brow furrowed in deep concentration, golden hair falling like a curtain around her face. She began systematically crushing caps between two rocks, collecting the juices and fibers.

Next, Leigh mashed goldenseal bulbs into the mix, releasing their earthy aroma. Her shoulders soon relaxed as she settled into the comforting trance of crafting. Diane and I remained perfectly still and silent nearby.

Humming softly, Leigh added the wispy spider silk, weaving the threads throughout the chunky paste until they bound it together. Lastly she worked in flecks of the lichen, its glittering particles lending an iridescent sheen.

Pinching off a walnut-sized lump of the finished mixture, Leigh rolled it between her palms, smoothing its surface into a flawless orb that gave off a hypnotic shimmer in the sunlight.

Finished at last, Leigh smiled proudly at the glowing lure resting in her palm. Its mystic qualities were palpable. She handed it to me gingerly. "There, that should entice our friend straight to us."

I turned the lure over delicately, admiring its pearlescent luster. Within its swirling depths, mesmerizing motes of light sparkled and danced. Its allure was undeniable. "Incredible work, Leigh," I said, returning it to her waiting hand.

Diane's blue eyes were wide with awe. "It's perfect," she murmured appreciatively. "I can already imagine the larroling being helplessly drawn to it." Her tail swished eagerly at the thought.

Safely securing the fragile lure, Leigh rose, brushing forest debris from her knees with a satisfied smile. "Many thanks for your help, you two," she said warmly. "Now, let's go find somewhere to set our trap."

Slinging our gear over our shoulders once more, our party set off through the sun-speckled forest, invigorated by our success crafting the lure and the thrill of the hunt ahead. Though we had to remain wary, our movements in the now-familiar stretch of forest were confident and quick.

Before long, we reached a small clearing surrounded by bramble thickets — an ideal location with plenty of cover. Working swiftly, we used vines to rig a clever snare trap beside a game trail showing larroling tracks.

In its center, Leigh gently wedged the glowing lure. Stepping back to admire our handiwork, we exchanged tense, exhilarated grins. Now came the true test of our woodcraft and Leigh's mystical bait.

Finding well-concealed vantage points nearby, we settled in to keep patient watch, ready to spring our ambush at the first sign of the larroling's lumbering approach. The forest seemed to hold its own breath in anticipation...

Shards of sunlight played over the empty snare as we peered out from hiding, ears pricked and hearts hammering with exhilaration. Now it was only a matter of time before the forest colossus arrived to take our bait. Our trap was set and the hunt was on!

# Chapter 2

Crouched in the underbrush, we scarcely dared breathe as the minutes crawled by. Any little sound seemed amplified as we waited tensely for the larroling to appear. Leigh's eyes blazed with anticipation where she hid, ready to spring her trap.

Before long, the bushes rustled up ahead. I froze, my pulse quickening. Was our quarry finally approaching? A bulky shadow lumbered into view between the brambles. Antlers swept low branches aside as a creature shuffled closer, snuffling curiously.

It was the larroling! Drawn by the lure's mystical emanations, the shaggy beast had returned. It halted mere steps from the cunningly concealed snare, small eyes fixed upon the glimmering orb. I could scarcely breathe as I watched that mythical beast drawn near. It had taken the bait!

With bated breath, we watched the enthralled larroling stretch its long neck toward the lure, tusks gleaming. It gave the strange object an experimental prod with its snout, then abruptly reared back, squealing in alarm as the snare's hidden noose snapped tight around one tree-trunk leg.

The larroling thrashed and flailed violently, roaring its fury as the vines held fast. Leigh sprang from hiding with a sharp cry, dashing straight for the tethered creature. This was her moment!

Nimbly evading the larroling's lashing claws; Leigh slipped beneath its defenses and laid both hands firmly upon its heaving flank. Closing her eyes, she began murmuring a mesmerizing chant. Gradually, the larroling's struggles eased as shining hearts appeared in the air around where she touched it, indicating she was using her Beastmaster ability.

Still murmuring soothingly, Leigh moved to stand directly before the subdued beast. Though it watched her warily, it no longer fought against its bonds. Leigh's taming spell was taking effect. Soon the creature would obey her will.

As Leigh communed silently with the larroling, I caught a glimpse of her eyes glowing emerald beneath shuttered lids. Wisps of verdant energy swirled around her fingers pressed to its hide. Her Class ability was a mystical sight to behold.

Bit by bit, the last of the larroling's tension drained away. Its thunderous roars softened to rumbling grunts. Leigh continued whispering gently until finally it quieted altogether, now fully bound to her will.

Letting her hands slip from its shaggy flank, Leigh turned to grin at Diane and me, the emerald light fading from her eyes. "It's done," she declared. "This gentle giant now answers to me alone."

The tamed larroling snuffled placidly at her shoulder, almost as if to confirm what Leigh had just said.

Moving slowly so as not to startle our new ally, Diane and I emerged from hiding to stand marveling beside Leigh and the docile colossus. Its small eyes followed us without alarm. Leigh's power had tamed its wild spirit entirely through the use of her Class ability.

"Amazing!" Diane gasped, daring to reach up and pat the larroling's furry snout. It chuffed at her touch but made no move to withdraw. "I can hardly believe this is the same beast we hid from in terror not long ago!"

I shook my head in awe. "Incredible work, Leigh," I told her sincerely. She had masterfully bent this massive creature to acceptance of her companionship with only her Beastmaster abilities.

As we lavished Leigh with praise, she waved it off modestly. "I've always had a way with animals," she explained. "With enough time and patience, just about any critter can become your loyal friend." The newly docile larroling proved her point.

While Leigh kept her soothing hand upon the great beast to reinforce their newfound bond, Diane and I quickly removed the snare still looped around its hind leg. It waited patiently as we loosed it.

Freed at last, the imposing creature rolled its bullish shoulders and shook itself before lowering its blocky head to signal submissiveness to Leigh. A deep rumble resonated from its barrel chest — not a roar of fury, but something akin to an immense purr.

Gazing fondly at the affectionate display, I said, "I think someone's made a friend for life."

Leigh beamed, burying her hands in the larroling's coarse pelt. "Let's head home and get him settled."

I laughed. "Yeah, I hadn't given that much

thought! Where will it sleep?"

"Oh, outside," she said, waving it away. "Larrolings don't need much care or comfort. It'll scrounge around for food, and I'll make sure it don't upset the farmin' and alchemy plots. Other than that, this beastie will guard the area and pretty much go its own way unless I tell it to do otherwise."

I nodded slowly, realizing we had won ourselves another powerful ally. Between my summons and the larroling, we could field a significant force...

Leigh elected to walk at the larroling's shoulder as we turned onto the forest path leading back to the cabin. Already, it responded readily to her subtle guidance, lumbering along docilely at her side.

Its rippling muscles and powerful frame hinted at what a formidable guardian it could become under Leigh's direction. With training, the larroling would surely develop into a loyal protector of our homestead.

When we arrived in the broad clearing surrounding the cabin, Ghostie and Sir Boozles immediately zipped over to investigate our huge new companion. To my relief, they seemed more curious than alarmed. Mr. Drizzles, the stupidly named storm elemental, kept its distance and impassively continued its rounds.

While I set out fresh water from the Silverthread for the larroling, Leigh patiently introduced it to each domesticant, soothing any concerns with calm reassurances. Soon they appeared to accept this newest addition to our motley crew.

Gazing proudly at our new companion, I slung an arm around Leigh's shoulders. "You've outdone yourself today," I told her sincerely. "Well done, Leigh."

I then smiled at Diane as I pulled her in for a hug as well. "And you, too! This is pretty impressive!"

Both girls leaned affectionately against me with happy sighs. "It was nice to be out there again," Leigh hummed. "It's been a while since I felt the thrill of taming an animal!"

I grinned and nodded. "See, life at the homestead is already growing on you!"

# Chapter 3

That evening, Diane prepared a hearty venison stew using meat from a recent successful hunt. The savory aroma filled the cozy cabin as she stirred the bubbling pot. I set the table while Leigh added more split logs to the crackling fire.

Soon, we were all seated around the wooden

table as Diane began ladling steaming bowls of stew. "Smells delicious!" I said, breathing in the fragrant vapors appreciatively.

Her frontier cooking never failed to rouse my appetite, and she knew how to whip any ingredients into a tasty and filling meal.

Diane smiled, brushing back a stray lock of raven hair that had escaped her braid. "Thank you, my love. We have so much venison from the hunt, I thought to use some of it for a nice stew." She passed Leigh and me each a bowl before taking her own seat.

We ate with relish, savoring the tender meat, potatoes, carrots, and onions. Diane's skills at seasoning were evident in the perfect blend of herbs and spices. Outside, daylight faded as we enjoyed the cozy meal together.

Over seconds, talk turned to making plans for the next day. "So," I began, "we all agree we need more funds for the cabin expansion, right?" I remarked.

The girls nodded vehemently. We had gone over the plans I had drafted with their help — Leigh especially had a head for numbers — and while we could source some of the materials ourselves and needed no labor other than ours and that of my summons, we would need to procure much. And that would not be cheap.

"Perhaps we could take a quest tomorrow? There may be some well-paying jobs available in Gladdenfield that play to our strengths. Even if there aren't, we can drop off some supplies with Randal at Leigh's store and earn some cash that way."

With Leigh part of my family, revenue from the store now benefited us all. However, in order to have Leigh with us more often, we needed to pay Randal fair wages for his work, and that left little coin for us — after all, Gladdenfield Outpost was only a small settlement; the store did not make *that* much.

Leigh nodded, pausing to wipe stew from her chin. "Yeah," she agreed. "I want to check up on Randal too. See if he needs any help. And I'm sure we could rustle up an adventure or two to stock the coffers! We make a pretty good team, after all."

Her blue eyes sparkled eagerly at the thought.

"We should go prepared for anything," Diane suggested pragmatically. "I can resupply our traveling packs with provisions tonight." Though more cautious by nature, she knew funds were short. We would need to get to work if we wanted to expand.

I gave Diane an approving smile. "Good thinking. And I'll make sure to bring some mana potions and some of the healing potions left over from our expedition to Nimos Sedia." Turning to Leigh, I asked, "What do you think would be our best bet for profitable quests?"

Leigh tapped her spoon thoughtfully against her chin. "Let me think... I reckon clearing out a low-level Dungeon could pay nicely. And caravan guard jobs sometimes have bonus pay. Oh! Or a bounty hunt — I know there's some critters with prices on their heads from time to time."

"A Dungeon could work," I mused. "Provided we find one well-suited to our levels and abilities." I was grateful to have these two capable women at my side to take on such challenges. "Not so sure about guarding a caravan. That sounds like we might be away from the homestead too long."

Diane got up to stir the pot on the hearth and refresh our stew. "I agree," she said, giving me a meaningful glance. "There is much we must do at the homestead. We can't be gone for weeks."

Leigh nodded soberly. "You both are absolutely right," she hummed. "We should have a chat with Darny at the Wild Outrider. He usually has a pretty good idea of what's goin' on in town and who's lookin' for what."

Diane smiled warmly and agreed with her friend. She refilled our bowls before retaking her seat. "There should be suitable opportunities that play to our strengths without undue danger."

Between bites, I said, "We make a good team, so something requiring scouting, tracking, or protecting could work well." Our varied skills complemented each other nicely for certain quests.

"Ooh, like a rescue mission!" Leigh suggested excitedly. "Good coin in savin' lost travelers or recoverin' stolen goods from bandits." Her enthusiasm for living the adventure was catching.

I laughed. "Well, let's see what's available first before picking anything specific." Taking quests blind could be risky. But Leigh's passion for our travels together was endearing.

We lingered over our meal, continuing to discuss potential jobs to pursue in Gladdenfield. Leigh's eyes shone as she described thrilling tales of past quests she had undertaken before we met. She had roamed the frontier for some time shortly after the Upheaval, and she had gone on a few quests before settling in Gladdenfield Outpost.

Diane and I listened with amusement to her colorful stories, enjoying seeing Leigh so animated. She waved her hands enthusiastically, nearly upsetting her drink in her eagerness to share each adventure.

The fire cracked merrily in the hearth as we talked. Our empty stew bowls sat forgotten while Leigh regaled us with an account of rescuing a carpenter's son from orcish river pirates.

"We tracked those orc rapscallions for three days through marsh and mire before finally cornerin' them in their den," she enthused.

Diane and I hung on every word. Leigh's affinity for daring exploits was contagious.

"I was with a party of five others back then," she continued. "A Paladin, a Tempest Mage, a Thief, a Berserker, and a White Mage... We made short work of them orcs, and the little kid was scared half to death when we found him."

After the conclusion of that particular tale, talk turned again to speculating what opportunities the job board in Gladdenfield might hold come morning. Our imaginations were eager to envision what might await.

"Regardless of what we pick, I'm just excited to be venturin' out with you both again," Leigh said warmly, reaching over to give my hand an affectionate squeeze. "Our little fellowship makes even the dullest job excitin'."

I smiled. "I feel the same way, Leigh. With you two at my side, I know there's no challenge we can't handle."

Diane nodded her agreement, tail swishing happily.

Our conversation and laughter continued late

into the evening as we enjoyed simply being together. When yawns finally came, we reluctantly declared it time to clean up for the night, calling on Ghostie and Sir Boozles to do most of the work. After that, we retired to the cozy sitting area to relax by the fire.

For lack of a large enough bed, we had made a little nest in front of the fire, and we spent the rest of the evening there. Soon, talk turned to touch, and we all fell asleep sweaty and satisfied when night was fully upon us.

# Chapter 4

Morning sunlight streamed in through the cabin windows as I stirred awake. Beside me, Diane and Leigh still slept soundly. Careful not to disturb them, I slipped from beneath the quilts and began readying for the day ahead.

After washing up and dressing, I gently opened

the door and looked outside. The property was quiet, and Ghostie and Sir Boozles slipped through the door, eager to be inside like cats after a night out. I peered until I saw both the storm elemental and the larroling were fine.

A quiet night, it appeared.

I lit the stove and put a kettle on to boil while I sliced some bread and cheese for a quick breakfast. The simple fare would fortify us for the ride to Gladdenfield.

As I ate, I mentally catalogued supplies to pack for the journey. We would need provisions, camping gear, and other essentials in case the quest took us far afield or delayed our return. We would also require alchemical provisions — mana draughts, healing potions, and some of the leftover antidote in case we came across venomous or poisonous critters.

By the time Diane and Leigh stirred awake, I had all our travel packs laid out on the table ready to be loaded up. The smell of fresh coffee finally coaxed the girls to join me at the table, yawning and rubbing sleep from their eyes.

"Morning, you two," I said cheerfully. "I let you sleep in a bit. But we should get an early start for town. There's coffee and some bread and cheese if you're hungry."

Leigh smiled sleepily, her golden waves of bed-tousled hair spilling over one shoulder. "Much appreciated, baby. Nothin' like coffee to get me going!"

"Oh, I know another way or two to get you going," I quipped, shooting her a wink.

The girls both chuckled at that before heading straight for the fragrant pot.

As we ate a quick breakfast together, I outlined the supplies I had assembled and my plan for securing the homestead in our absence. The girls listened and offered suggestions as we finalized preparations.

Before long, we were carefully stowing gear in our packs — dried rations, bedrolls, cookware, hunting knives, rope, and other essentials. I added a couple potions, carefully wrapped in soft furs, and a first aid kit.

Finally, we strapped on weapons and other

combat essentials. I took my rifle and handgun, while Diane had her crossbow and Leigh had her revolver. Each of us carried a long knife as a backup.

Stepping outside into the crisp morning air, I whistled for the domesticants and my storm elemental. Ghostie, Sir Boozles, and Mr. Drizzles dutifully appeared.

I issued them firm instructions to guard the homestead diligently in our absence and keep it clean and well-tended. After that, I did a quick imbuement of the soil and the crops with my earth and woodland spirits and disarmed the traps for our time away.

Meanwhile, Leigh made Colonel ready. She would be riding him to Gladdenfield while Diane and I took the Jeep with our supplies. Our new larroling companion plodded up and snuffled Leigh's hair affectionately.

Chuckling, Leigh gave the beast a few pats. "You be good and stick close now," she told it with a smile.

The tame creature rumbled agreeably. It would

shadow us through the forest.

"Won't people in Gladdenfield be scared of him?" I asked.

Leigh shook her head. "He'll get a look or two, but people know Beastmasters and a couple other Classes have pets. It'll be fine."

After locking up the cabin securely, we piled our packs into the Jeep. Diane claimed the passenger seat beside me. Engine rumbling to life, I steered us onto the winding trail leading away from the secluded valley.

Glancing beside us, I saw Leigh trotting on Colonel to the side of the path — not behind us as we were kicking up a lot of dust. She sang a jaunty frontier tune, blonde braid swinging. The bulky larroling brought up the rear, lumbering along at its own steady pace.

Diane fiddled with the radio dial as I drove, but static was all that came through out here. The frontier had a way of meddling with electronics, and it was a miracle that the thing would even turn on. Instead, she contented herself with watching the vibrant greenery slide by our windows.

Birdsongs and sunlight accompanied us on the peaceful journey.

Each bend in the shady trail revealed new vistas of the woodlands awakening to the morning. Diane inhaled deeply of the fragrant air flowing in, a dreamy smile on her lips. Our wheels kicked up puffs of dust that drifted lazily in shafts of golden light.

My thoughts wandered happily as I tapped the steering wheel in time with a melody in my head. It felt good being on the move again to new adventures after working the homestead. A change of scenery renewed the spirit.

In the side mirror, I could see Leigh keeping easy pace astride Colonel. The handsome roan's gait was smooth and untiring. Leigh's golden hair fluttered in the morning breeze, her posture relaxed and confident atop her mount.

The larroling bulled its way steadily through the underbrush paralleling the twisting trail, relying on its raw power rather than agility. But the creature kept up admirably despite its lumbering gait and massive frame. It followed Leigh like a loyal puppy, and I marveled at the power of the Beastmaster.

Soon enough, the seemingly endless forest began yielding gradually to open country. Grasslands flecked with wildflowers rippled in the breeze. A hawk circled high overhead, scanning for prey.

Distant specks hinted at farms and homesteads nestled around Gladdenfield's outskirts. Those people were like us — carving out a living from the beautiful but dangerous environment of the frontier.

Before long, the timber palisade walls of Gladdenfield came into view. The gates stood open, allowing travelers and traders easy passage in and out of the lively community. Guards waved in friendly recognition as we rumbled past.

As Leigh predicted, the guards gave the larroling a second look but did not seem alarmed. The beast was allowed to enter, but Leigh made it clear she would have to stable it together with Colonel. Apparently, there were a few special stables for pets.

I navigated the dusty main thoroughfare slowly

to avoid kicking up too much grit. Townsfolk strolling the boardwalk waved to Diane and me as we passed. The settlement was beginning to stir to life as the day commenced.

Up ahead, Leigh had already dismounted and stood stroking Colonel's neck outside the livery stable. As I parked the Jeep and turned off the engine, the larroling settled onto its haunches with a ground-shaking thud to await further commands.

Hefting our packs, Diane and I made our way over to join Leigh while stable hands saw to securing Colonel. "Well, we made it," I remarked. "Where should we start? The tavern?"

Leigh nodded, shielding her eyes from the sun as she gazed up the bustling street. "Sounds perfect," she agreed. "Give me a sec to stable Colonel and the larroling, and let's go rustle up some adventure!"

Leigh secured Colonel and the larroling in

neighboring stalls with fresh hay and water while Diane and I waited outside the livery. Soon, she rejoined us, dusting straw from her hands.

"All set!" Leigh said brightly. With a wave, we set off down the bustling main thoroughfare toward the familiar facade of the Wild Outrider. The tavern's doors stood propped open, inviting patrons escaping the morning heat.

Stepping into the dim, cool interior, we were greeted by the familiar mingled scents of ale and smoke. Despite the early hour, a handful of trail-worn regulars already sat nursing drinks. A couple of them looked like they had sat there all night, but I knew that couldn't be the case. After all, Darny usually closed up around midnight, barring festivities or the chance for some serious extra revenue.

Behind the long counter, Darny looked up from wiping glasses and broke into a broad grin beneath his bushy mustache when he spotted us. "Well, look who it is!" he bellowed in his usual jovial manner. "My favorite adventurers return!"

We exchanged smiles as Darny came over to

greet us with hearty handshakes. His eyes twinkled merrily at seeing us again.

"What brings y'all back to town so soon?" he asked. "More tales of derring-do to share, I hope? Y'know the offer for y'all to tell the tale of the tournament is still open?"

I chuckled at his enthusiasm. "Perhaps soon, Darny. For now, we're just here to restock provisions and see what interesting opportunities there might be on offer. We're looking to make some extra coin as we want to expand the homestead."

Darny's expression grew suddenly somber. Rubbing his bearded chin, he gestured for us to take a seat at the bar while he poured three mugs from a pot of coffee he kept for those patrons that didn't like alcohol in the morning. I sensed he had news to share.

Clasping his meaty hands on the counter, Darny met our eyes gravely once we had settled onto the stools. "Well now, funny you should mention work opportunities," he began. "We've got ourselves a bit of a situation, you see..."

"What is it, Darny?" Diane asked with concern, her ears lowering. Beside me, Leigh also looked apprehensive. The barman's serious demeanor was unusual.

Darny grimaced. "It's Clara..." he said heavily. "Seems she and her party have gone missing somewhere out in the Shimmering Peaks while expeditioning to old Hrothgar's Hope."

I blinked in surprise, immediately recalling the grizzled adventurer who had stopped here some time ago. She had been pursuing that dwarven Dungeon with her companions and had told us all about it the last time we were in town. Unease trickled down my spine.

Clara had told us that Hrothgar's Hope was a dwarven Dungeon, built shortly after the Upheaval by dwarves of the Forgeheart clan. Kobolds infested the place three years ago, and Clara had said the Dungeon was supposed to be level 4 to 5. She was taking several adventurers I knew from Lord Vartlebeck's tournament at the Aquana Festival — Branik Storsson of Ironfast, Karjela of the foxkin, and a human called Ergun.

"When did this happen?" Leigh asked with a frown, voicing my own question.

Darny sighed. "It's been nearly a week now since they were expected back. No word or sign of 'em since they left." He shook his shaggy head. "Something's gone wrong out there for sure."

My mind raced, picturing the dangers that could have waylaid such an experienced party. She told me and Leigh that they expected kobolds, drakelings, goblins, and maybe even a young dragon. A serious challenge, but she had seemed confident in her and her party's ability to handle it.

"There's a reward posted by the mayor for anyone who can discover their fate," Darny went on. "Pretty hefty sum, too. I know Clara, she's too stubborn to go down easy. But them dwarven Dungeons in the Shimmering Peaks can be mighty treacherous..."

I nodded somberly, understanding his unspoken request. If anyone could pick up Clara's trail, it was us. We had a Scout, after all, and we were capable of dealing with a Dungeon of that level — assuming Clara's intel had been right.

I turned to Leigh and Diane. "What do you two think? We're capable trackers, and we know our way around."

Diane bit her lip anxiously. But Leigh's eyes blazed with resolve. "Clara's from Gladdenfield," she declared. "We gotta look out after our own. Plus, she's a good soul. We gotta try and find her." She then gave a light shrug. "And we could use the coin — no sense lyin' about that..."

"It's the right thing to do," Diane agreed after a moment's hesitation. I knew tracking down Clara's unknown fate would be dangerous. But fortune often favored the bold.

I met Darny's hopeful gaze. "We'll see what we can uncover," I told him.

If Clara still lived, we would track her down. If not, at least we could return her to rest with honor. The frontier was a rough place despite its beauty; it would not be the first life claimed.

Relief broke across Darny's careworn face. He reached over to clasp my shoulder. "Thank you, my friend. You're Clara's best hope if she still lives. And her party deserves a proper burial if..." His voice faltered gruffly.

I patted his shoulder. "Whatever their fate, we'll find them," I said simply but sincerely.

Beside me, Leigh and Diane nodded solemnly. Come what may, we would discover the truth and return tidings to Gladdenfield. I did not know if Clara had any relatives in town, but I knew Branik was of the Silverheart clan — the clan that Lord Vartlebeck ruled.

Darny quickly outlined all he knew regarding the route Clara's group had planned to take toward Hrothgar's Hope.

"As y'all know," he began, "the Shimmering Peaks are north of here. 'Bout a day or three should get you to the sloping path up Hrothgar's Hope. It's gonna be cold up near the summit where the entrance is, but the trail should lead ya straight there!"

I nodded along as he spoke, then let him point out the route on my map, memorizing each detail.

"I've been that way before," Diane said, "so we should be able to make our way. But it's a dangerous stretch of the frontier."

I nodded. "We'll be careful then, and we'll get some extra warm clothes from Leigh's shop. But let's travel light — no pack animals. We should move swiftly and be mobile, especially if we run into any threat we can't handle."

The girls nodded agreement, and Darny too seemed to think that was wise.

"We'll leave at first light tomorrow," I told Darny.

If fortune favored us, perhaps we could still pick up Clara's trail before it faded completely. Time was of the essence. After all, who knew if she and her party members were being held captive or trapped somewhere with dwindling supplies?

"Travel safely," Darny rumbled. "And thank you again." He squeezed my shoulder gratefully before turning to give Leigh and Diane's hands an affectionate pat as well. "But please, don't get lost yourselves, alright?"

I nodded. "Don't worry," I said. "We know what we're doing."

Over the next hour, we lingered at our table finalizing plans between swigs of coffee while

Darny kept our mugs filled and brought us a filling lunch.

Our conversation was lively but determined. With our course set, we would prepare this day to depart on the morrow. Before that, we would pack our extra supplies, purchase what rations we needed, and get ready.

But before we would leave, there was someone else I wanted to pay a visit in town…

# Chapter 5

After finishing up at the tavern, the three of us moved our supplies from the Jeep to Leigh's house and began making preparations. Of course, I wanted to see Celeste, who was staying at the Wild Outrider, but I wanted to help my girls before I headed back there to speak to the elven beauty.

Once we had unloaded, I told Diane and Leigh I wanted to go pay Celeste a brief visit before we began preparations. They smiled knowingly and said they would take care of getting supplies while I went to see her. We would all meet again at Leigh's place above the store for dinner and final preparations.

I made my way through the busy streets of Gladdenfield, returning friendly greetings from townsfolk along the way. My victories at the Gauntlet Run and Lord Vartlebeck's tournament at the Aquana Festival were still fresh in their minds, and I was becoming more known by the day.

And while Waelin had never revealed to others why he had sent us to Nimos Sedia, it was a known fact that I had conquered that Dungeon and braved the Blighted Land along the way, aided by my women, and that was building my fame as well. Children watched me with big eyes, and adults paid me respect as I passed them.

Soon, I once again arrived at the Wild Outrider where Celeste now had a permanent room performing nightly. Darny waved as I passed by the counter and shot me a wink, knowing full well who I was here to see.

Climbing the creaking wooden steps, I came to Celeste's door and gave a firm knock. After a moment, I heard light footsteps approach before the door swung open. Celeste's eyes lit up when she saw me standing there.

"David! What a lovely surprise," she exclaimed. "Please, come in." She ushered me eagerly inside the cozy room. I smiled; always glad to see her radiant beauty again. Her melodic voice was like music.

As I stepped into the modest space, I saw Celeste's elven harp resting in the corner near the window. She bade me take a seat at the small table by the cold hearth while she prepared tea.

Soon, we were settled across from each other, steaming mugs in hand. I studied her fair features in the soft morning light streaming through the curtains.

"You look well," I remarked. "How have you been finding things here?"

Celeste smiled shyly. "Oh, the people are kind

enough, if loud at times. But I cannot complain. Darny and his wife have been so very generous." Her pointy ears flushed slightly. "And you visited at just the right moment... I was feeling rather lonely."

I reached over to squeeze her delicate hand reassuringly. "Well, I'm here now," I said gently. "Actually, my companions and I are in Gladdenfield to resupply and seek out a new quest."

As we sipped our tea, I explained about the missing adventurer Clara and our intent to pick up her trail come morning. Celeste listened raptly, concern creasing her smooth brow. My heart swelled just looking at her.

"It is noble of you three to undertake such a dangerous mission," Celeste said gravely once I had finished. "But please exercise caution in those peaks. Many perils lurk. My people of old have a vendetta with the orcs and goblins, but those wretches will just as happily slay humans or foxkin. They are murderous, and the kobolds are no better."

"We'll be careful," I assured her. "And hopefully return with good news."

I decided not to mention the equally likely prospect that Clara and her friends were already dead. But Celeste read the grim possibility in my eyes regardless.

She bit her lip pensively. "Might I ask a favor? It... It is a big favor." Celeste ventured almost timidly after a moment.

I blinked in surprise but nodded for her to continue.

Celeste took a deep breath. "Would it be permissible if... Might I come along with you?" She rushed the request out in a nervous tumble of words.

I stared, caught wholly off guard. Bringing Celeste along had not even crossed my mind. She had never accompanied us beyond Gladdenfield's walls.

Moreover, I knew nothing of her abilities to survive the harsh frontier. She seemed delicate, and she had only just awakened from a long, comatose slumber. The nature of her illness —

other than that it was magical — had never been revealed to me.

As I floundered for words, Celeste hastily added, "You need not decide right away. But please consider letting me join you. I am restless here in town, and I feel my skills would be of use."

I regarded her solemnly. "What skills do you have, Celeste?" I inquired gently. She averted her gaze.

"I am afraid I cannot say just yet," she replied cryptically. "Only that I am capable of holding my own on such a quest as this. I can fight. You have my word for it."

Her eyes were guileless. I sensed no deceit, only hope, and I had learned over the years to trust my senses. Often, the heart spoke wisdom before the mind.

But what Class would she have? We had touched on the subject of Classes before, and something about Celeste had turned wistful at that. She had not yet revealed her Class to me, and I was, in fact, unsure she even had one. And people without a Class — even elves — should not venture into the

Wilds.

My instincts warred within me. The frontier's dangers were not to be underestimated. I cared for Celeste too deeply to risk her lightly. And yet, denying her outright felt equally wrong. Accompanying us clearly meant a great deal to her.

And unlike any other, I knew what it felt like to be left behind. In the days after the Upheaval, I had been one of the people who had not — by some luck or divine boon — received a Class.

As such, while there was a whole magical world to explore, I had been confined to the Coalition-protected cities because it was simply too dangerous out there.

And I knew the feeling of being left behind was terrible. My parents got Classes, and they went adventuring. It led to their disappearances, but still, they got to see the world...

I didn't wish for anyone else to suffer the sheltered fate of my previous life in New Springfield.

I chose my next words carefully. "If you truly feel you can handle the hazards we'll face, I won't refuse you outright," I said slowly. "But I must consult with my companions first."

Relief broke across Celeste's delicate features. Impulsively, she leaned over to plant a soft kiss on my cheek.

"That is all I can ask," she said warmly. "You are wise not to decide alone on this."

My pulse quickened pleasantly at her affectionate gesture. I found myself wondering again what hidden talents Celeste might possess if she was so keen to venture into the frontier wilderness with us. But further questions would have to wait.

Glancing out the window, I saw the sun was on its way down. "I'm afraid I have to go prepare and talk to the others," I told Celeste regretfully as I finished my tea. "But I will return with our decision by tonight, alright?"

She nodded, and I could see the hope in her pretty expression.

Rising, I clasped her hands and met her vibrant green eyes. "Whatever is decided, please know your company means more than I can express," I said earnestly.

Celeste's answering smile outshone the high noon sun.

After a farewell embrace, I took my leave. My thoughts swirled as brightly as the warm sun overhead and I went down the tavern steps and along Gladdenfield's bustling avenues. Though caught off guard by Celeste's request, a part of me now hoped she might join our fellowship.

But before that, I would need to talk things through with Diane and Leigh.

# Chapter 6

That evening, after a long day of preparations, Diane, Leigh, and I gathered in the cozy dining room above Leigh's store for a hearty dinner. The table was laden with freshly baked bread, vegetable stew, apple pie, and mugs of ale from the settlement's bakery. Despite the savory spread, my mind kept turning to Celeste's unexpected request from earlier.

As we began eating, I decided it was time to broach the subject. Clearing my throat, I began, "I spoke with Celeste today. She had an interesting request — she wants to join us on our mission to find Clara."

Diane paused, her spoon halfway to her mouth. "Celeste wants to come with us on an adventure?" she asked incredulously. "Did she say why?"

I shook my head as I tore off some bread. "Only that she's restless in town and feels her skills could aid us. But she didn't specify what those skills are."

"Hmm..." Diane's brow furrowed pensively as she set down her spoon. "It seems rather sudden. And we know so little of her abilities."

Leigh wiped her mouth and chimed in eagerly. "Aw, give the gal a chance! She's been cooped up here for ages. I reckon she just wants a taste of adventure with pleasant company."

Diane shot Leigh a wry grin. "Ever the adventurous spirit! But remember, the peaks harbor untold dangers. We'll need clear heads and ample skill just to track Clara. Also, we're a team — we've done this sort of thing together before. She's new, and we're unsure what role she can play."

I nodded soberly, sipping my ale. "You both make good points. And we can't make this choice lightly." I turned to Diane. "You know these lands better than any. What perils do you foresee for someone as green as Celeste?"

Diane considered the question seriously as she tore off a hunk of bread. "Well, just the Shimmering Peaks alone... I mean, the elements pose a threat — frigid winds, thin air, avalanches on those slopes."

She ticked each hazard off on her fingers as she spoke. "And orcs and goblins roam there as well. Celeste may be naive to their bloodlust."

"She seems to know orcs and goblins hate her kind," I said. "But she did not tell me if she had any prior adventures."

"Every elf knows orcs hate their kind," Diane said. "We simply don't know enough about Celeste to accept her."

"Well, we can bundle up and be her guides," Leigh countered, gesturing with her spoon. "And we'll be with her if any beasties appear. Ain't gonna be the first time a greenhorn comes along to learn a thing or two..." But she shot me a questioning look, seeking my thoughts.

I pondered how best to voice my conflicted feelings. "I want Celeste to feel included, to experience life beyond town walls. She craves it deeply. I know that longing all too well."

Leigh and Diane nodded full of empathy, understanding my past isolation.

"Yet, I worry for her safety also," I continued after a swig of ale. "This will be her first time in the wilderness, and we three are still learning how best to survive out there ourselves."

Diane reached over and gave my hand an understanding squeeze. "You want to grant her freedom without undue risk. A wise perspective." Her blue eyes were compassionate.

"Maybe we start her off easy?" Leigh suggested, gesturing with her fork. "Have her join us on the trip to build experience? If we ain't sure about her skills, we can tell her to stay outside and not enter the Dungeon. She could guard the base camp or somethin'?"

I smiled, appreciating Leigh's effort to find a compromise. "That's a fair point..." I mused, stroking my chin.

With training, perhaps Celeste could handle the frontier's challenges. And if she came along, we could gauge her experience and power before we would let her get into the thick of things with us.

"Still, that means exposing her to the dangers of the Shimmering Peaks themselves," Diane remarked. "Hrothgar's Hope might be more dangerous, but the Shimmering Peaks are nothing to shake a stick at."

I nodded. "I agree," I said. "Guarding the camp will also come with perils of its own. But she guaranteed me she can fight."

Diane nibbled her lip thoughtfully. "Provided that's true, I suppose it could work." She met my gaze over her stew bowl. "Celeste clearly means a great deal to you. We should at least try to make her inclusion possible."

Impulsively, I reached out to clasp both their hands. It was sweet of her to say so, because I knew well enough she harbored a few reservations when it came to elves. Allowing her to come along was sweet, and I understood it would be a test in more than one way — combat ability, but also if she could get along with Leigh and Diane and fit our dynamic.

"You two are the best," I said earnestly. "I want all of us to venture forth together. But only if we agree it's safe."

"We'll look out for her same as we do for each other," Leigh declared stoutly, giving my hand a squeeze.

Diane finally smiled again. "You're right, Leigh. If we stay alert and vigilant, Celeste will learn the ways of the Wilds under our guidance." She gave my hand an affectionate squeeze.

My own smile broadened at their show of support. With these two exceptional women at my side, I knew we could achieve anything, including mentoring a newcomer to the frontier life.

And I would not lie about it: I was hoping that,

in time, Celeste would come to mean more to us than just a friend and companion; but that all depended on if she would fit the unconventional little unit that our family made up.

As we continued eating, curiosity about Celeste's mysterious skills kept nagging at me. "Do either of you have any guesses as to what Class Celeste might have?" I asked before taking a bite of stew.

Leigh hummed thoughtfully. "Well, she's an elf, so maybe an alchemist like her uncle? Though that doesn't really seem to fit her love of music."

Diane shook her head. "I don't think so. I don't know her personally, but there's one potential direction for a fellow music lover." She tore off some bread, considering. "Perhaps a Bard?"

I nodded slowly as I took another sip of ale. "A Bard? That's a very good point. Her music was very moving. Although I wouldn't call it magical..." I thought back to her grace and poise. "Still, you may be onto something."

Leigh's eyes lit up. "Ooh, I'll bet she's got a sneaky Class like a Rogue! It'd fit with her lithe build and whatnot."

"Hmm, also possible," Diane mused. She glanced at me curiously. "Celeste didn't even give you a hint?"

I shook my head ruefully. "She remains tight-lipped for now. But the mystery just deepens my interest." I chuckled.

The girls laughed in response. "Well, one thing's sure — she's got you plenty intrigued," Leigh teased.

I felt my cheeks flush but laughed along. Their gentle teasing was affectionate. I was fortunate to have their support in this matter.

"Then it's settled," I declared, steering us back on track. "I'll inform Celeste she can join us, but she must heed our guidance and wisdom in all things. Does that sound fair?"

Diane and Leigh both nodded firmly. "Just promise you won't let your feelings cloud your judgment where she's concerned," Diane added gently.

I met her earnest gaze. "You know me better than that, but point taken," I assured her.

Raising my mug, I proclaimed, "To our first

fellow traveler on the long road ahead."

"To Celeste!" Diane and Leigh chorused, touching their mugs to mine.

The rest of dinner passed cheerfully as we discussed preparations for the days ahead. Despite the uncertainties around Celeste, I felt confident that together we could help her in the Wild, and that she would become a valuable member of our fellowship.

# Chapter 7

Evening shadows descended over Gladdenfield as I made my way back to the raucous facade of the Wild Outrider. Inside, the tavern was already bustling with patrons eagerly awaiting Celeste's nightly performance.

Weaving through the lively crowd, I spotted

Darny behind the counter and exchanged a wave and a grin with the jovial barkeep. He gestured wordlessly toward a small table near the makeshift stage that he had kindly reserved for me.

Settling into the rickety chair with a nod of thanks, I allowed my gaze to roam appreciatively over the motley assortment of frontier folk who filled the tavern. Though rowdy, their cheerful camaraderie was welcoming.

Before long, the stool and violin were carried onto the modest stage, signaling the imminent start of Celeste's set. An anticipatory hush rippled through the crowd, followed by enthusiastic applause as the elf girl glided gracefully into view.

Celeste's sheer presence captivated all eyes the instant she took the stage. Clad in a gown of flowing emerald silk, her alabaster skin seemed to glow ethereally in the lantern light. The crowd's din softened to reverent silence as she raised the violin to her sculpted shoulder.

Closing her eyes, Celeste drew the bow slowly across the strings. An achingly beautiful melody soared out, infused with longing and sorrow. I was struck by the haunting edge she brought to even a simple folk tune. Her skill, entrancing, I forgot the bustling tavern.

"O, mist-veiled land of ancient lore,
*Where elven ships sail nevermore.*
*'Neath lonely stars that vigil keep,*
*Your storied shores in slumber deep."*

"Once loud with joy and sorrow rang,
*Meet songs of mariners who sang,*
*While dancing light on breakers gleamed,*
*Now only seagulls' cries are screamed.*

"Tannoris, beloved home,
*For you my exiled people roam,*
*Bereft of hearth and harmony,*
*That graced your soaring canopies."*

"Within each heart an aching dwells,
*For verdant groves and mossy dells.*
*Gone are the birdsong, scent of pine.*
*Naught left but memory's feeble shrine."*

"Across the void sundered apart,
*Still woven in each exiled heart,*
*Remembrance of your beauty pure,*
*Shall all our days of exile endure."*

*"Until at last when we reclaim,*
*Our lost and most beloved domain,*
*In joy, each tear-dimmed eye shall see,*
*Dawn break on far Tannoris' sea."*

As the last plaintive note faded, the rapt silence lingered a breath longer before the crowd erupted into thunderous applause. Celeste's pale cheeks colored prettily as she inclined her head in gratitude before launching into a lively jig.

What followed was a dazzling showcase of repertoire from sprightly fiddle tunes to mournful elven ballads. The bawdy frontier folk were uncharacteristically respectful, captured wholly under her spell. Watching Celeste lose herself to the music, I could scarcely draw breath.

The minutes flew by too swiftly; each melodic piece Celeste performed imprinting itself on my heart. Her talent transcended mere technical skill. That violin was simply an extension of her soul given voice through song. Hearing her play birthed dreams of what bliss we might create together.

All too soon, Celeste's fingers alighted gracefully on the violin strings for a final time, as her closing number came to an end. The rapturous applause shook the very rafters. Beaming, she curtsied delicately before gliding off stage, where men raised their mugs and tankards to her.

It was endearing to see that the elven beauty still struggled with the rowdy patrons of the Wild Outrider. She had told me as much during one of our earlier conversations — how she had a cultural barrier to overcome because elves usually did not mingle with the other creatures of Tannoris or Earth. But she had shown she had a spine, resolving to change her ways before they would turn her lonely.

My pulse still thrummed with the exhilaration of her performance as I weaved my way through the crowds toward her. When she caught sight of me approaching her, she took a steadying breath and smiled, waving me over — as if I hadn't yet spotted her dazzling beauty in this crowd of bearded frontier men.

Our eyes met as I made my way past a few admirers, and in hers, I glimpsed a kindred passion that kindled my heart afresh. "Celeste, you were magnificent tonight," I said earnestly.

A pretty blush graced her sculpted cheeks at the praise. "Oh, thank you, David," she hummed. "It is sweet of you to say so!"

Smiling, I took her by her arm and led her to a quieter corner of the Wild Outrider, as the men began drinking and shouting, launching into bawdy frontier songs of their own.

"Really," I told her once I had her alone. "Every time you sing, your words transport my spirit."

As I held her arm, Celeste's eyes shone vulnerability and hope, both apparent in her voice when she said softly, "And you have given flight to mine by coming this eve."

I treasured those simple yet profound words, sensing well that we were growing closer.

Gently clasping both her delicate hands in mine, I gathered my courage before gazing into her vibrant eyes and saying, "Celeste, I spoke to the others, and we would be honored if you would accompany us on our quest."

Her answering purr of delight and fierce embrace needed no further translation. When, after a moment, we parted, joyful tears glimmered on her flushed cheeks.

"You have granted my heart's desire this night," she whispered.

I tenderly brushed a crystalline droplet from her sculpted cheekbone, overcome with emotion myself at her naked elation.

"We'll set out at first light," I told her gently. "It will be a long journey. So, for now, you should try to rest."

She gifted me with a radiant smile that outshone even the moon's soft glow. "I shall play the sweetest melodies when we make camp," Celeste promised, clasping her hands. "You shall hear music such as you have never known!"

I chuckled. "Well, we might have to be quiet so as not to attract attention to ourselves…"

She blinked, touching her plump lip with a slender finger before nodding. "Of course, you are right. But pray tell, are there any specific preparations you would ask of me?"

I quickly told her of the route north toward the Shimmering Peaks and of the icy winds on the flanks of Hrothgar's Hope. She quickly picked up that she would need to pack warm clothes, and I told her that Leigh would pack victuals from the store. If she had anything else that might be of value on an expedition such as this, I recommended her to bring it along as well.

She listened attentively, and I got the feeling from her questions and conclusions that she had been out in the wilderness before. That gave me hope — there was likely more to her than met the eye.

At length, I reluctantly bid her goodnight, knowing we both required sleep. Celeste saw me to the door, standing framed in firelight. We exchanged one final, lingering glance, speaking of dreams unvoiced, before I descended into the now quiet streets.

My heart felt buoyant as my boots echoed off the cobblestones. Celeste would join our fellowship come dawn. Though her class remained a mystery, her passion was unmistakable. Together, we would help her find her courage.

I lifted my face to the blanket of glittering stars

overhead. The heavens themselves seemed to wink in portent of adventure. Somewhere out there, our destiny waited. There would be combat and peril, but I was looking forward to it and to the bonds it would forge between us.

When I arrived back at Leigh's, I found her still awake, unable to fully settle on the eve of our departure. She sat gazing pensively into the dying embers when I entered.

At the sight of me, she stirred from her reverie. "So, how did it go?" Leigh asked, eyes searching mine for a clue. "What did she say?"

I could not restrain a radiant smile as I gave her the news. "Celeste is coming with us."

# Chapter 8

The next morning, the first blush of dawn was just creeping over the eastern forest as Leigh, Diane, and I made our way through the quiet streets of Gladdenfield. A chill still clung to the morning air, our breath fogging faintly, but the towering timber palisade walls already cast long shadows across our path.

We first made our way to the stables, where a sleepy attendant was helping those who — like us — were leaving town early and needed to get their mounts ready. There, we found Leigh's larroling, and the creature gave a happy huff at the sight of its mistress.

She made sure it had been well tended before we moved on together, heading toward the gates.

Up ahead, the gates stood closed and barred, the night watch still on duty. We would need to wait a bit yet until they opened for morning departures. Shifting my pack, I glanced around for any sign of Celeste joining us.

Diane walked silently beside me, her expression pensive. Though supportive of allowing Celeste to accompany us, I sensed her unease. Bringing a newcomer into our close-knit group was no small matter, and she had expressed before that she often found elves arrogant. But I had faith Celeste would find her place.

On my other side, Leigh seemed to share none of our hesitance. "Maybe we should check on

Celeste?" she suggested brightly. "Wouldn't want her to sleep through our grand adventure!"

I nodded. "We're a bit early. I'll go to the Wild Outrider and see if she's up."

It seemed a good idea to check up on her and walk her to the group, rather than let her come without introduction.

Handing Leigh my pack, I pivoted and made to leave for the tavern. But at that moment, a figure rounded the bend in the street and headed straight toward us.

There, haloed in the morning's early light, came Celeste.

She had donned a cloak and sturdy traveling clothes, though her beauty was undimmed. Slinging a pack over one shoulder, she hurried to join us, cheeks flushed delicate pink. There was a long object wrapped in furs that might have been a blade. My curiosity was piqued, but I decided to wait a while before I would ask her.

"Apologies for my tardiness," she said breathlessly. "I did not know you were already here." Those brilliant eyes found mine, radiating warmth and anticipation.

I smiled reassuringly. "You're right on time. We were just about to come looking for you."

Celeste then turned to Leigh with a gracious smile. "Thank you again for your kindly offer of provision, Leigh. I shall return all in good time."

Leigh waved off her thanks cheerfully. "Any friend of David's is a friend of mine! No need to repay — we're doing this together!"

At last, Celeste's vibrant gaze moved to Diane standing silently beside me. I watched them size one another up discreetly, feeling the undercurrent of uncertainty swirling around this first true meeting.

Gently, I made the introduction. "Celeste, this is Diane, my steadfast companion. We have weathered much together. Diane, meet our new fellow traveler, Celeste."

Politely, Diane extended a slender hand in greeting. "Well met, Celeste. Any friend of David and Leigh is welcome company." Though her words were gracious, her tail swished warily.

Taking Diane's proffered hand with porcelain

fingers; Celeste gave a cordial yet reserved smile. "The honor is mine, Diane." For all her musical talent, the elf maiden's voice rang slightly stilted in that moment.

Though subtle, the undercurrent of reservation flowing both ways was palpable to me. But such was only natural, I reasoned, for two strangers cautiously taking the other's measure.

And the two girls were, after all, very different. Celeste came from the elven culture, where art and magic reigned supreme against a backdrop of luxurious living.

Diane, however, came from the rougher and grittier foxkin who struggled for survival on the frontier. I hoped that, given time, they would grow to understand each other's ways, and their unease would fade.

Eager to break the awkward tension, Leigh sidled over and threw a friendly arm around Celeste's slender shoulders. "Aw, we're gonna have a blast together out there," she enthused, giving the elf girl a playful squeeze. "Just you wait and see!"

Giggling, Celeste's stance relaxed, the ice broken. Even Diane had to chuckle softly at Leigh's antics. The bubbly blonde had a knack for lifting spirits that never failed.

Satisfied the initial meet-and-greet had gone smoothly enough, I gestured toward the gates where more people were now congregating in anticipation of departure at gates open — merchants and travelers eager to be on their way.

"Shall we?" I proposed.

Together, we four mismatched wanderers fell in step making our way toward Gladdenfield's timber gates as the night watch prepared to open them for the day's ventures.

The guards eyed our group and Leigh's larroling with interest but offered respectful nods of acknowledgment in my direction. My victories had cemented some reputation.

As we waited, I caught Celeste gazing wide-eyed all around, taking in each detail of the frontier settlement she had seldom ventured out of during her stay. A hint of wonder softened her elegant features. She was a beauty.

When at last the gates creaked ponderously open, we were among the first travelers to pass beneath the archway onto the winding dirt road beyond. Diane took up a position leading us northward, relying on her natural Scout instincts.

With a glance back at Gladdenfield's walls receding into the distance, our party set off toward adventure together for the first time in this new composition.

Though Celeste lingered silently at the rear for now, I hoped in time she would open up and find her place among us. Diane and Leigh chatted amiably about possible campsites ahead along the route, feeling the excitement of this new venture.

I purposefully fell back to walk beside Celeste, letting the girls take the lead. "How are you feeling so far?" I asked gently.

She offered a brave smile. "Eager for the journey ahead," Celeste replied, though her luminous eyes betrayed a hint of trepidation.

Gently I said, "You're in good company. We'll watch out for one another." My steady tone seemed to reassure her.

As Diane and Leigh's lively banter floated back, mingling with birdsongs, I matched my strides to Celeste's. Together, we followed the twisting trail onward through dappled sunshine toward the azure silhouette of the Shimmering Peaks beckoning in the distance.

For now, our fellowship was united by purpose and the open road ahead. What mysteries awaited us, what strength we would find in each other, the coming days would tell.

# Chapter 9

The morning sun shone through the leafy roof overhead as we made our way along the forest trail. Diane led confidently, ears pricked for any sounds out of the ordinary. At her side, Leigh hummed a wandering tune, bright and cheerful as a songbird, and the larroling lumbered behind.

I walked a few paces behind with Celeste, glancing her way now and then. She moved with innate elven grace, yet her eyes held a guarded wariness I had not seen in Gladdenfield's sheltering walls. Each little forest noise made her subtly tense.

By late morning, the pleasant chill had burned off, and a muggy heat descended. We were all growing weary and ready to rest our feet. Up ahead, the faint gurgle of a woodland stream reached our ears.

"Let's stop and take a break up ahead near the water," I suggested, seeing the others' fatigue. "We can refill our canteens and have a bite to eat."

Diane glanced back and nodded in agreement, relief flashing across her delicate features at the prospect of a break from the sun's relentless assault. Even the tireless Leigh gave an exaggerated sigh.

"Now that sounds mighty fine to me!" she declared, fanning herself dramatically beneath her hat. "My feet are fixin' to rebel if I walk another mile in this heat. Why don't we make a lil' fire, and

I'll cook us up some eggs — somethin' to fortify us for the rest of the day?"

"Great idea," I agreed. "Though I won't be sitting too close to the fire."

The girls chuckled as we plodded on. Soon enough, we reached the gurgling stream and gratefully shrugged off our packs and sat down in the shade of a towering elm to rest our dusty legs.

While Leigh helped me gather kindling, Diane moved off on her own through the trees, scouting the area. We needed to be sure there were no unseen threats out there — these were the Wilds, after all.

Celeste perched gingerly on a fallen log, looking unsure what to do with herself. I caught her eye and smiled reassuringly.

"Why don't you help me get a little fire going?" I suggested.

Looking relieved to have a task, she came over to assist. Yet when I handed her the flint and steel to try sparking a flame herself, uncertainty flooded her expression once more. Her porcelain cheeks flushed in embarrassment.

"I am afraid I do not know how," Celeste admitted, eyes downcast. "Such skills were never required of me before."

Gently, I showed her how to strike at just the right angle to produce sparks. After several tries, she succeeded in igniting a little tongue of flame in the kindling. Pride lit up her face at this minor accomplishment.

As we worked, Diane returned to report the area secure. Yet I noticed her tail bristle slightly seeing Celeste at my side by the growing fire. Wordlessly, she moved off again to refill our canteens downstream.

Soon enough, our small fire crackled merrily. Gathering around it, we ate dried meat and fruit from our packs, with Leigh making some eggs in the skillet. The fare was rich, the eggs especially good, and it was a pleasant respite. The canopy overhead warded off the worst of midday's heat.

When we had eaten our fill, I instructed Celeste how to safely douse and stir the embers to prevent the fire from rekindling. As she set dutifully to work, I watched Diane observing her from across our makeshift camp, blue eyes inscrutable.

Once satisfied the fire posed no risk, I thanked Celeste for her help. She gave a gracious nod, looking pleased to have gotten it right. A smile touched my lips seeing her try so earnestly to learn basic skills foreign to her upbringing. I hoped with time she would gain wilderness wisdom.

While the girls rested a while longer, I decided to try my hand fishing in the creek, hoping that a fresh dinner at night would smooth things over a little. Wading out into the shallows, I managed to spear three fair-sized trout with my hunting knife.

"A fine catch!" Leigh enthused when I returned with the flopping fish. Diane, too, cracked a smile at the prospect of freshly cooked fish for our supper, and Celeste happily clapped her hands.

Soon enough, we were ready to move again. A gentle breeze rustled the leaves pleasantly, bringing a breath of cool air, and our break had reinvigorated us. Diane stood, declaring it was time we moved on.

As we prepared to depart, I held up the three plump trout I had caught earlier. "Who's looking forward to a delicious trout dinner tonight?" I asked cheerfully.

"Oh, me!" Leigh exclaimed, rubbing her smooth tummy. "Nothin' better than fresh fish cooked over the campfire."

Diane gave a slight smile. "Yes, the trout will make a nice, fresh dinner," she agreed. Though she remained reserved, I could tell the prospect of hot food appealed to her.

"And we'll find some wild onions and tubers we can roast up as a side," I added. Diane relaxed further at the thought of foraged vegetables to accompany the fish.

As we discussed the meal, Celeste listened quietly, seemingly hesitant to interrupt our planning. But I noticed a wistful look enter her vibrant eyes.

After a moment, she ventured softly, "Your meal sounds wonderful. Perhaps... after we dine this eve, if you are amenable, I would be honored to perform a song for you beneath the stars."

Leigh's face lit up at the suggestion. "A song around the campfire sounds perfect!" she enthused, giving Celeste an encouraging smile. "And if we scout our location well, we can risk just a little soft-voiced singin', right David?"

I nodded, looking forward to the idea. Celeste's voice was beautiful, and if she got to show her skills, it might help make her feel more at home among us.

Diane pondered the idea, absently swishing her tail. I could tell she was wary of potential delays. But the promise of a hot meal and music ultimately swayed her.

"I suppose we've made good time today," Diane conceded. "We can afford to relax this evening and enjoy Celeste's singing before bedding down."

Celeste's shoulders relaxed in relief at Diane's acquiescence. I reached over and gave her hand a gentle, reassuring squeeze.

"It's settled then," I said brightly. "A delicious trout feast and a song beneath the stars before we turn in."

Shafts of amber sunlight slanted through the canopy of rustling leaves as we arrived at the forest clearing Diane had selected for making camp. Evening was fast approaching, and we had marched through most of the afternoon in silence.

The spot was well found. Here, a babbling brook murmured nearby, providing fresh water. Dropping my pack with a grateful sigh, I surveyed the tranquil glen.

"This is perfect," I remarked, smiling at Diane.

She returned a subtle smile, already moving off to gather firewood and scout the area. Leigh eagerly began unpacking cooking gear for our trout dinner.

I turned to Celeste. "Why don't you help me clean the fish?" I suggested. Looking relieved to have a task, she joined me by the stream.

Kneeling on the mossy bank, I demonstrated how to descale and gut the trout with smooth strokes of my hunting knife. Celeste watched my technique closely before attempting it herself. Her slender hands moved gracefully despite being unaccustomed to wielding a knife in this way.

It was clear that the elven beauty had little experience with survival and living in the wilderness. It made sense as she had lived a sheltered and urban life with her uncle.

By the time Leigh had a crackling fire going, we had six plump fillets ready to cook. Seasoning them with herbs from her pouch, Leigh soon had the trout sizzling merrily in her iron skillet, their savory aroma filling the glen.

While the fish cooked, I gathered wild onions and tubers to roast as I'd promised. I had already spotted plenty of them nearby, so it wasn't much work. Diane returned from her perimeter check and wordlessly took over tending the fire. Celeste refilled our canteens upstream.

Soon we were all seated around the popping fire as afternoon's gold faded. Diane passed out bowls, and we ate eagerly. The trout's flavor paired perfectly with the roasted vegetables.

Around mouthfuls, Leigh chatted about her larroling, who was snuffling contentedly nearby, trying to find some tubers of its own.

"I'm thinkin' about teaching it some tricks," she said. "Maybe I can get it to fetch me things, like... I don't know, slippers?"

I chuckled. "Or you could have it man the store."

She laughed. "What? And put poor Randal out of a job? Never!"

The mood lightened. Only Celeste remained mostly silent as she picked delicately at her food. She was new to the group and didn't know Randal, of course, but she laughed along, understanding it from the context.

When our plates were clean, we sat sipping coffee Leigh brewed, letting the hearty meal settle as the evening fully descended on us. The evening felt peaceful, but there was an undercurrent of unease centering on Celeste.

And I understood why.

Diane was still wary, from time to time eyeing our elven companion discreetly across the flickering flames. For her part, Celeste stared pensively into the fire, withdrawn. An idea struck me.

"Perhaps you could sing your song now if you're willing, Celeste?" I suggested gently. "Your music would be a perfect end to this lovely evening."

Diane shot me a subtle look, curiosity lighting up her features. She loved music, and she was undoubtedly curious to hear the elven maiden perform.

Leigh nodded eagerly. "Oh yes, please do!" she encouraged Celeste. "We'd love to hear a song! Songs around the fire are always good."

Celeste hesitated only a moment before rising gracefully to her feet. "It would be my pleasure," she said with a smile. Moving nearer the fire's warmth, she folded her hands and closed her luminous eyes.

A hush fell over the glen. Then, in her clear melodic voice, Celeste began to sing.

*"Come away, o wanderer weary,*
*Let the forest soothe your tired heart.*
*Lay your head beneath the silent stars,*
*And let their light impart…"*

*"… solace for your heavy sorrows,*
*Balm for all that causes pain.*
*Let the whispering trees enfold you,*
*Until you smile again."*

*"Be still and feel the heartbeat,*
*Of the slumbering wood.*
*Hear it murmur comfort,*
*To spirits old and good."*

*"Let the burdens that you carry,*
*Sink down to the forest floor,*
*While magic songs the nightbirds sing,*
*Lull you to dream once more."*

*"Come away, o wanderer weary,*
*Lay your restless mind to rest.*
*Leave the world you know behind you,*
*And let the wildwood bless…"*

*"… your tired eyes with wonder,*
*Your wounded soul with peace,*
*Till all that brought you sadness,*
*Fades like shadows cease."*

*"Come away, and wander here,*
*Where leaf and starlight gleam,*
*And find within this ancient wood,*

*A peace of mind serene."*

The haunting elven ballad seemed woven from moonlight and shadow, transporting us wholly. As the last eerie note faded, we sat enthralled.

"My goodness that gave me chills!" Leigh exclaimed, breaking the silence.

Diane's eyes were wide with wonder. Even she could not hide her admiration. As a fellow musician, I expected that in music their bond might strengthen.

Celeste inclined her head graciously, cheeks flushed. "You are too kind," she demurred. "It is an old lay dating back centuries. I am pleased you found beauty in it." She chuckled. "Although it is perhaps a trifle melancholy — as the songs of my kin often are."

Diane spoke up. "Few can invest such feeling into song. Is that a skill of your particular Class?" Though polite, her question probed for information we were all curious about.

Celeste smiled softly at Diane. She understood well enough what Diane wanted to find out, and she chose her words with care. "My skills were honed under many fine elven tutors." Then, she winked. "But I'm not a Bard, if that's what you're asking."

We all laughed at that, even Diane. The elven maiden had known well enough what Diane was after, and Diane was a good enough sport to deal with Celeste's quick mind and wit.

Soon enough, we were laughing and talking as loudly as we dared out here. Leigh sat forward, deftly changing the subject to recount a colorful story from her days roaming the wilds.

She regaled the tale of a dwarven Rune Singer named Breki, who sang so false that his companions preferred he held his tongue, even if that meant they did not receive the magical buffs from his singing. As she talked and imitated the dwarf's rough and coarse singing, we all laughed freely.

But as dusk deepened and Leigh's hilarious tale concluded, we began preparing for sleep. After all, we had another day of journeying ahead. I extinguished the fire while the girls made sure the cooking utensils were clean.

Still chuckling over Leigh's tale, I was happy that we had all grown a little closer over Celeste's beautiful song. Building friendship takes patience and care, of course, but the first steps had been taken.

After I took extra care to make sure there were no embers left glowing, I gazed up through the leafy boughs overhead. The velvet sky beyond shimmered with countless stars.

Feeling small beneath their ancient light, I drew a happy breath to be out in the wilderness. I loved the homestead, but being out here was something I greatly appreciated as well.

"I'll take first watch," Leigh said, rousing me from my ruminations. "You should get some sleep!" She nodded at the two tents we had pitched — one for Celeste and another for me and the girls.

I gave her a thankful nod and headed over to our tent, eager to get some rest.

# Chapter 10

I made my way to the tent, a little tired at first. It was dark, so I saw only by the grace of the dim glow of the campfire.

My heart pounded for a moment when a shadow moved, and before I knew it, Diane had tackled me. I laughed as I lay in the grass under her, her black hair burying me.

"Got you!" she purred playfully.

"You're a sneaky one, aren't you?" I teased, my fingers tangling in her silky black hair that shimmered in the starlight.

Her sapphire eyes sparkled in the dim firelight; her cheeks flushed with excitement. She tapped my chest playfully before jumping up and darting towards our tent, her bushy fox tail playfully swishing. She threw me a coy look over her shoulder, daring me to follow.

I pushed myself up and did just that, making my way into the tent. It was cozy but small. The faint scent of lavender, a hint of her presence, teased me. She was already inside, her giggles echoing softly as she shot me a blazing look.

"What are you up to?" I said, grinning.

"Oh, *nothing*," she stated, her tone teasing as she drew out the word. "But it's so hot in here."

With a playful smile, she started to undress. Her clothes fell away, revealing her athletic build, her curves, and her skin glowing in the dim light that filtered through the tent's fabric. She was a vision, lithe and sensual, and my body responded to her at once.

She saw what she was doing to me, of course, and she quickly zipped open her sleeping bag, shooting me a naughty look. She slid into it, her naked body hidden from my view.

"Ready for bed!" she claimed, her voice feigning innocence, and her eyes large. My arousal stirred, a reaction to her teasing.

"Is that so?" I asked, my voice low.

She nodded, her eyes twinkling with mischief as she continued teasing me. "Aren't you going to sleep?"

"Not in my clothes," I said, pinning her in place with my eyes.

"Oh," she hummed innocently, continuing her little game. "Well... Do you need some help undressing?" she offered, her gaze drifting down my body.

I chuckled, my hands moving to the buttons on my shirt. "Sure, but if you come close to me with no clothes on..." I gave her a grin. "There's no telling what might happen next."

Her laughter filled the small tent as she climbed out of her sleeping bag, her eyes watching my every move, as she came over to me on all fours. Her delicious naked body was all I could see, her lithe movements revealing what a pleasure she was in bed.

"I'll just have to be extra careful," she hummed.

Diane's hands met mine, stopping my own movements as I was still working on my shirt.

"Let me," she whispered, her fingers working diligently on my buttons. Her touch was soft, delicate, and it sent shivers down my spine.

I let her do the work, her hands exploring my body as she undressed me. The touch of her fingers on my chest made my heart race, her fingernails grazing my skin, leaving trails of heat in their wake.

Every button undone was like a small victory, her hands sliding over my bare chest, her touch growing bolder. She traced the lines of my abs, her fingers dipping into the grooves of my muscles. The soft gasp that escaped her lips made me grow harder.

I had to fight myself not to grab her up, but I knew she was playing a little game to build desire. And I was going to play along.

My heart pounded in my chest as she lowered herself to her knees, her fingers moving to my belt. I watched as she unbuckled it, her movements slow, teasing.

With a deftness that surprised me, she unzipped my jeans and pulled them down, along with my boxers. I was left standing naked in front of her, my erection visible in the dim light.

She took a moment to admire my body, her eyes traveling over my muscular form. Her gaze lingered on my cock, her lips parting slightly. I could feel my arousal building, fueled by her appreciation.

"You look so good," she whispered, her eyes meeting mine. I could see her desire, mirrored in my own, burning in her sapphire gaze.

I reached out and pulled her towards me, my hands moving over the curves of her body. Her skin was soft, warm under my touch, yielding. I traced the lines of her figure, my fingers lingering on the swell of her breasts, the dip of her waist, the curve of her hips.

She let out a soft sigh as I explored her body, her eyes closing in pleasure that only the touch of a trusted and familiar lover can rouse. I could feel her body react to me, her nipples hardening under my fingers, her body arching into me.

My hand moved lower, tracing the line of her thigh, moving upwards. Her breath hitched as my fingers brushed against her wetness, a soft moan escaping her lips.

She reached out and touched my cock, her fingers wrapping around my girth. Her touch made me grunt with desire, my cock twitching in response.

She gave a soft giggle as she slowly teased my weapon with the tips of her fingers, her eyes sparkling with mischief.

"I can't wait to feel you inside me tonight," she purred, her voice a whisper. Her words made my arousal spike, my desire for her overwhelming.

"Sweet Diane," I hummed, my voice thick with desire as I pulled her closer. "You're going to get just that."

She responded with a teasing smile, her hand stroking my cock, her touch driving me wild. Already, a bead of precum gathered on my tip, and she scooped it up with a finger and lapped it away as I kept kneading her delicious breasts, losing myself in her slight lavender scent.

I pushed her back onto the bedroll, her body laid bare beneath me. Her breathing was heavy, her chest rising and falling rapidly.

Diane's fox ears twitched, a sign of her anticipation. There was always something innocent about her, even as she teased, and that only served to drive me wilder.

I moved over her, my body hovering above hers. I could feel the heat radiating from her body, her tail brushing my leg with its softness.

As I kissed her deeply, her heart pounded against my chest, her body trembling beneath me in anticipation. Her fingers tangled in my hair, pulling me closer.

As we kissed, Diane's hands roamed my back, her nails digging into my skin. I groaned at the sensation, my cock throbbing against her thigh. She replied by writhing her perfect body beneath me, her moans encouraging me — she wanted me to enter her, but I needed this moment to last.

I moved my hand down her body, my fingers finding her wetness. She gasped and moaned my name, her body arching off the bedroll. I watched as pleasure washed over her face, her eyes fluttering closed.

Watching her surrender like that, I allowed my fingers to dance over her, my touch light and teasing. Her body responded to my touch, her legs spreading wider, inviting me closer. I could feel her heat, her desire matching my own.

"Please," she whispered, her voice filled with need. "Oh David... It feels so nice."

I could feel her body tighten, her breaths coming in short gasps. I slowed my movements, my fingers leaving her. Her eyes fluttered open, her gaze meeting mine, filled with desire and anticipation.

"I'm going to give you everything you want," I said, my need taking control. "And more..."

She grinned and bit her plump lower lip.

"Good," she purred.

Diane lay on the bedroll before me like a prize, naked and waiting to be claimed. Her skin shone with the dim glow that crept into our tent, and all I wanted was to kiss every inch of her delicious body.

Her sapphire eyes were wide and filled with anticipation, her lips slightly parted as she watched me with an intoxicating mix of love and lust.

I crawled towards her, my eyes roving over her form. Her breasts, firm and round, were teasing me, their pink nipples hardened with arousal. I took one into my mouth, flicking my tongue over the sensitive peak, eliciting a gasp from her.

"D-David..." she whimpered, her fingers tangling into my hair. Her fox ears quivered, and her tail twitched with each lick, each suckle.

I continued to lavish my attention on her chest, alternating between her breasts with a wicked grin.

The taste of her skin was intoxicating, sweet and slightly salty.

Moving lower, I traced a path down her tummy with soft kisses. My hands glided over her flanks, feeling the smooth texture of her skin, the gentle curve of her waist. Her lower tummy was soft and warm, my lips peppering it with kisses, making her squirm.

I parted her legs slowly, revealing her to my eager gaze. Her pussy was wet and inviting, the sight making my cock twitch in anticipation. I leaned in, inhaling her scent, my tongue darting out to taste her.

Diane let out a sharp gasp as I kissed her pussy, her body arching off the bedroll.

"David!" she cried out, gripping the sleeping bag tightly. Her knees trembled, her thighs quaking as I pleasured her.

I moaned against her, the taste of her driving me wild. I lapped at her, my tongue swirling around her clit, my fingers delving into her warmth. Her tail thrashed wildly behind her, a testament to her pleasure.

Diane's moans filled the tent, the sound making me harder. Her breasts jiggled as her body convulsed, her hands moving to tease her nipples. Her eyes were half-lidded, her lips parted in a silent moan.

I took my time, savoring every whimper, every twitch of her body. My tongue played with her clit, flicking it, sucking it, while my fingers explored her depths. The feel of her was intoxicating, her muscles clenching around my fingers, her body writhing in pleasure.

"David... oh gods, David..." she moaned, her fingers curling into my hair. Her breath hitched as I picked up my pace, her body arching off the bedroll.

I could feel my own arousal growing, the taste of her, the sounds she made, all driving me to the edge. But I held back, wanting to fulfill her pleasure first. My tongue delved deeper, my fingers curling up within her to tease her G-spot.

Diane's moans turned into cries, her body shaking as her climax neared. Her thighs tightened around my head, her hands gripping my hair.

"Yes…" she stammered, her breath coming in ragged gasps.

I didn't let up, my tongue continuing its assault on her sensitive flesh, my fingers pumping into her. She was close, so close. I could feel her walls clenching around my fingers, her body trembling with the intensity of her pleasure.

"David!" she cried out, her body convulsing. "I'm… Ahnn! I'm cumming!"

It only made me speed up. Her climax hit her hard, her muscles spasming around my fingers as I lapped her into submission. Her cries echoed in the tent, her body shaking with the force of her orgasm.

I didn't stop until her tremors subsided, my tongue teasing and stimulating her until she could only mumble my name. Finally, as she gave her last spasm, I pulled away and surveyed the result of what I had done.

She lay before me, panting and exhausted, her body glistening with sweat. Her fox ears were flat against her head, her tail limp under her. Her eyes were glazed with satisfaction, a small smile playing on her lips.

"David," she purred, reaching for me. "That was too good…"

Her fingers traced down my chest, over my abs, stopping just short of my throbbing cock. The sight of her, naked and spent, was too much.

I moved up, pressing my body against hers, capturing her lips in a heated kiss. She tasted wild and fresh, a heady combination that made my head spin. I could feel her body relaxing under me, her hands roaming over my back.

My cock throbbed against her thigh, my body aching for release. She shifted her position, and the tip of my cock touched her pussy. She was warm against my cock, her juices coating me.

"You feel so good," I groaned, my voice hoarse.

Diane moaned into my mouth, her hips shifting against mine. She was tempting me, teasing me, her eyes filled with desire. Her fingers trailed down my back, making me hiss in pleasure.

I pulled away from her lips, my breath ragged as my hands moved to cup her breasts. Her nipples were still hard, her skin hot to the touch.

"David," she breathed, her eyes locked onto mine. "Take me," she whispered, her voice thick with desire. Her eyes were pleading, her body trembling with anticipation.

She was driving me crazy, making me lose control. My cock throbbed against her pussy, my body aching for release.

But I held back, wanting to hear her beg, to see her eyes filled with desire. And so I rose, shooting her the most teasing look as I severed the connection between our bodies.

Diane whimpered, her body arching off the bedroll as if she would impale herself on my cock. Her tail twitched; her ears quivered.

"David," she whimpered, her eyes pleading. "Please..."

I kissed her again, my tongue delving into her mouth. The taste of her was intoxicating, her body pressing against mine. I could feel her warmth, her softness, her desire. Her body was writhing beneath me, her hips shifting against mine.

I could no longer postpone my own desires. She squirmed before me, ready to be claimed, and I would not refuse that call.

Diane yelped and giggled as I grabbed her ankles and pulled her toward me, my eyes a possessive fire raking her beautiful body.

"David," she squealed, her fox ears twitching with anticipation, "I need you. Please, fuck me." Her voice was desperate, a raw yearning that twisted my guts with lust.

I could only grunt in response, my brain short-circuiting at the sight of her laid bare before me. Her body was a symphony of curves, her black hair spilling over her shoulders, shimmering in the dim light. Her sapphire eyes sparkled with desire, and I shared the sensation deeply.

I moved the tip of my weapon to her entrance; my body now poised to claim hers. My cock, rock hard and aching, nudged against her wetness once more.

Her tail twitched, brushing against my thighs,

and I felt her shudder beneath me.

"Yes," she moaned, her hand reaching down to guide me in. "Fuck me. Breed me." Her words were a command, a plea, a sweet surrender.

I pushed forward, the tip of my cock parting her folds. A gasp left her lips as I entered her, her tight warmth enveloping me. She was so wet, so ready for me. I slipped deeper and deeper, making her enclose me in her embrace.

And after I had bottomed out, I began to move, each thrust sending a shiver through both our bodies.

Her body bounced beneath me, her breasts swaying with each thrust. The sight was intoxicating, driving me to push deeper, harder. The sounds she made were music to my ears, each moan, each gasp, feeding my desire.

Her hands roamed my back, her nails digging into my flesh. The pain was sweet, a sharp counterpoint to the pleasure coursing through me. I groaned, the sound vibrating through her.

"David," she whimpered, her eyes glazed with lust. "Harder. Please… Ahhnn… Give it to me!"

I obliged, picking up the pace, pounding into her with reckless abandon. She was mine, and I was going to make her feel it. With every thrust, I bottomed out inside her, making her yelp with delight.

Her body arched beneath me, her muscles tightening around me. She was close, so close. I could see it in her eyes, could feel it in the way her body responded to mine.

My own pleasure was rising as well, a furious desire to empty myself inside her. But still, I fought it off, wanting the play to last.

Suddenly, a sound pierced through the haze of pleasure. A rustle, a gasp.

I turned my head, my gaze landing on a silhouette outside our tent, drawn in moonlight. It was a female figure watching us, decidedly so. For a moment, I considered it was Leigh, having a little fun of her own...

But then Diane's hands were on my cheeks, turning my head to look at her. "David," she breathed, her eyes wide and filled with need. "Don't stop."

I didn't. I couldn't. Not when she looked at me like that, not when she felt so good around me. I thrust harder, faster, driving us both to the brink, the female figure outside the tent forgotten.

Her body convulsed beneath me, her nails digging into my back as I drove her over the edge and made her cum.

"David," she cried out, her voice a sweet symphony that sang of pleasure and release. "Oh! Gods! I'm cumming!"

Her pussy tightened on me as I slammed into her again, the wet sound of our skin slapping together all I could hear, the scent of our sex all I could smell. I watched her as her second orgasm of the night undid her, my heart pounding in my chest as she rode out the wave of pleasure.

Her body tightened around me, drawing me in deeper, her arms pulling me closer. Her legs wrapped around me, pushing me as her body desired my seed. I could feel her walls pulsating around me, milking me for all I was worth.

"Ahhn... Breed me, David," she begged, her voice a desperate whisper.

With a grunt of lust, my body moving on its own accord. I thrust into her, again and again, each movement bringing me closer to the edge. Sweat trickled down my forehead, my muscles aching with exertion.

"Diane," I groaned, my voice raw with pleasure. I could feel the pressure building, my body tensing in anticipation.

"Yes, David," she urged, her hands clutching at my shoulders. "Give it to me, my love. Cum in me!"

I thrust one last time, my cock buried deep within her as I came. I could feel my release, hot and potent, filling her. She gasped, her body arching beneath me as I painted her insides with my seed.

My mind emptied as I filled her up. In that moment, my whole world was in Diane's arms, wrapped around her, pressed against her, giving her my all. Kissing her neck as she hummed sweet words, I gave one final push, and then remained on top of her, our bodies entwined.

We remained like that for a moment, her body

still trembling beneath mine, my cock still twitching inside her. I could feel her heartbeat, steady and strong against my chest.

At length, I brushed a stray lock of hair from her face, my fingers trailing down her cheek. Her eyes fluttered open, meeting mine. They were filled with contentment, with satisfaction, with love.

"David," she murmured, her voice barely a whisper.

I leaned down, capturing her lips in a tender kiss, as I pulled out of her, some of my seed trickling out of her. She gave a small whimper, her body missing the connection.

I moved to her side, pulling her into my arms. She snuggled into my chest, her tail curling around my waist. I could hear her soft purrs, a soothing melody that lulled me into a sense of peace.

With a delighted moan, I pulled the sleeping bag over our naked bodies for warmth, and she gave a pleased little purr as she looked up at me with loving eyes.

Naked, sweaty, and panting, Diane and I huddled under the sleeping bag together. Her fox tail brushed against my bare skin, eliciting a shudder from me. Her sapphire eyes sparkled in the moonlight, mirroring the lust and satisfaction that were evident in mine.

"David," she whispered, her voice husky from our lovemaking, "that was... really hot." Her fingers traced the muscles in my chest, causing my heart to pound louder.

The corners of my lips curled up into a grin. I liked hearing her admit how much she enjoyed it, especially when she looked so shy and demure.

"I loved it too," I replied, tugging her closer to me. Her tail coiled around me, the soft fur tickling my skin pleasantly. I let my hand trace over her soft belly. "I can't say I mind all this work we put in to get you pregnant," I joked.

She laughed and gave me a playful swat before

her eyes turned dreamy. "I can't wait to have your kits," she murmured, resting her head against my chest before she let out a long yawn.

"Neither can I," I agreed.

Her fox ears twitched slightly, a sign that she was slowly drifting off to sleep.

I spent a few moments watching her as she drifted into sleep, her breasts rising and falling with each breath. The dim light spilled over her body, highlighting her curves, making her look even more beautiful.

Satisfied, I pulled on my pants and slipped out from the tent, the cool forest air nipping at my bare skin. Nature called, and I wanted to check with Leigh about the silhouette I'd seen.

The forest was alive with the sounds of the night. The gurgling of the nearby creek was a soothing melody, accompanied by the rustling of the leaves and the hooting of distant owls.

Leigh was standing guard, her voluptuous figure bathed in moonlight. She had my rifle with her, and she kept it close as she peered at the trees. Her blonde hair, reflecting the silver rays of the moon, hung loose around her shoulders.

"See anything interesting?" I asked, my voice breaking the silence of the night.

Leigh turned towards me, her blue eyes sparkling with mischief. A blush spread across her cheeks as she bit her lower lip.

"Well, first off, I *heard* somethin' interesting," she hummed.

I laughed. "Yeah, Diane had a little plan for tonight."

"Hm-hm," she hummed. "Well, you two had a sneaky lil' spectator," she said, her eyes twinkling with amusement.

I raised an eyebrow at her, trying to suppress the grin that was threatening to spread across my face. "Who?" I demanded, playing along with her teasing and still fully expecting it had been her.

Leigh leaned closer to me, her ample breasts brushing against my arm. Her scent, hinting of the wilderness we had braved today, was intoxicating.

"It was Celeste," she whispered, her voice barely audible over the sounds of the forest.

"*Celeste*, huh?" I hummed.

I couldn't help the grin that spread across my face. The thought of Celeste watching Diane and me was intriguing, to say the least.

"And, baby," Leigh continued, her voice dropping to a low whisper, "I believe I saw her… *touching* herself."

She pulled back, a triumphant smile on her face. Leigh loved to tease, and she knew exactly how to push my buttons.

"Really?" I asked, a hint of surprise in my voice.

Leigh nodded, her smile never faltering. The thought of Celeste pleasuring herself to the sight of Diane and me was both surprising and exciting.

"Well," I said, "That's certainly some interesting information."

Leigh let out a throaty laugh, her eyes dancing with excitement. "I'll say, baby. I think she's got the hots for ya!"

I shook my head at her, trying to suppress my own laughter. "We'll see!"

She shot me a wink. "Now go on, join that poor Diane before she gets cold!"

I nodded, still chuckling. With a lingering glance

at Leigh, I stepped out of the radius of the camp and did my business.

My mind was buzzing with thoughts of Celeste. I could almost imagine her, kneeling in the verdant grass, her slim fingers dancing over her body while watching Diane and me.

I couldn't help but feel a sense of satisfaction. Celeste was always so reserved, so elusive. It was a thrill to know that she had a carnal side, that she was affected by our lovemaking.

I entered the tent and slid back into the sleeping bag next to Diane. Her breaths were slow and steady, a clear sign that she was deep in sleep. I wrapped an arm around her, pulling her closer to me.

As I lay there, I found my mind wandering back to Celeste. The thought of the elven maiden, of her lustful side, was intriguing. It was a side of her that I hadn't seen before, a side of her that I wanted to explore further.

Still smiling, I closed my eyes, my mind filled with thoughts of Celeste and of the possibilities that lay ahead.

# Chapter 11

The next morning, we awoke energized and eager for another day of marching through the verdant forest. A light mist still clung to the underbrush as we stirred to leave our cozy nests of blankets. The day's march beckoned, so after a quick breakfast we doused the fire and prepared to depart.

Diane took the lead once more as we hiked briskly to warm up stiff muscles, picking up yesterday's route north. Droplets of dew spangled each fern frond and leaf, glittering like countless tiny jewels in the sunshine. The beauty of the living forest never failed to lift my spirits.

We spoke little, voices hushed so as not to disturb the serene woodland ambiance. Our footsteps seemed to blend harmoniously into the surrounding wildlife's subtle rhythms.

At times, Celeste softly hummed wandering melodies that complemented the tranquil atmosphere. When I caught her gaze, she blushed and looked away, no doubt recalling what she had done yesterday, but I decided not to confront her... at least, not yet. Let her have her little pleasures.

By midmorning we reached more open country. Sun-warmed meadows rippled under fleeting cloud shadows and stands of timber gradually yielded to rolling grassland. Far ahead, the jagged Shimmering Peaks jutted skyward, but still lay distant.

"We'll arrive tomorrow evening," Diane said,

shielding her eyes from the sun as she peered at those majestic peaks.

I nodded. "According to schedule, then. That's good. You've done well leading us, Diane. You're a great Scout."

She smiled at me. "Things will get more dangerous once we touch the foothills," she said. "And we should keep our eyes open for any traces of Clara's party."

"We will," I agreed. "For now, let's continue."

When the path dwindled to little more than a faded furrow amidst the waving grass, Diane paused, tasting the breeze with pricked ears. Apparently satisfied with the direction, she continued on confidently, and we matched her tireless pace.

Around noon, dark clouds began roiling on the horizon as a storm approached. Hurrying, we took shelter in a rocky gorge flanked by outcroppings of granite just as the first raindrops began to fall.

Huddling beneath the natural stone overhang, we watched the gathering gale lash the meadow grass violently. Thunder rumbled overhead, making even Leigh jump nervously. Lying beside her, the larroling yawned, nonplussed by the tumult.

The tempest's fury soon diminished to a steady downpour, and we decided to resume our trek. After all, we didn't know how long the storm would last, and there was a sense of urgency to our mission — who knew what Clara and her party members were going through?

And so, we set out in the rain. Before long, even our water-repelling clothing was drenched. Diane still took the lead, furry tail dripping, and seemed the least put down by nature's show of force.

Leigh and Celeste, however, were no fans of rain, it seemed. Even the normally so optimistic blonde seemed a little down as she walked along, drenched to the bone.

By late afternoon, only sporadic drizzle remained. With one final thunderclap, the clouds began breaking up, revealing watery shafts of sunlight. We continued our soggy hike across the meadows, making for a craggy bluff in the distance that would provide dry shelter for the coming night.

Wading through the marshy grass left boots soaked, and water trickled annoyingly down my collar. But the storm's fury had passed overhead, leaving the landscape scrubbed clean. Birds sang tentatively as the sun reemerged.

Reaching the bluff as dusk fell; we assessed its pockmarked surface until Leigh spotted a likely cave. A quick search revealed the shallow cavern to be unoccupied, so we gratefully shrugged off our packs and began making camp.

While I gathered more firewood along the bluff's drier base, finding good pieces that were relatively dry, Diane disappeared to scout our location, making sure that there would be no surprises at night. She soon returned, indicating that we were in a safe place.

That night we feasted happily on our provisions, enjoying pasta with a sauce of tomatoes and dried meat. The cheerful firelight danced over the stone walls as we talked and laughed together. The mood seemed lighter now that we were getting to know each other, and Celeste sang us another song that definitely won Diane's admiration.

When the embers had burned low, I offered to take first watch for a few hours beneath the glittering swath of stars visible through the cave's mouth. We would be safe here, but it never hurt to keep eyes peeled. The others gratefully rolled into blankets, tired muscles craving rest. I watched our camp with the larroling, although the beast was soon asleep itself.

The following dawn brought clear blue skies with barely a wisp of cloud marring the horizon's serene expanse. Sunlight spilling into the cave roused us one by one to begin breakfast. I smiled seeing Diane offer Celeste an apple as they started breaking down camp together.

Bellies full, we continued along the bluff studying the sweeping vistas all around for landmarks. The Shimmering Peaks now dominated the northern skyline, bold and imposing. We were drawing steadily nearer to their lower foothills.

When the bluff petered out, our path led down into a shaded hollow spanned by an ancient stone bridge over a rushing stream, undoubtedly a relic from Tannoris, placed here during the Upheaval. Though worn by centuries of weathering, the elegant arch still felt reassuringly solid underfoot.

By day's end, foothills began rising around us in place of the grassy lowlands. These were the leading edge of the Shimmering Peaks' vast domain. Scanning them, I glimpsed specks wheeling in the distance that might have been eagles riding the thermals. The scale of this place was daunting.

"We should be on our guard," I cautioned the women. "This is the domain of the kobolds, the goblins, and the orcs. When we set out on the trail to Hrothgar's Hope tomorrow, I want Diane scouting ahead at all times."

The girls nodded agreement, each of them taking on a more grim countenance at the realization that danger could easily find us here.

We searched until Leigh spotted a suitable cave set into one stony ridge side. A small fire kindled in its mouth helped ward off the evening's chill.

Tomorrow we would ascend into the peaks proper, climbing treacherous slopes. But tonight, it was enough to share a warm meal beneath the glittering sky and listen to Celeste quietly sing once more, warming our hearts for the task to come.

# Chapter 12

The next morning, I was on watch as the girls awoke to a crisp chill in the air. Dawn's light was just creeping over the jagged horizon as I stirred the embers of last night's fire, coaxing a cheery blaze. We would need hot coffee and food to fortify us for the arduous hike into the peaks.

While I prepared breakfast, the girls broke camp swiftly and efficiently, with the larroling patrolling. Diane scouted the trail ahead, ears pricked for any sounds of danger. Leigh hummed merrily as she rolled up blankets despite the early hour.

Even Celeste had begun pitching in without hesitation, slowly finding her rhythm in our group. As I had predicted, song and time spent together would forge the bond we needed.

Soon we were gathered around the crackling fire sipping steaming mugs of coffee and watching strips of dried meat sizzle in the skillet. Our breath fogged in the brisk foothill air. Above, the lightening sky heralded a clear day ideal for hiking.

Diane returned just as Leigh began dishing out breakfast. "All's quiet ahead for now," she reported, tail swishing cautiously. "But keep weapons close. We're nearing the domain of less friendly inhabitants."

Nodding grimly, I checked my rifle and handgun while Diane and Leigh ensured their own weapons were easily reachable and ready for use. Celeste still carried the long object wrapped in furs, but she did not check on it.

Stomachs full and weapons ready, we set off up the steady incline. The rising sun lent strength to tired legs. Before long, the cave's dark mouth receded into the distance behind us. Aside from the birdsongs and distant cries of eagles, a brooding silence surrounded our small party as we finally approached the Shimmering Peaks.

The larroling brought up the rear, plowing steadily upwards despite its stocky bulk. Leigh at times placed one hand lightly atop its shaggy head, reinforcing their bond. At times the great beast huffed uncomfortably in the thinning air.

By late morning, jagged peaks loomed all around, framing a magnificent but unforgiving landscape. We paused to gulp water from our canteens. The thin air left me winded. Looking back, the sweeping grasslands now seemed a lifetime away.

Diane scouted ahead once more while we caught our breath. My eyes roamed warily over the rocky terrain. If enemies lurked nearby, we would be vulnerable. Every nerve felt taut as a bowstring.

At last, Diane returned, her expression grave. "There's a crumbling watchtower just over the next ridge," she reported tersely. "And shapes moving that could be goblins or kobolds. Almost a dozen."

I swore under my breath. Goblins and kobolds already. It made sense that they were watching the trail up Hrothgar's Hope.

"Did they spot you?" I asked.

Diane shook her head.

"Then we have a moment to strategize."

I turned to the others. "If we engage, I can summon allies, and I'm hoping it will be enough."

Leigh grinned fiercely, one hand falling to rest on her revolver's grip. "My larroling is gonna help us make short work of those little bastards!"

Despite the threat, her brazen spirit seemed undimmed. The larroling gave a throaty grunt that seemed to signal it agreed with its mistress.

Celeste remained silent, porcelain features taut. I offered what I hoped was a reassuring smile. "Stay behind us, and you should be safe," I told her.

She shook her head. "But I can fight," she said. "I

may not be very good at all this wilderness survival, but I have combat skills."

I studied her for a moment. The elven maiden had a sprightly build — certainly not the muscular frame that I would expect from a melee combatant. If the thing she had been lugging around was a sword, it would be a large one, and I wondered if she would be able to use it.

Leigh and Diane eyed Celeste with curiosity as well, and I saw a measure of skepticism in their eyes. They, too, struggled to accept that the dainty elf would be capable of dishing out much damage in melee.

"Celeste," I said gently, "if you want us to allow you to fight alongside us, we will need to know what exactly you are capable of."

She considered my words for a moment, weighing them as she pursed her lips. Finally, she gave a resolved nod and retrieved the long item wrapped in furs.

With delicate care, she unwrapped it, revealing a beautifully adorned longsword that would have taken quite the burly knight to wield in combat.

"You can't possibly mean to say that's your weapon?" Diane objected, voicing what we were all thinking. "Can you even lift it over your head?"

Celeste's cheeks flushed, but there was strong conviction in the way she nodded her pretty head.

"I can," she assured us. "I know I may not look the part, but... there are Class abilities in play that make me a capable combatant."

I exchanged a look with Leigh and Diane before returning to Celeste. "So, what *is* your Class?"

"I... I cannot say," she hummed. "It is a forbidden Class."

"A forbidden Class?" I echoed, eyebrow raised.

She nodded. "Yes, my kin — the elves — do not look kindly upon it. That is all I can say."

"Alright," I said, running a hand over my stubble.

It was a difficult position. On the one hand, I needed to know who was fighting alongside us. But on the other, I did not want to violate her wish to keep her Class to herself. If she wanted to keep it private, then that was her right.

I glanced at Leigh and Diane. Leigh shrugged,

signaling that she was willing to accept Celeste's explanation. Diane, however, seemed a little more reserved, narrowing her eyes at the elf.

There was one way to resolve it.

"Celeste," I said. "I can accept you wanting to keep your Class secret. But if you want to fight alongside us, you will have to show what you are capable of."

She gave a solemn nod and rose slowly, and my eye was at once drawn to how easily and casually she held that big sword in one hand.

"Very well," she hummed. "I will demonstrate my weapon skill to you."

Celeste walked a short distance away from the group and took up a ready position, holding the longsword at her side. She closed her eyes for a moment as if mentally preparing. When she opened them again, her green eyes seemed to glitter with an inner light.

In a blur, she launched into motion, swinging the heavy blade in precise arcs and thrusts that would have taken immense strength to control. Yet Celeste handled the sword as if it were an extension of her own body, never faltering. The sword gleamed dangerously as it sliced through the air.

We watched in awe as Celeste demonstrated flawless swordsmanship, the long blade moving with grace and speed that seemed impossible for her slender frame. She performed lunges, parries, ripostes, and more in quick succession, showing perfect form and finesse.

With a fierce cry, Celeste leapt into the air far higher than any normal jump and brought the sword crashing down in a powerful overhead slash. The impact when the blade struck the earth sent out a visible shockwave and left a small crater behind.

"Good gracious!" Leigh exclaimed, wide-eyed.

The rest of us were too stunned to speak. Celeste's dainty appearance hid shocking combat abilities.

Turning to face us, Celeste neatly sheathed the enormous sword across her back once more. Her cheeks were only slightly flushed from the exertion of her dazzling demonstration.

"I know it seems improbable," she said softly. "But I assure you, I am able to fight."

"I'd say that's putting it mildly," I managed, shaking my head in continued disbelief. "You clearly have extraordinary talents. That was... incredible swordsmanship."

Beside me, Diane and Leigh nodded mutely in awed agreement.

"But how..." Diane began when she found her voice again. "You wield that blade with such power and precision. How is that possible?" She eyed Celeste with newfound respect mingled with puzzlement. "You shouldn't even be able to lift it so high and so long!"

Celeste gave a cryptic smile. "Let us just say that my class provides certain battle enhancements that allow me to use this sword to its full potential." She rested one hand lightly on the hilt where it protruded above her slender shoulder.

I studied Celeste thoughtfully. It was obvious now that she harbored impressive martial abilities and the restraint to keep them hidden until the need arose. Though I would have never taken her for a melee class, I felt a touch of guilt for doubting her word.

"You've more than demonstrated your skills are up to the task," I acknowledged sincerely.

Beside me, Leigh and Diane nodded agreement.

"Please forgive my skepticism," Diane said. "You're clearly a good ally to have in battle."

Celeste inclined her head graciously. "You had fair reason to question. But I am thankful you allowed me to prove myself." Her luminous gaze met mine. "All I ask is that you continue to trust me, going forward."

I reached out and clasped her slender shoulder. "You've earned that trust today. We would be honored to have you fighting at our side." Leigh gave Celeste an approving thumbs up.

Diane stepped forward next. Though she still eyed Celeste cautiously, she extended a hand. "My apologies for doubting you," she offered sincerely.

"I can admit when I'm wrong."

After a brief hesitation, Celeste shook Diane's hand with a hint of a smile. I grinned at the sight, knowing that the two were growing closer still.

With Celeste's fighting abilities no longer in question, we gathered to discuss strategy. A dozen enemies lay just over the next ridge, but the advantage of surprise was ours. Together, we devised a cunning plan of attack.

"If we strike fast, they won't have time to flee and alert others," I reasoned, outlining a simple but effective plan of ambush. Celeste and Leigh would take the left flank, using the larroling to break their ranks. Meanwhile, Diane and I would assault from the right with my summoned allies. In this way, we would divide their defenses.

Diane traced a rough map in the dirt with a stick, showing lines of attack converging on the crumbling tower where she had spotted them. "We'll have to hit hard and fast once we engage," she cautioned. "No hesitation."

"We approach in silence," I said. "Try to stay out of sight so we can surprise them."

"There is concealment along this line," Diane said, pointing with her stick at the map she had drawn. "Bushes and rocks. It should work."

Celeste nodded grimly, her sword at the ready. "I will charge in," she said, "as is my style."

I nodded. "My summons and the larroling will aid and protect you," I said, "and we will focus our fire on the goblins not in melee with you."

"Yeehaw, we've got this!" Leigh cheered, pumping a fist.

Beside her, the massive larroling grunted as if in agreement. Its huge claws scraped the earth impatiently.

Checking my rifle and handgun one final time, I gave the others a resolute nod. My heart hammered with adrenaline, but we had the element of surprise.

"Let's go then," I said. "We end this quickly."

Moving in swift silence, we approached the last ridge separating us from our quarry. Tension mounted with each step. I summoned an Aquana's avatar and a guardian in preparation as we neared the crest and the first glimpse of the ruined tower.

Diane sank low, crossbow at the ready as we crept nearer using available cover — shrubs and boulders. To my left, Celeste moved with scarcely a whisper of sound despite the enormous sword across her back, every muscle coiled in readiness.

Eyes blazing, Leigh kept one hand atop the crouched larroling, holding it in check until she would unleash it as a wrecking ball against the unsuspecting raiders. Step by careful step, we closed in.

The larroling's snarls were muffled by Leigh's restraining hand. It could sense the coming mayhem. My own fingers tightened around the rifle stock as we reached the ideal ambush point and prepared to strike. The moment to unleash chaos was nearly at hand...

# Chapter 13

With bated breath, we slowly crept up the ridge toward the goblins' camp, moving with utmost care to remain hidden. My heart pounded adrenaline through my veins as the crumbling watchtower finally came into view just over the crest.

Those goblins had no inkling of the doom about to descend upon them.

Gesturing for the others to hold position, I slowly raised my head above the crest just enough to glimpse the enemy camp. There, clustered lazily around a smoky campfire surrounded by scattered refuse and bones, were nearly a dozen goblins. The creatures were preoccupied gnawing noisily on the grisly remains of some recent kill, oblivious to our presence.

Their crude spears and rust-pitted blades lay discarded within easy reach should an alarm sound. But for now, the brutes seemed lost in their repast of stringy, blood-slick meat. Yellow eyes glinted with malice beneath jutting brows as they hungrily tore at sinews with jagged teeth.

The light etched their rotund, warty faces in flickering illumination that lent their features an even more sinister cast. Guttural snarls and grunts carried faintly as the loathsome creatures quarreled and jostled among themselves between ravenous bites. The gory feast fueled their naturally violent natures.

My lip curled in disgust at the vile display, but I lingered a moment more, carefully double-checking their numbers and studying the camp layout for tactical advantages. Through hand signals, I indicated for the others to be ready. Our moment to strike was nearly at hand.

Sensing their anticipation, I met each of my companions' eyes in turn. Celeste's delicate brows were drawn together with quiet focus, both hands resting on the long hilt of her sheathed blade as she awaited my signal. The light flickered across her smooth features, but no hesitation showed in her luminous gaze.

Leigh crouched beside the restless bulk of her larroling, keeping one calming hand upon its shaggy neck to hold the eager beast in check. But her own blue eyes blazed with readiness, every line of her frame taut with coiled energy like a drawn bowstring. At my word, she would release the beast, and then fire with her revolver.

Lastly, I glanced at Diane, taking strength from her closeness where she knelt poised beside me. Her delicate profile was etched with grim purpose, eyes narrowed intently upon our unsuspecting quarry. Sensing my gaze, she gave a subtle, confident nod. We were ready.

With a final deep breath, I gestured sharply and rose swiftly from concealment. Leigh released her grip on the larroling with a jubilant cry as we broke cover. The great beast lunged over the crest of the ridge with a thunderous roar, barreling down the slope straight towards the startled goblins.

My guardian and Aquana's avatar followed closely behind, the water elemental sloshing as it raised its fists. Celeste followed them, unsheathing her great blade with a dexterous swoop.

Shrieks of shock and dismay split the air as the larroling smashed through the goblin camp with the force of an avalanche. Gnawed bones flew wildly, and the cook fire scattered in an explosion of embers as the beast plowed through, a whirlwind of rending claws and crushing bulk.

Before the goblins could even gather their scattered wits and weapons, Celeste descended upon them with blinding speed. The ornate blade seemed to take on a life of its own as she drew it forth, the steel burning with a cold blue light to match the battle fury blazing in her eyes.

With lethal grace, she spun and sliced through their ranks in a scintillating dance of death. Dark ichor sprayed wildly as the singing sword cleaved limbs from bodies and opened broad swathes of red ruin across flesh and armor alike. The goblins fell in pieces around her, powerless before her onslaught.

My guardian took position beside her, protecting her from the rusty blades and spear tips of the goblins. At the same time, Aquana's avatar brought its fists to bear, smashing into the goblins as they shrieked and scrambled for their weapons.

From my position, I brought my rifle to bear upon the first goblin trying frantically to crawl away from Celeste's whirlwind assault. It collapsed with a bubbling shriek as my shot pierced one bulging eye — the first kill of our combined volley raining mercilessly down.

All around me, the ridge exploded with violence. Diane's crossbow sang again and again, each steel-tipped bolt unerringly finding its mark in goblin flesh while Leigh whooped with wild abandon, emptying her revolver's chambers into the roiling fray.

The larroling rampaged unchecked through the heart of the camp, each swipe of its claws now leaving ragged red arcs across the darkness. Shrieks rose in pitch and agony as it crushed writhing bodies beneath its massive bulk, churning the hard earth into a slurry of gore and trampled filth.

Mere heartbeats had passed, yet fully half the goblins already lay dead or dying. But still, the survivors rallied desperately, brandishing crude spears and axes as they charged towards Celeste's graceful silhouette, murder in their beady eyes. It was time to tip the scales further.

Raising my left hand, I summoned a storm elemental with an effort of will. The air crackled as motes of light coalesced into the towering form of a living thundercloud. Without hesitation, it surged forth, blasting arcs of lightning.

Celeste leapt agilely aside as the elemental plowed into the remaining knot of goblins seeking to overwhelm her, scattering them like leaves as it crackled with the fury of a storm. Cursing and flailing wildly, the creatures were helplessly electrocuted and fried by the elemental's raw power.

Triumph rising within me, I took aim once more and picked off a goblin attempting to desperately scale the crumbling watchtower's facade in search of refuge. It did not reach the top alive, my shots driving it down to sprawl twisted on the hard ground below.

The last of the goblins died swiftly in the closing moments of our ambush — one with a round from Leigh's revolver through its heart, and the final survivor with Diane's crossbow quarrel sprouted between its shoulders. None would escape alive.

As the last wails and whimpers faded upon the wind, quiet descended over the charnel scene. I rose cautiously, scanning the surroundings through the drifting smoke. No further movement stirred upon the gore-slick ground.

Complete victory was ours, hard-won. We had been swift, merciless, and brutal. But such was the way of survival upon the frontier.

With a grin of satisfaction on my lips, I moved up to join my companions surveying the grisly remains. Leigh whooped exultantly, throwing a companionable arm around me as her larroling rumbled proudly.

Meanwhile, Diane meticulously moved among the tangled dead, ensuring each body had crossed the veil. Finding no lingering signs of life, she turned at last to give me a subtle, satisfied nod. Between all of us, not one goblin had slipped the noose. Our coordination had been flawless.

Lastly, I turned my gaze toward Celeste. She stood silently apart from the gruesome tableau, head bowed. Only the slightest tremors in her blood-slick hands betrayed that behind the serene mask, emotions still stormed brightly from her first true test of arms at our side.

Yet not a single drop of gore marked her flawless ivory skin and garb. Only the crumpled, rent corpses scattered at her feet gave testament to her ferocity and sublime skill. She was untouched, seemingly untouchable.

Stepping carefully through the wrack of the slain, I came before her. Gently reaching out, I tilted her downcast chin up until our gazes met. Her eyes burned still with the fires of recent violence yet softened as they found mine seeking to console.

"You did well," I told her sincerely. "This work is grim, I know, but take pride in your courage and skill."

At my words, the last of the tension ebbed from Celeste's taut frame. Slowly she nodded, the wisdom in my words touching some deep part of her spirit. Again, she graced me with a tremulous but luminous smile.

# Chapter 14

As the haze of battle fury lifted, we took stock of our situation. The crumbling watchtower was strewn with goblin corpses, testimony to the ruthless efficiency of our ambush. I met Leigh's eyes across the gory tableau, and we exchanged fierce grins.

"Hot damn, we sure laid the smackdown on those ugly bastards!" Leigh whooped, punching the air. Her eyes shone with exhilaration in the wake of our hard-won victory.

Beside her, the massive larroling grumbled happily at the praise. It scuffed a clawed foot through the dusty earth as it started to look around for something to eat.

I chuckled, glad to see her indomitable spirit undimmed by the grim work just completed. Leigh's lust for adventure never failed to lift my own mood. Together with Diane, we had proven ourselves a force to be reckoned with.

Speaking of Diane, I glanced over to where she was meticulously retrieving spent bolts from goblin corpses, nose wrinkled delicately in distaste. Catching my eye, she gave a subtle but satisfied smile. We had fought seamlessly alongside one another.

Celeste still remained slightly apart from our exultation, gazing silently down at the carnage her own blade had sown. Though she hid it well, I sensed the roiling emotions still storming beneath her serene exterior. This had been her trial by fire.

"You never saw actual combat before, did you?" I asked her.

She looked up at me with her emerald eyes and shook her head. "Once," she said. "I fought once before..." She hesitated for a moment. "Do not think that I mourn these goblins... But fighting stirs a wicked memory within me."

Stepping carefully through the littered bodies, I moved to stand before her.

"You fought brilliantly," I told her sincerely. "Whatever you feel now, know that you have my pride and gratitude."

Slowly, she inclined her head in thanks, though her luminous gaze remained clouded by doubt. Sensing her inner conflict, I drew Celeste into a comforting embrace. She clung to me tightly, trembling almost imperceptibly.

At length we parted, and I was relieved to see some of the shadow had lifted from Celeste's eyes. She offered me a small smile that warmed my heart. I gave her shoulder a reassuring squeeze.

By then, Diane and Leigh had wandered over to

join us. "You sure sent those ugly devils straight back to hell!" Leigh declared, clapping Celeste heartily on the back. "Can't imagine a better ally to have watching my hide."

Celeste flushed at the praise. "You honor me," she demurred modestly. "Though in truth, I fear my skills remain yet unpolished..."

Diane waved off her modesty. "Nonsense," she countered evenly. "The precision and power of your sword strokes was breathtaking. You have rare talent indeed."

I smiled to see Diane extending sincerity despite her reservations toward Celeste. It seemed the crucible of shared combat had fused us closer together. Celeste returned Diane's words with a gracious dip of her head.

"Yeah, remind me not to get on your bad side!" Leigh added cheekily, winking at Celeste. Her levity finally coaxed a small chuckle from the elf maiden. The mood lightened as we reveled in our victory together.

But noon was coming, and we should not linger long amidst the grisly scene. With the ruined tower temporarily secured, we set about searching the goblins' ransacked belongings for any clue to Clara's fate. Maybe this was where their expedition had ended?

I rifled through a moldy pack, grimacing at the rancid pouches of goblin snuff tucked inside alongside various petty treasures looted from unwary travelers. Meanwhile, Leigh checked the perimeter for tracks while Diane sorted meticulously through the debris.

Among gnawed bones and soiled rags, our efforts unearthed a handful of coins, some scattered provisions, and other odd trinkets. But nothing definitively linked to Clara's party emerged. If the goblins had encountered them, there was no sign of it here.

"No weapons or gear belonging to Clara's group," Diane reported once she had combed over every inch of the abandoned camp. She shook her head in frustration. "Just the spoils from other victims."

I nodded. It seemed there was still hope they were alive. Unless other clues awaited somewhere ahead along the path, the goblins had not interacted with Clara's party.

"We'd best press on soon as we're able," I said grimly. "I don't like losing daylight. And the odds are that Clara and her party made it to the Dungeon. Although I wonder how they passed by these goblins..."

"They haven't been here that long," Leigh said, inspecting the tracks. "These critters moved in a couple days ago... And I can see here that there was a fire predatin' their camp... Not in the careless way goblin make 'em, neither."

"So... Clara?" I asked.

She looked up from the tracks with a small smile. "Likely," she confirmed.

We exchanged hopeful looks. Quickly we gathered up our scattered gear and weapons, preparing to depart. The larroling snuffled curiously at some bloodied bones before lumbering to Leigh's side, ready to march on.

Within a few minutes, we had left the site behind, eating lunch straight from our packs, for we were unwilling to stop now.

The further we climbed the Shimmering Peaks, the colder and more inhospitable the environment became. Icy winds howled between sheer cliff faces, cutting through our warm clothing. We huddled together against the biting chill, our breath coming in faint puffs of vapor.

The winding path grew ever steeper and more treacherous as we ascended. Loose shale shifted precariously under our boots, threatening to send us skidding over the sheer precipices that plunged into the mist-shrouded valleys far below. We picked our way carefully, wary of twisted ankles or worse.

Diane took the lead, scanning the rugged landscape for any signs of Clara or her party having passed this way. But if they had come before us, the ever-present winds had scoured away all trace of their passage. The higher we climbed, the more remote and untamed our surroundings felt.

As the last light faded from the slate grey sky, we paused in the lee of a towering cliff face to catch our breath and take stock of the situation. Night was falling swiftly, and the temperature had plummeted to dangerously frigid levels that pierced even our layered garments.

"We need to find shelter and get out of this biting wind," I said through chattering teeth. The girls huddled close together for warmth, nodding agreement. Exposed on the open mountainside after dark would be a death sentence.

"There," Diane said after a moment, pointing toward a rocky overhang just visible through the deepening gloom. It was not an ideal refuge, but it would shield us from the worst of the elements.

Stumbling the last few yards over the slick terrain, we gratefully ducked beneath the overhang. Though cramped, it provided respite from the shrieking gale outside. Dropping our packs, we sank down onto the cold stone, exhausted but relieved. After a moment's rest, we set up a single tent and prepared for the night.

"We should try to get some rest while we can," I said wearily. "We'll need our strength for climbing the steepest parts tomorrow." Despite my bone-deep fatigue, sleep felt unlikely in this inhospitable place.

Huddling close for warmth in the tent, we managed to doze fitfully through the long night, our empty bellies grumbling. We did not dare light a fire or eat, afraid its light might draw unwelcome eyes. The mountain's dangers felt ever-present in the oppressive darkness.

By the time the sky lightened to gloomy predawn grey, we were all awake and shivering uncontrollably. "Here, quickly eat this," Diane said, passing out jerky and hard crackers. The meager rations took the edge off our hunger pangs but did little to alleviate the numbing cold.

As the brittle light strengthened, we packed up swiftly and continued picking our precarious way up the frozen slope. Our progress slowed to a crawl in places where the path narrowed along crumbling ledges slick with ice. We shuffled like the elderly, bent against the wind.

I glanced back periodically to make sure Celeste was keeping pace. The harsh environment was taxing even her elven endurance, but she persevered without complaint. Leigh trudged steadily ahead beside the unperturbed bulk of her larroling. Its thick pelt served it well against the cold.

By late morning, the wind had picked up to a howling gale that drove frozen needles of sleet into our exposed faces with unrelenting fury. It was nearly impossible to catch our breath in those thin, frigid gusts that threatened to tear our very footing loose and send us plummeting over the sheer precipice.

Pressing into the side of the cliff, I waited for a brief lull in the screaming wind. "There's a small cave up ahead!" I shouted over the gale's roar. "We have to wait out the storm there!" If we lingered here exposed much longer, the relentless cold would claim our lives. A fire and shelter were now our only hopes of surviving this ordeal.

Staggering the last few feet, we collapsed in an exhausted, shivering huddle just inside the cave's mouth. The meager outcropping provided some respite from the slicing sleet but did little to stop the bone-numbing chill from sinking deep into our bodies. Violent tremors wracked our frames as we clung to one another for warmth.

"I'll g-get a fire s-started," Leigh chattered through blue lips, fumbling with numb fingers in her pack.

She was right. Making a fire brought the risk of detection, but even goblins would not venture out in this icy gale. And if we did nothing, we would likely freeze.

Soon she had managed to ignite a small pile of kindling, coaxing the fledgling flames higher. We huddled desperately close, holding our frigid hands to the blessed warmth.

As our ice-stiffened clothing began to gradually thaw, I took out the maps to examine our progress. We were still likely several hours' climb up the slopes from Hrothgar's Hope if the weather permitted it. And somewhere along this inhospitable route, Clara and her party may have met their ends. The thought sent a shiver through me unrelated to the cold.

The storm kept us pinned in the cave through the remainder of the day, and I paced the rock surface impatiently, frustrated at the loss of time. When evening came, the storm finally settled. Of course, it was growing too dark to go out by then.

We reluctantly allowed the meager fire to die, wary of the light drawing unwelcome eyes now that things would go a-prowling again. In the cave's pitch blackness, we had only our lantern light. Luckily, our blankets provided plenty of warmth, and our rations sustenance and energy.

When night truly fell, I took first watch and let the girls sleep. Those hours of standing guard in the dark cave were not comfortable. The echoing hollow amplified the slightest sound, and I was on my toes the entire time, occasionally making my way to the mouth of the cave to see if anything lurked outside. If there was, I could not see it.

After several hours, I woke Leigh, who relieved me. Despite being tired, I lay awake for a while. But at some point, exhaustion had claimed me, for when I opened my eyes again, the faintest predawn glow suffused the cramped cave. It seemed that only the larroling had slept well.

As we prepared to resume our slow, agonizing ascent, I made sure to clasp each companion's shoulder in wordless support. Their answering nods, despite the grim situation around us, rekindled my determination. If we stuck together, we would prevail.

Diane took the lead once more as we emerged stiffly from the cramped cave to face another bitter day. Though the previous storm had subsided, the wind retained its vicious chill. We pulled our collars tighter and bent into the gusts, breath fogging. Without the fire last night, our clothes were still damp, sapping body heat.

The creeping light revealed no traces left by Clara's party either. If they had passed this way, the elements had long since erased their footsteps. I prayed we were on the right path, that somehow they yet lived. But as the sheer drops and endless waste of rock and ice stretched out around us; hope felt far away.

We trudged on in grim silence as the morning

wore on. Even Leigh's irrepressible spirit was subdued by the bleak, barren majesty all around. The Shimmering Peaks in their harsh beauty cared nothing for our lives. They ground down hardier beings than us daily.

Still, we would persist, and we would find Hrothgar's Hope...

# Chapter 15

Up in the mountains, the light was pale and deadly, offering no warmth. Morale was low after the brutal storm, but we were determined to press on. If Clara and her party had made it this far, so could we.

I took the lead for a time, rifle at the ready. The

winds had died down, but a bitter chill still clung to the air.

Our boots crunched on gravel and patches of old, slurry snow. Overhead, slate grey clouds threatened more wintry weather to come, and I had no doubt that another storm would soon pour its vengeance down on us.

We climbed doggedly onward and upward, each footfall a small victory against the increasing slope. I could feel my muscles burning with exertion beneath the layers of clothing. The thin air made each breath a struggle.

Around mid-morning, the path ahead took a sharp turn between two towering pinnacles of stone. As I rounded the bend, a glint of color in the rocks below caught my eye. I paused, peering down the steep incline. "Wait. I see something."

The others halted behind me. I pointed down to a narrow defile about 50 yards off the main trail. There, fluttering among the boulders, was a scrap of faded green fabric snagged on the rocks.

Exchanging tense looks, we carefully picked our way down the treacherous slope using handholds in the stone. Reaching the bottom, I crouched and tugged the scrap free. It was a torn piece of embroidered fabric, stuck between two stacked stones of impressive size.

"This was placed here on purpose," Diane said. "To signal the return path. Kobolds and goblins don't do this — they have an innate sense of direction in the mountains."

"This was Clara's party's doing, then," I said grimly.

"They must've passed through here before the storms hit," Leigh reasoned, studying the surrounding rocks.

I nodded. If we continued up this defile, it might lead us to where they had sheltered.

We moved slowly, watching every step on the uneven terrain. The defile twisted steeply between close cliff walls before opening up into a wider basin surrounded by sheer rises of stone. I sucked in a breath at the sight that greeted us.

There at the basin's edge, partially buried in snow, sat the burned-out remains of a small campsite. There was a mess of abandoned gear and collapsed tents. Ice had frozen over the dead fire pit in the center.

"A base camp," I muttered.

"Yeah," Leigh agreed. "One that didn't get packed up again…"

"Oh my…" Celeste breathed, concern marring her fine elven features.

"Let's see what we can find," I said. "Maybe they're still around somewhere… or a trace of them."

While the others searched for any further sign of the party, I moved slowly through the abandoned campsite. Everything was still — frozen in time. A pot lay upended near the fire pit, its contents long spilled. The fine layer of snow covering each item made it clear no one had been back here for at least a day.

Leigh was studying old tracks at the camp's edge. "Looks like they headed on up the mountain from here," she reported.

I nodded, casting my gaze up the sheer cliffs hemming us in on all sides.

Somewhere above, the Dungeon of Hrothgar's

Hope awaited. And I was certain that they had entered it.

"Should we follow?" Diane asked uneasily, ears flat against the wind's shrill whistling through the rocks.

I considered a moment. "I'm guessing the entrance to the Dungeon is close by. They probably built this camp as a base of operations, but they didn't return to it."

The girls nodded in agreement. "That does seem the most likely scenario," Celeste agreed.

"We still have some daylight left, so I want to scout the path up with Diane," I said. "We can search for any further traces and the entrance to the Dungeon. If we find it, we'll enter it tomorrow, with renewed energy."

I knelt, brushing snow off one of the abandoned packs. "Let's use their beginnings and make camp here. It doesn't look like it was attacked or scavenged, so the location is still safe."

The girls murmured agreement. There were a few more hours until darkness would find us here in the mountains, which left us time to gather firewood, melt snow for drinking water, and explore the trail to the entrance of the Dungeon.

There was another advantage too. I could have a talk with Diane and gauge how she was getting along with Celeste, while Celeste and Leigh could bond a little while cooking Diane and me a meal for when we returned.

With the quick summoning of a domesticant to lighten our workload, we got to work bringing the base camp in fine order.

As the fading sunlight filtered through the gorge, Diane and I set off to scout the path leading up from Clara's abandoned campsite. Our boots crunched on gravel and crusts of old snow as we walked, our senses alert for any signs of the lost expedition.

I kept one finger resting lightly on the trigger guard of my rifle, though no threats had emerged yet. Still, in a place like this, one could never be too cautious.

Beside me, Diane's keen eyes continuously scanned our surroundings. Her ears twitched now and then at some distant sound.

Before long, the narrow defile we had been ascending opened into a wider, bowl-shaped depression hemmed in by towering cliff faces. I halted, peering upward. There, perhaps fifty yards above, a dark fissure was visible in the rock — likely the entrance Clara's party had used to access Hrothgar's Hope.

"That must be it," I murmured.

Diane followed my gaze and nodded in agreement, her bushy tail swishing pensively.

"We should check the area directly below it for any signs left behind," she suggested. "But carefully. The rockfall danger is high here."

Moving slowly, we began searching the steep slope of scree and boulders directly beneath the cave entrance. If there were traces of Clara's group, the ever-present winds had long since scoured them away.

It was looking more and more like the party had

entered Hrothgar's Hope and simply not returned from their venture. What fate they had found inside we would soon discover.

As we searched, an opportune moment arose to broach another matter that had been weighing on my mind.

Turning to Diane, I asked gently, "So what are your honest thoughts about having Celeste along so far?"

Diane's delicate brow furrowed slightly in thought. "She's been an asset in combat," she acknowledged after a moment. "And I can admit I misjudged her abilities on that count."

I nodded encouragement, sensing Diane still had reservations she was reluctant to voice. "Go on," I prompted. "I value your open perspective."

She hesitated before continuing slowly. "It's just... so much remains unknown about her. Why the secrecy over her Class? And she lacks basic survival skills. I simply find it... odd." Diane bit her lip. "But perhaps I'm being unfair."

I chose my response carefully, sensing Diane's caution came from a place of care for our group's safety; I knew that she was not a jealous lover, and that my obvious interest in Celeste did not vex her.

"You may have a point," I acknowledged seriously. "Celeste is an enigma in many ways. But I believe her intentions are good. She seems to have a kind heart."

Diane absently flicked her tail as she pondered my words. "I hope you're right. She'll have to be truthful to us if she... well, if she wants to be a part of our group. And we barely know each other. I could be misjudging." She sighed softly. "I'm likely just slow to trust. My instincts tend toward suspicion."

Reaching over, I gave her shoulder a reassuring squeeze. "You've kept us alive more than once out here using those instincts," I said earnestly. "I would never dismiss your judgment. If you feel Celeste endangers us, say the word."

Diane managed a small, grateful smile in response. "I don't feel that way," she conceded after pondering a moment. Then, she sighed. "I... I'm just not really accustomed to elves, I suppose, because she doesn't answer to what I would expect of an elf."

I smiled. "Maybe you should let go of those expectations. Just let Celeste be Celeste. Give her a chance."

Diane nodded softly. "You are right, of course. If she proves herself trustworthy, I'll gladly call her a friend. My concerns may turn out baseless."

"I'm happy to hear that," I said. "We'll stay vigilant together, and Celeste will get the chance she deserves."

With our discussion resolved for the time being, we turned our focus back to scouring the area for any last traces of Clara's party. As the light faded toward dusk, our fruitless search ended of necessity. The gloom beneath the distant cave entrance had deepened impenetrably.

"The only option left is that they entered the Dungeon," I said.

"Maybe they got lost or trapped."

"Or killed," I added. "It's an option we must consider."

She nodded grimly. "Indeed."

"We'd best head back while we still have light," I

remarked reluctantly as the shadows stretched ever longer across the icy gravel.

"We should," she conceded with a frustrated flick of her tail. "I just hope we'll find a sign of them inside the Dungeon..."

Together we began picking our way carefully back down the steep gorge as twilight descended. The temperature was already plummeting, our breath puffing out in faint mist. I shivered, longing for the warmth of the campfire Leigh, Celeste, and the domesticant had hopefully gotten started by now.

When we finally stumbled back into camp, I was relieved to see a cheery blaze already crackling. Leigh waved in greeting as she tended a bubbling pot of stew that filled the air with savory aroma.

Celeste sat quietly beside her, her gaze lost in the leaping flames. But she glanced up and favored us with a subtle smile as we entered the flickering light. The warmth raised my spirits, and I was feeling better already.

Settling gratefully beside the fire, Diane summarized our findings — or lack thereof — over bowls of steaming stew. The others absorbed this news solemnly. The fate of Clara's party remained a mystery for now.

As we lingered over our meager but welcome supper, I met Celeste's luminous eyes across the flames. She said little, but I sensed her gratitude for being included. However this mission ended, I was glad she was here, sharing the journey with us.

When the cold night deepened and stars kindled sharp and bright overhead, we reluctantly set aside lingering doubts and concerns until daylight. For now, rest and preparation for tomorrow's venture took precedence.

Banking the fire against the night's chill, I volunteered for the first watch. My companions gratefully rolled themselves in their blankets close to the sputtering warmth.

# Chapter 16

The next morning, we awoke to find the winds had calmed and an eerie stillness lay over the mountain basin. After a quick breakfast, we gathered our gear and approached the cave mouth, yawning darkly ahead.

I felt a prickle of apprehension, gazing up at that

lightless entrance, but pressed it down. Answers waited within Hrothgar's Hope, however grim.

I clicked on the flashlight I retrieved from my backpack. The bright beam pierced the gloom, revealing a crumbling staircase carved into the rock face.

Old torch sconces lined the walls, long cold and empty. Our boots scuffed noisily on gravel and dust as we descended single file into the mountain's depths, senses straining.

The air grew steadily colder and danker as we wound our way deeper along the carved passage. Roots protruded from cracks in the stonework, and rivulets of icy water trickled down the walls. The worn, stone-wrought architecture hinted at the bustling activity this dwarfhold had witnessed just a few years ago.

Now, all was dark and still.

At intervals, side tunnels branched off into fathomless blackness. I swept my flashlight beam down each in turn, wary of anything lurking in those dark veins. But nothing stirred save whispering drafts. The entire complex felt like a tomb. Unease coiled tighter in my gut with each step.

Before long, we emerged into a high-ceilinged chamber with intricately carved pillars flanking the room's edges. Dwarven runes adorned the walls, their meanings lost to the years. Two archways yawned on the opposite sides of the chamber, leading into unknown depths.

"Which way?" Leigh whispered, voice hushed. The room's stale air seemed to swallow sound itself.

Diane's ears swiveled slowly. "This way, I think," she murmured finally, turning toward the left-hand arch.

I trusted her instincts and matched her cautious stride as we passed beneath its crumbling edge into the passage beyond.

This hall was not of careful make. Crudely chiseled from bare rock, it angled steadily downward. Veins of glinting ore snaked through the walls.

The larroling's bulky shoulders brushed both sides as it lumbered behind Leigh and Celeste.

Leigh soothed the great beast with a murmur.

The crude tunnel terminated abruptly in a natural cavern, its uneven floor studded with stalagmites. Bioluminescent fungus speckled the ceiling, casting everything in sickly greenish light. The others tensed as we stepped out onto the spongy, moss-strewn ground.

"Stay alert," I warned softly. This seemed an ideal lair for mountain predators. We picked our way between the stone spikes bristling from the floor, boots sinking into the soft loam. The occasional plink of water droplets echoed eerily around us.

Reaching the far wall intact, we discovered a low opening half-concealed behind a stone outcropping. I shone my flashlight into the void, but the beam fell short of piercing its depths.

Wordlessly, I gestured for Diane to take the lead once more. She slipped through the gap, crossbow raised.

The rough-hewn passage beyond sloped ever downward at a steep angle. Loose rocks shifted treacherously under each step.

We were forced to proceed slowly, bracing our hands against the walls. Dust and debris rained down continuously from cracks in the poorly supported ceiling. I struggled to calm my pounding heart. One misstep could send this whole section crashing down atop us.

After an agonizing descent, we stumbled awkwardly into a cavernous chamber crisscrossed by rickety rope bridges spanning a yawning chasm. Dank mist rose from the void's unseen bottom. Rotting planks groaned beneath our cautious steps. Vertigo clutched my senses.

We were halfway across one swaying bridge when an earsplitting screech rang out. The cavern walls themselves seemed to tremble from the force. My blood turned to ice. That cry was inhuman. Leigh's eyes were wide with fear beside me. Even the stoic Diane looked shaken. Something ancient and deadly inhabited these depths.

"Hurry, quietly," I rasped. We moved as swiftly as the rotting ropes allowed toward the far ledge. The shriek did not repeat, but its chilling echo lingered. I could not tear my gaze from the abyss on either side. Darkness there seemed to roil and seethe just out of sight.

Reaching solid ground once more, we staggered past crumbled masonry toward a wound in the cavern's far wall — the only exit. Rivulets of water glistened as they trailed down the weathered carvings flanking the arched portal. Beyond, steps receded into the earth. There was nowhere left but further down.

Our feet scraped deafeningly loud on the time-worn stairs no matter how gingerly we trod. The flickering glow of Diane's lantern did little to pierce the oppressive gloom shrouding our descent. How many more fathoms deep would Hrothgar's Hope extend?

Just as the weary thought crossed my mind, the claustrophobic stairwell opened unexpectedly into a vast natural cavern, its dimensions lost in darkness.

We huddled together at its precipice, peering out over the abyssal expanse. A bone-chilling draft sighed up from those unseen depths.

"We should turn back," Diane whispered. "This

feels too dangerous..."

I pondered her words in silence. Every instinct screamed to retreat from this nightmare place. Yet if any flicker of hope remained for Clara's party, it lay somewhere ahead in the impenetrable dark.

Before I could respond, another soul-shattering shriek resonated up from the void below. Pebbles skittered over the cavern's edge, dislodged by the force of that eldritch cry. The creature lurking in these depths was not far off now.

"We've no choice," I said grimly. "We press on."

Leigh's jaw was clenched, knuckles white around her revolver's grip. But she gave a terse nod. Together, we moved away from that dread precipice into the maze of stone deeper inside the mountain.

The darkness seemed to thicken palpably as we descended unevenly carved steps ever downward. Our flashlight beams began flickering erratically as we moved.

A frigid draft clawed through our garments, leeching body heat. But still, we pushed on through the stillness. To turn back now might leave us blind in the dark.

At the bottom of the stairs, we entered a final low-ceilinged cavern. A faint phosphorescent glow outlined a small fissure in the far wall. Icy rime coated the stone floor, crunching under our boots. No sound carried from the outside world this deep beneath the mountain's roots.

It was the eerie limbo before chaos.

Halting before the gaping fissure, I met my companions' frightened but resolute eyes one final time. "Stay together," I enjoined them softly.

Gripping my rifle, we pressed as one through the rime-slick cleft. Whatever lurked ahead in the stygian dark, it was our fate to meet it.

The fissure opened into a small cave lit by a soft azure glow. Stalactites hung from the ceiling, dripping water that echoed faintly. Diane moved ahead on silent feet, crossbow raised as she scanned for any threat. The rest of us fanned out, senses strained for the slightest sound.

But only the plink of water and our own hushed breaths stirred the heavy air. The luminous fungus on the walls cast everything in an ethereal blue-green light. Cautiously, we picked our way across the uneven cave floor toward an arched opening on the far side. Diane reached it first, gesturing for us to wait as she slipped through alone.

Tense minutes passed as we stood frozen, ears pricked. Leigh shifted nervously beside me, casting anxious glances toward the way Diane had gone.

Meanwhile, I kept my rifle trained on the dark entrance, finger resting lightly on the trigger guard in case of an ambush. But the subterranean silence remained unbroken.

At last, the faint scuff of a boot on stone signaled Diane's return. I released a pent-up breath as her lithe shape materialized out of the gloom. Wordlessly, she beckoned us to gather close so she could share her report in hushed tones.

"There's a larger cavern beyond this one," she whispered tersely. "I glimpsed movement in the shadows that looked like kobolds. Perhaps a dozen or more." Her tail lashed in agitation. "We need to form a plan before proceeding."

I swore under my breath. Kobolds were vicious, tribal creatures that dwelled in mountain tunnels. Often, they laid claim to dwarven ruins once they were abandoned or if they felt like they could overtake its inhabitants. Their packs could number in the dozens.

"Did they spot you?" I asked Diane urgently. She shook her head.

The element of surprise remained on our side, however slim that advantage might be. The others absorbed the news like me — grimly but without panic. We had faced worse odds together before.

"If we move fast, we can ambush them," I reasoned in hushed tones. "Hit hard before they can rally."

Beside me, Leigh nodded fiercely; eyes alight with battle-readiness. Her massive larroling rumbled deep in its throat, sensing the brewing conflict.

Meanwhile, Celeste remained silent, porcelain features schooled into tranquil focus beneath her drawn hood. She, aided by my summons, would need to swiftly cut down any kobolds that slipped past our frontline while Leigh and I engaged them head-on.

"I will summon a guardian and Aquana's avatar to aid Celeste in melee," I said before turning to Diane. "Provided there is enough room for a melee like that?"

She nodded. "But knowing kobolds, there could be side tunnels concealed nearby with more waiting to join the fight. Our ambush risks being surrounded." Her eyes were clouded with doubt.

I hesitated, acknowledging her point. My instinct had been for a direct attack, but these twisting caverns likely held unknown variables — hidden numbers, traps, and escapes. A stealthier approach might serve us better here.

"You're right," I conceded after a moment's thought. "A full assault is too risky without knowing what else lurks nearby." The others murmured agreement, tension coiling tighter. We needed a revised strategy, quickly.

"What do you suggest, Diane?" I asked.

Though I often took the lead in combat, her wisdom and scouting experience shone here in unknown territory teeming with threats. She had skills and instincts that gave her a better insight into places like these.

Diane considered carefully before responding. "The corridor opens unto a ledge that skirts the cavern," she whispered. "Between that and the many fungi, we might skirt around the edge unseen. If we can do that, there may be a way to flank them and get a quick look down the other corridors to make sure there aren't any reinforcements."

It was dangerous, but likely our best path forward. "Lead on then," I said simply. "We'll follow your guide."

Diane gave a terse nod before turning back toward the shadowy tunnel mouth, crossbow at the ready. Together, we slipped into the darkness on her heels.

The flickering glow of scattered mushrooms provided our only light as we crept single-file deeper into the winding passage. Our breaths and the scuff of boots on stone seemed deafeningly loud, but no cries of alarm rose ahead yet.

Before long, we emerged onto a ledge overlooking the larger cavern Diane had scouted before. Dim shapes milled and scrambled about the fungus-choked floor far below.

Guttural snarls echoed off the walls as the kobolds proceeded about their business, and the occasional glint of steel betrayed crude weaponry. The situation was precariously balanced... for now.

With utmost care, we picked our way along the cavern's uneven walls, seeking a suitable ambush point and to quickly scout those other corridors. The kobolds below remained oblivious, preoccupied with their snarling disputes. They were not expecting an ambush, and they seemed preoccupied with arguing amongst themselves, sleeping, and gorging on strips of meat from a source I did not wish to consider.

As we moved, Diane quickly ducked into each corridor we passed, scouting ahead on behalf of our party. Although my heart raged in my chest, she returned shaking her head every time. It

seemed there were no other kobolds in the halls —
at least, not nearby.

That, however, left the source of the shriek we
had heard earlier. It had been too loud for kobolds,
and there was another beast somewhere around.
An open attack risked rousing it.

At last, Diane signaled we had reached the spot
she found ideal for opening the attack. The dense
growths and the ledge should hide us from view
below until we struck, letting us draw out the
element of surprise as long as possible. I peered
down, gauging angles and distances as I mentally
prepared our assault. The moment of reckoning
was nearly at hand...

Yet just as we readied ourselves, a thunderous
rumble shook the cavern foundations. Dust rained
down as the quaking intensified, and startled cries
rose from the kobolds.

"What's happening?" Leigh hissed, struggling to
keep her balance. Before I could hazard a guess, the
deep tremors subsided as quickly as they had
started. An eerie silence followed in their wake.

One by one, the kobolds fell to their knees and

began chanting as if they were caught up in worship, weapons discarded at their sides for the moment.

"Now," I hissed. "This is our chance!"

# Chapter 17

Our ranged assault from the ledge above began swiftly. With the kobolds distracted by their strange worship of the shrieking roaring in the Dungeon, they were ripe targets. Taking aim with my rifle, I quickly dropped one of the creatures with a clean shot to the neck. Beside me, Diane's crossbow sang out, her bolt finding its mark.

On my left, Leigh whooped fiercely as she emptied her revolver's chambers into the panicked throng. The cavern echoed with shrieks, snarls, and gunshots. Our surprise attack was brutally effective, the ledge providing us ideal elevation to shoot down into their midst.

The kobolds shrieked and flailed as our coordinated volley rained down death. Shook up from their worship, they scrambled for weapons and cover.

Meanwhile, nimble as a mountain cat, Celeste rapidly descended the slope, blade strapped across her back. The larroling followed close behind, claws gouging handholds in the crumbly rock face. Together, they dropped into the chaos erupting below.

Now it was time for phase two. While Celeste drew her sword, I focused my will. With a burst of light, my guardian manifested beside her. Aquana's shimmering avatar coalesced into being a moment later.

My spells set me back 18 mana and left me with

25. The two summons stood ready to engage and defend.

Seeing new foes suddenly in their midst, half the remaining kobolds broke from their cover and charged toward Celeste with murderous intent. They raised crude axes and spears as they converged, beady eyes alight with bloodlust.

But my guardian rushed to meet them, massive shield raised. Spear tips and axe blades glanced off its armor in showers of sparks as it slammed bodily into the throng. Behind its bulwark Celeste stood untouched, blade poised in flawless form.

At the same moment, Aquana's avatar swept its watery fists into the kobold mob with incredible force. The concussive impacts sent one of the kobolds flying like a rag doll, armor rent and shattered. The kobolds' guttural battle cries turned to yelps of dismay and pain.

And then, Celeste joined the melee. She wove her deadly dance. The ornate blade carved crimson arcs through the gloom as she spun and sliced through their ranks with lethal precision. None could stand before her whirlwind fury.

From our elevated position, we continued raining death down upon the creatures still twitching and writhing where they had fallen. It was an execution, our combined firepower decimating the last of their ranks before any could regain their feet.

Meanwhile, the larroling — a little late to the party because of its clumsy descent of the slope — joined the fray with thunderous fury. The cavern shook with its roars as it plowed through the creatures, swatting them aside like insects beneath its massive bulk and rending claws.

In mere moments, the last kobolds lay in hacked, gory pieces on the blood-soaked cavern floor. Celeste flicked dark blood from the sword almost disdainfully before turning to calmly survey the gruesome scene we had wrought. My summons took position on either side of the elven maiden, ready for my next command.

Above, as the echoes faded, we rose from our positions on the ledge. Though the cavern floor was strewn with carnage, my companions appeared untouched, having cut down the creatures with flawless coordination before even one could draw near.

"That was some sweet shootin'!" Leigh whooped, pumping a fist exultantly as we regrouped. Only the faintest flush of exhilaration colored Celeste's porcelain cheeks. But her eyes shone with a fierce pride in her capabilities.

"You all performed flawlessly," I said sincerely. I felt staunch pride in my comrades as we stood together surveying the victory.

However, there was little time for celebration. Now that the kobold threat was neutralized, we needed to press on swiftly in search of Clara before something else lurked forth to investigate the sounds of slaughter. And there was that thing that had shrieked and roared somewhere within the Dungeon.

Moving quickly, we began searching the tangled mound of corpses and debris for any clues potentially left behind by Clara's party. It was grisly work picking through filthy bedding and other refuse among the bloody dismembered limbs.

"Here!" Diane called sharply, beckoning us over. Half-buried nearby, an ornate dagger glinted in the dirt. I carefully extracted it, brushing off the blade's engraved roses.

"This was Clara's," Diane said confidently. "I remember her showing it to me after one of her earlier Dungeon runs. It must have gotten knocked free when they were taken."

My pulse quickened as I turned the blade over in my hands. This was a definitive sign we were on their trail, and that they had gone into Hrothgar's Hope.

"Then there's a chance some escaped deeper within," I reasoned.

After all, if Clara had dropped it during a struggle, perhaps she and some others had slipped away alive.

"We should move swiftly but cautiously," Diane advised.

She was right. Somewhere ahead, the lost party might be languishing wounded, with dwindling supplies. Proceeding recklessly could ruin any hope of reunion. Their situation remained dire.

Thus resolved, we gathered our scattered equipment and pressed onward with renewed vigor. The answers we sought lay somewhere in the black depths ahead. Step by step, we delved through the maze of twisting passages, focused solely on finding Clara's group.

The darkness steadily drained our flashlight beams as we wove deep beneath the mountain's roots. The deathly silence weighed oppressively. We strained each sense for the slightest sign of life, but only spectral echoes answered back.

Still, we persisted through the network of shadowed tunnels and sprawling caverns. The eldritch chill seeped into our bones, but we moved on.

# Chapter 18

Further exploration of the shadowy Dungeon proceeded haltingly. Our flashlight beams seemed feeble against the endless dark pressing in all around. Any rubble or loose stone turned treacherous underfoot, forcing us to watch every step lest the noise of a fall echo too far through the tunnels. We spoke only in terse, muted whispers.

So far, no new threats had emerged after the slaughtered kobolds. But something ancient and deadly yet lurked somewhere in the stygian depths around us. Its bone-chilling roars had long since faded, but its brooding presence lingered. The hairs on my neck prickled at the thought.

Diane scouted a little way ahead, her eyes keen for the slightest sign of Clara's group. But time and darkness conspired to hide their trail.

The rocky floor revealed little, and the stale air carried only our own sounds. All we could do was search methodically, passage by passage.

The unwelcoming gloom seemed to press in from all sides the deeper our search carried us. Even our lantern light appeared dim and frail against the vast dark. Any shred of proof that Clara or her companions had passed this way before us now would have been a relief. But thus far, the rocky tunnels remained obstinately devoid of clues.

When the twisting passage we followed opened into a high-ceilinged chamber, Leigh froze and held up a halting hand.

Cocking her head, she stood motionless for several taut heartbeats. "You hear that?" she finally whispered.

We shook our heads mutely, exchanging looks. None of us had heard a thing.

Keeping her revolver ready, Leigh crept forward into the expansive chamber, boots scraping softly on the gravel-strewn floor. I gripped my rifle tightly, poised to back her up.

Step by cautious step, Leigh approached the chamber's far wall. There, in the wavering lantern light, a small crevice about shoulder height was visible.

Leigh paused before it, frowning pensively. Then her eyes widened.

"It's flowing air," she gasped. "Could be a way through!"

Joining her swiftly, I pressed my palm against the opening and felt a steady current of frigid air flow over my skin from some space beyond. This could signify a route Clara might have taken. The gap looked barely large enough to squeeze through.

"I'll slip through and scout it out," Diane volunteered when I shared my conjecture.

I nodded. "Be careful."

She smiled at me, blew me a kiss, and slithered into the crevice headfirst with a lithe wriggle. The bushy tip of her tail disappeared last.

We waited and watched that narrow opening, our weapons at the ready in case anything would show up. I tried to ignore my pounding heart. Leigh shifted her weight nervously from foot to foot, casting anxious glances toward the crevice.

Each second Diane was out of sight stretched intolerably. We had to place faith in her skills.

After some fraught minutes, one slender hand reappeared, beckoning urgently. Diane had returned unharmed.

"Hurry, come look what I found!" she whispered sharply when we approached the crevice.

We squeezed through one after the other — me, Leigh, Celeste, and finally the larroling. The beast barely fit and grumbled a complaint as it squeezed in.

The hidden tunnel beyond steadily widened as we stumbled along it half-bent. Diane clutched my hand, guiding me onward until the constricting walls abruptly fell away, depositing us in a small cave lit by ghostly fungi. My breath caught at the sight that greeted us as I swept the flashlight over the new room.

There, slumped against a massive boulder, was a crumpled form in tattered mail and furs. Diane hurried to the motionless figure as I raised my flashlight, playing the harsh beam over the ugly gashes marring their torso and limbs. But the bearded face seemed miraculously untouched.

Kneeling swiftly, Diane pressed gentle fingers to the fallen man's neck in search of a pulse, but we already knew what the result of that would be — she was just making sure.

Leigh, Celeste, and I watched mutely, hardly daring to breathe. The dripping sound that permeated the caves turned unnaturally loud. Diane lifted her eyes to mine, sorrow gleaming there even in the poor light.

"He's gone," she murmured heavily after a

moment. My shoulders sagged. Though not Clara herself, this man had almost certainly been one of her companions. We had been too late to spare him from his lonely death in the pitiless dark.

Grimacing in sympathy at the severity of the poor soul's wounds, I stepped closer to inspect his leather armor and gear — all of fine dwarven craftsmanship by the look.

"Can either of you identify him?" I asked Diane and Leigh solemnly. There might still be clues to pursue.

Diane circled the crumpled form slowly, brows knitted as she searched her memory for the details. But she soon sighed and shook her head in defeat.

"Can't say I've seen this man before," she admitted regretfully.

Crouching, Leigh reached with delicate care to tilt the man's head into the full light of the flashlight. Her eyes clouded with sorrowful recognition.

"It's Lander," she said heavily after a moment. "He was one of the warriors often lookin' for a group for Dungeon runs in Gladdenfield. I know him from the shop. Pretty sure he joined Clara on the regular."

My pulse quickened at this first concrete evidence of the lost expedition's fate. Grim as it was, Lander's demise proved we walked in their footsteps.

"He must have gotten cut off or separated somehow," I reasoned.

But if he had succumbed, what dire straits might Clara and the others now face?

"And look at those cuts on the torso and limbs," I continued. "Claws. And bigger than those of a kobold. It looks like they cut straight through the links of the chainmail…"

"Must've been a real big critter," Leigh said. "Maybe the thing we heard growl earlier?"

I nodded. "It does seem that way."

While Leigh and I stood guard, Diane swiftly searched Lander's remains for anything potentially useful. But she eventually shook her head in defeat. "Just his weapons and a little food." She closed his lifeless eyes gently. "No further clues about Clara."

I swore under my breath. While finding Lander's

final resting place provided some tragic closure, it still left Clara's ultimate fate, and that of her other companions, a mystery.

Most likely, they had been forced to leave him behind here after he succumbed to his wounds. All we could do was press deeper into the mountain's treacherous maze of tunnels.

The search resumed, our sense of grim purpose renewed. Lander's lonely end was a cautionary tale. If injured, lost, or out of supplies, Clara's predicament could be dire indeed. The attackers might have overwhelmed her; either foes that already were here or they ran afoul of the thing that made the shrieking noises.

Step by determined step, our fellowship delved on through the winding passages, bereft of daylight. Perhaps somewhere ahead, our lantern beams would at last reveal Clara and her surviving companions.

Or perhaps we would recover only cold bodies to bear back in sorrow. Either way, we would find out.

The twisting passage narrowed as we pressed deeper into the mountain's hollowed roots, forcing us to proceed single-file. Rocks underfoot turned slick with strange lichens and subterranean fungi, treacherous to the unwary step. Each breath seemed to echo too loudly in the dead air, as if the very stones listened to betray our presence.

Holding up a halting hand, I paused to sweep my flashlight beam over the uneven walls and stony debris littering the cramped tunnel floor ahead. Some dwarven delving seemed to have exposed a natural fissure here that still breathed its chill, tomblike air into the passage from unknown depths. The beam's harsh glare revealed no movement, but my every nerve felt taut as a bowstring.

Behind me, Diane stood poised on the balls of her feet, ears swiveling slowly to catch the faintest disturbance upon the air. Leigh shifted her weight restlessly, her finger resting lightly upon her revolver's grip while the silent bulk of her larroling loomed at her shoulder.

Celeste seemed composed, her hand resting with deceptive casualness on her sword hilt. Yet I knew that like us, she strained each sense into the darkness ahead. We were nearing something. The shadows' uneasy weight whispered warnings no words could articulate.

Inch by tense inch, we crept forward across the uneven terrain until the cramped passage abruptly spilled out into a high vaulted cavern. Sweeping my flashlight in a slow arc, I glimpsed tumbled columns and carven walls that spoke of hard work in merrier days.

Now, their craft lay in ruins, lost like their makers to the feral fury of kobold and goblin. All was still but for the insistent plink of water somewhere in the dark.

The larroling lowered itself a little closer to the ground, and its nostrils flared as it caught a whiff of a scent from somewhere nearby — something that we did not detect. The great beast rumbled softly to Leigh, who signaled that we should exercise caution.

"This guy smells something," she whispered.

I gave a firm nod. "We'll be careful," I said.

Scanning the uneven ground, I spotted markings that might have been claw prints in the dust. I stepped forward to follow their trail before turning my light abruptly downward as if on instinct. There, almost lost amidst the jumble of stone, gaped a sheer cleft.

Cold air sighed up softly from that lightless opening, and with it rose the unmistakable stench of some creature's filth. My heart hammered against my ribs, and I gestured for the others to draw near and observe my troubling find in silence.

"That's the stink o' goblins," Leigh muttered, wrinkling her nose. "Ain't no mistake about it."

"Indeed," Celeste agreed. "Like orcs, they are the enemies of old of my kin. I know their filthy stink anywhere."

Wordlessly, I directed my flashlight into the gaping void. Steps spiraled down into the pit, vanishing into pitch darkness within a few yards. Some side passage the dwarves had once carved to reach precious metals or stones and abandoned when the veins ran dry.

The steps were crudely hacked from bare rock, definitely rushed work. The stench that billowed up from below was almost overwhelming. Their lair surely lay nearby, reachable through this exposed opening we now hunched over.

Exchanging a tense look with my companions, I knew that we had found a goblin den. Their vile stench seemed to cling to the very walls. But the risks of proceeding blindly into such a viper's nest were immense.

We would need to formulate a plan before undertaking any reckless assault.

I gestured for the others to retreat from the gaping pit so we could confer in hushed whispers and decide our next course of action.

Back within the relative shelter of the ruined colonnade, we gathered close with weapons and light sources in easy reach. Though no goblin cries had yet raised an alarm, the advantage of surprise hung by the thinnest thread.

Our voices never rose above the barest murmur as we swiftly debated strategy. The steps downward confirmed the goblin lair lay below, but we could only guess at its size or defenses.

I suggested summoning additional allies before we ventured into their midst, but Diane cautioned that my summons might announce our approach if unleashed too soon. They were not stealthy, after all, so she made a good point.

After tense debate, we settled on sending a scout ahead to gather more information before committing ourselves irrevocably to open battle.

"I will go," Diane volunteered without hesitation.

Much as I hated sending her into danger once more, I could not deny that she was an excellent scout — she had the Class and the talent. "Very well," I said. "Go on, but take no risks. Return to us the moment things get hairy."

She nodded, gave me a quick peck on the cheek, then turned toward the stairway down. Then, with scarcely a sound, she melted into the shadows and was gone.

We crouched on anxious watch as the minutes crawled by. The waiting clawed at my nerves. Though outwardly still, my companions' tense postures gave proof that they shared my unspoken anxiety.

When at last Diane's lithe shape materialized silently from the gloom, I gave a sigh of relief. Our whispered conference was brief, and dire.

Diane confirmed a veritable warren existed below, teeming with goblins. Exact numbers were unclear, though they certainly numbered two dozen at least. And worse, their lair showed signs of captives — including a woman matching Karjela's description.

"Karjela," I hummed. "The foxkin I fought in Lord Vartlebeck's tournament at the Festival of Aquana…"

Diane nodded. "I'm certain it's her. She is alive but wounded."

Our path forward was now clear but dangerous. We would need the fury of the storm itself to scour this nest of vipers and free those unfortunates trapped below.

My mouth was dry as I outlined the plan. A full frontal assault relying on spell and shot to carry swift confusion into their midst, while blade and claw wreaked havoc within the same heartbeat.

"If luck is with us, the chaos will overwhelm them. We try for the cage to free Karjela. If we are overwhelmed, I will summon a guardian or two to halt them while we fall back."

Celeste volunteered to spearhead the liberation effort if the larroling and my summons could keep her flanks clear. The rest of us would harry them from the shadows, denying the creatures the opportunity to effectively rally their full numbers against those darting into their lair.

"Sounds like a solid plan," Leigh said. "The best one we can make."

I nodded agreement, and we made our final preparations. Then, approaching the pit mouth once more, we gazed down into its depths, braced shoulder-to-shoulder.

From below, the shuffling and snarling drifted up to us.

"Let's go," I said.

# Chapter 19

My pulse thundered as I led the silent descent into the goblins' reeking lair, my companions close behind. Our boots scarcely whispered on the steps worn smooth by countless filthy feet. The creatures had no inkling of the doom about to descend upon their wretched heads.

Reaching the bottom, I swept my eyes over tangled mounds of refuse filling the low cavern as guttural snarls and grunts drifted from the shadows. Then, with a quick spell, I summoned my allies — a towering guardian and Aquana's shimmering avatar — even as Diane and Leigh opened fire, Celeste gingerly advancing and getting ready to charge.

Cries of dismay greeted the sudden blinding flashes and blast of Leigh's revolver as my summons arrived, ready to do my bidding. Still shrouded safely in darkness, I commanded the burly guardians to flank Celeste and plow into the confused throng at her side, carving us a path toward the cage.

From the rear, Leigh released her massive larroling with a fierce command. The beast advanced at Celeste's side, ready to tear a swathe of devastation through the milling goblins, its thunderous roars echoing off the walls. With her pet released, Leigh fired with vicious enthusiasm into the fray.

Like a deadly breeze, Celeste slipped past

toward the crude prison holding a wounded foxkin woman, likely Karjela. The elf's blade carved crimson arcs through all who dared block her path. My guardian shielded her slender form, while Aquana's avatar slammed into the goblin with fists that carried the power of the enraged seas.

Hard on Celeste's heels, I blasted away with my rifle, dropping two goblins seeking to cut off her advance. The thunderous shots left my ears ringing painfully, but the goblins fell in spurting ruin before me.

From the relatively protected elevated opening, Diane rained down death on those creatures still reeling in our wake. Her bolts unerringly found their marks even amidst the roiling chaos. Not one goblin could stand before us.

Though rage and desperation fueled them, the fiends fell in pieces beneath our ruthless onslaught. Celeste's blade sang a cruel song as it cleaved through armor and bone. Beside her, my guardian blocked all goblins who dared attack with spear or curved sword. The creatures, cowardly and overwhelmed, darted in all directions.

Reaching the prison, Celeste slashed through its lock in fierce strokes, and I stood amazed for a moment to see the elven steel cut through the crude and rusty padlock like it was butter. Surely, she had some kind of Class ability that allowed her to do that?

Inside, a bruised foxkin woman — Karjela — turned her face toward the light at last, eyes widening in disbelief. Her cracked lips muttered something, but she lacked the strength to speak.

As Celeste cut Karjela's bindings, I glimpsed Leigh laying waste on the goblins, keeping her fire up just like Diane to prolong the confusion among their ranks as long as possible. The larroling crushed and rent until naught remained but mangled meat. None could stand against them.

Howls of agony mounted to a deafening cacophony within the cramped cavern. The shocked survivors began a desperate retreat, scrambling over the dead and dying in their panic to escape our whirlwind assault. The fight had gone out of them.

But no mercy awaited the wretched creatures

here this day. Diane picked off the stragglers from above with ruthless precision, and I followed suit after slamming home a fresh mag and directing my guardian to block off their escape route. Meanwhile, Aquana's avatar smashed apart those goblins fleeing our blades into the deeper warrens.

They were unable to escape, and the dozen or so of remaining turned in despair and rallied together, snarling hate and insults in their vile little language as they made ready to give a final stand.

We gave them no quarter. First, a salvo from me, Leigh, and Diane cut into them, halving their number. Then, Celeste slammed into them, flanked by the larroling and Aquana's avatar.

The goblins gave a bloody account of themselves, but their weapon skill paled in comparison to that of Celeste and the ferocity of the summons. They were cut down, the world free of their wretched hatred.

Soon, the final wails fell silent beneath the attack, and Celeste overlooked the field with a satisfied smile. Diane slid down to join us, tail lashing fiercely. No spark of life stirred upon the blood-slick ground now but our own. Against all odds, we had carried the day unscathed.

"We sure served up somethin' for those gobbos!" Leigh said with a grin. Beside her, the massive larroling grunted in satisfaction, claws dripping red.

Wordlessly, Celeste stepped over entrails and severed limbs to stand before Karjela. With delicate care, the elven maiden helped the battered prisoner from her fetid cell, while Karjela muttered words of thanks.

Joining them, I quickly checked Karjela for serious injuries while Diane kept sharp watch for any remaining goblins drawn by the commotion.

When she saw me hover over her, Karjela narrowed her eyes before managing a wry chuckle. "You, of all people," she muttered hoarsely.

I smiled. She knew, of course, that I had won the tournament, wresting victory from her, but she didn't seem the least grudgeful as we freed her from captivity. "Where are the others?" I asked. "Are they here, too?"

She shook her head, wincing with pain. "Not

here…"

Seeing she had no serious injuries, I turned to the others. "Let's get out of here," I said. "Who knows what the clamor might awaken? We'll talk once we're safe."

The girls nodded, and we quickly prepared to leave. Karjela leaned on me, and we helped her into the least foul-smelling of the corridors leading away from this goblin nest.

Skirting crude pits and deadfalls, our party moved as swiftly as our bodies allowed through the maze of twisting passages. When at last I considered us to be at a safe distance from the site of the battle, we conceded a brief respite.

I set my rifle within easy reach and stood watch as the girls provided Karjela with refreshments, allowing her to regain strength for the continuing ordeal ahead. It seemed the goblins had starved her in her cage.

I was eager to learn more, and when Karjela had recovered enough, I nodded for Leigh to take over the watch. It was time to get some answers.

# Chapter 20

Once Karjela had regained some strength, I walked over and crouched down beside her. "I know you've been through an ordeal, but any information you can provide about what happened to your group could help us find the others," I said gently.

Karjela took a shaky breath and nodded. "There were six of us — myself, Ergun, Clara, Branik, Lander, and Talia. We came seeking treasure within Hrothgar's Hope, but the place was infested with kobolds and those wretched goblins. But there is something worse..."

"Worse?" I asked, eyebrow raised.

She winced and nodded. "We managed to fight our way past the kobolds. But we didn't realize a *dragon* had taken up residence in the depths! The kobolds alerted it to our presence. Apparently, they worship the thing! It attacked during the night, killing Lander before we could even react." Karjela's voice quavered at the memory.

"The rest of us tried to flee, but the narrow tunnels gave little room to maneuver or escape the dragon's flames. We became separated in the chaos and panic. Talia and I raced ahead, but she fell behind..." Karjela trailed off, blinking back grief. "I saw her scream as the dragonflame enveloped her and consumed her."

"Go on," I urged gently. "We found Lander's body in a cavern. What happened to you after that?"

Karjela took a deep, steadying breath. "I doubled back to try and find the others, but a band of goblins captured me and threw me in that wretched cage. They must have snatched me up in the aftermath once the dragon withdrew."

I nodded. Her account lined up with what we had seen so far. "We know Talia and Lander have fallen. Did you see or hear anything about what became of Clara, Ergun, and Branik after the attack?" I pressed.

She shook her head regretfully. "Nothing definitive, but knowing them, I'm certain Clara would have pressed onwards seeking the treasure we came for. She's stubborn and fearless, sometimes to a fault."

"Ergun would protect her with his life if needed. And Branik..." Karjela trailed off, fresh anguish creasing her brow. "He was badly wounded shielding us from the flames. And Lander was our Cleric. We have little means of healing. If he still lives, it's by his sheer dwarven determination alone."

My pulse quickened at this first concrete news. If Karjela was right, some of the party may yet live deeper inside the mountain's treacherous maze of tunnels. But their situation grew more dire with each passing hour.

"Do you have any idea where they might have gone?" I asked urgently. "Or where the dragon's lair lies?" Any scrap of information could aid the search.

Karjela worried her lip as she wracked her memory. "The main treasure vault should lie much deeper, in the lowest levels near the mines. That's where Clara was headed. As for the dragon..." She shivered. "Its roars seemed to come from below."

That matched my own dark suspicions. The eldritch shrieks that had echoed through the tunnels likely heralded the same dragon that had attacked Clara's party. Likely, its lair was somewhere on the paths leading down.

"We have to go after them," Leigh broke in fiercely. Her eyes blazed. "If they're trapped down there injured, who knows how long they can hold out against that beast?"

I nodded grimly. Though the risks were great, we could not in good conscience abandon Clara's group to their fate. We were on a quest to find them and find them we would.

"You're right," I said. "We press on." Turning back to Karjela, I asked gently, "Are you strong enough to travel if we aid you? Or do you need longer to recover your strength?"

Bravely, she pushed herself up on one elbow. "I can make it with help," Karjela said stubbornly.

Though she still looked haggard, determination shone in her eyes. "I owe it to the others not to falter now." She then let her eyes dwell over us. "You came for us?"

"We did," I said.

Emotion colored her face — very different from the stoic and scarred warrior woman I had seen her as during the tournament. "Thank you," she said, voice broken.

Admiration for her grit swelled within me. I clasped her shoulder. "We'll get you out safely," I vowed. "But first, we must make one last effort to find the rest of your party before we abandon this place."

Diane fetched water for Karjela while I double-checked her injuries to ensure she was fit for further travel. She seemed the type to downplay her injuries, and I needed to be sure.

Though clearly exhausted, the foxkin woman seemed stable and in less pain now. When we had done what we could, I signaled Leigh it was time.

We forged onward down crumbling stairs and treacherous passages seemingly etched by dragon claws with Karjela supported between us. Deeper into the mountain's suffocating dark we ventured, ears straining for any sound of life. The stifling air tasted of dread, and we all knew we were drawing closer to the dragon's lair.

When we reached a sprawling cavern carved by an underground river long run dry, our lights finally reflected off a body in brass armor half-buried in the rubble. With a cry, Karjela broke free of our support and staggered to the body's side.

It was Ergun, his body pierced through by some massive talon. Though his empty eyes stared sightlessly upward, a hint of defiance still hardened his face, and I knew he had fought until the bitter end.

Sobs wracked Karjela as she cradled her fallen companion. We averted our gaze to grant what little privacy the gloom allowed.

Ergun's death, though grievous, ignited fresh hope within me. If he had fallen here, Clara and Branik perhaps yet lived and had gone on ahead.

My eyes scanned the cavern's yawning mouths eagerly seeking some hint of her passage. If we hurried, perhaps we could still find her — provided the vengeful dragon hadn't found them first.

Laying Ergun reverently down, Karjela rejoined us with red-rimmed eyes now blazing with renewed purpose. "She went that way," Karjela rasped, indicating a tunnel sloping deeper into the earth. "I can feel it."

Gripping our weapons tighter, we plunged into the waiting darkness without hesitation. The final confrontation lurked somewhere ahead in the stygian depths. But we would face it together, to whatever end.

# Chapter 21

The twisting passage descended at a steep angle, forcing us to slow our urgent pace lest the crumbling floor give way. Jagged rocks and broken masonry littered the uneven ground, treacherous to hurried steps. A heavy stillness permeated the stale air, untouched by any breath of life. The flashlight beam seemed feeble against the oppressive dark.

Before long, the claustrophobic tunnel opened into a high-ceilinged cavern, its far wall lost in shadow. Charred skeletons — perhaps goblin or kobold — were scattered amidst the rubble, hints that the dragon had not always been as worshipped by those creatures as it was now. Perhaps it had fought its way to supremacy.

We picked our way cautiously over the battle-scarred ground, senses straining for any sign of Clara and the remaining members of her party. With all the death surrounding us, hope was feeble.

Near the cavern's center, the loose rocks and debris gave way to a scorched clearing surrounding a yawning pit. The edges were blackened as if by intense heat.

My light revealed the sheer walls plunging endlessly into the mountain's roots far below. A sulfurous exhalation drifted up, tickling our throats. This abyss surely led toward the dragon's lair.

Signaling a halt, I knelt to examine gouges marring the sooty ground — fresh claw marks. The dragon had passed this way recently, and the sinking feeling in my gut whispered that it had descended seeking prey. We needed to move swiftly if any hope of finding Clara remained.

Skirting the sulfurous pit's crumbling perimeter, we pressed on toward a tunnel mouth gaping at the cavern's far edge. The uneven floor turned slick with strange lichens, treacherous to hurried steps. We were forced to slow our pace to prevent injury or accident.

The rough-hewn passage twisted erratically, occasionally splitting into multiple lightless veins. We were forced to pause repeatedly as Diane scouted each branch in turn, seeking some hint of Branik and Clara's route. But the warriors' steps had long since been swallowed by the dark. With no trail to follow, our progress felt maddeningly random.

When the path forked yet again, faint noise echoed from the leftmost tunnel, raising our hackles. Silently, Diane stole forward, crossbow poised until she reached the bend obscuring the sound's source. Breath bated, we awaited her report, ears straining futilely to identify the scraping and guttural snarls.

At long last, she reappeared and waved us over urgently. A small band of drakelings was clustered around a sputtering fire, oblivious to their impending doom.

Exchanging grim nods, we readied weapons and prepared to ambush them. If swift and thorough, their deaths should not draw undue attention.

Our surprise attack went flawlessly. Before the drakelings even fully grasped our presence, their blood soaked the rocky ground. A few managed to loft spears or curved swords, but clumsy fear ruined their aim.

It was over in less than a minute, the victors never wounded. We swiftly moved on, leaving corpses to cool in the shadows.

The unrelenting darkness quickly swallowed all traces of the brief skirmish. Our boots scuffed softly on the dusty floor, ears straining for any sound in the tunnels around us.

Before long, the stale air took on an acrid scent that stung the eyes and burned in the chest — sulfur. The gradually increasing temperature and coppery tang upon the tongue whispered that somewhere ahead, volcanic fire and ash awaited. The dragon had clearly chosen its lair with care.

When at last the narrow tunnel spilled into a towering cavern filled with hellish light and heat, we all froze in dismay at the sight. Far below, a churning magma pit roiled, thick fumes spewing up endlessly to wreathe the uneven walls in noxious yellow haze. Any unprotected flesh would blister instantly upon contact.

But there was a way across: the sprawling chamber contained a maze of rope bridges spanning the roiling lava pit below. The bridges led to ledges, platforms, and outcroppings, but all seemed to converge on a tunnel on the far side of our current position.

The rickety walkways swayed erratically in the updrafts from the churning magma. The blistering heat made the air shimmer and scorched our lungs.

In a place like this, one misstep would send us

plunging to a fiery end. The rope bridges themselves seemed to hold despite the heat, but it stood to reason they were weak.

I outlined the plan — we would traverse the bridges carefully, moving one by one. Though desperation urged speed, I knew balance and caution were essential in navigating this deadly abyss. Focus would be our key to crossing safely.

Once across, the tunnel on the far side appeared our best route forward. Karjela's directions indicated Clara was likely pressing deeper down that path toward the abandoned mines and vaults. The ancient dwarven runes flanking its entrance seemed promising. The claw marked that had defaced some of them, however, did not.

With muscles tensed, we approached the first swaying bridge spanning the bubbling pit. The wooden planks creaked ominously beneath our cautious steps. We proceeded inch by inch, arms outstretched for balance on the slippery ropes. Gusts of hot air buffeted our bodies.

Agonizingly slow, we felt our way across the precarious ropes and rotting planks linking a series of tiny stone outcroppings together. The bridges swung wildly with every step. We froze whenever the walkways bucked too violently, waiting for them to steady.

Agony pounded at my skull from smoke and fumes by the time we stumbled into the far tunnel's shelter, dripping sweat. We sagged against the blessedly cool stone, gasping raggedly until the sting of sulfur began to fade. Fortune had smiled upon us. We had crossed the volcanic pit intact through skill and care alone.

But as we moved to resume the pursuit, a resounding roar shook the very walls — the dragon stirred once more, and it seemed to be angry. All color drained from Karjela's face at the bone-chilling cry. Gripping our weapons tighter, we pressed deeper into the crumbling tunnels, hearts hammering an urgent rhythm.

The carved passage twisted erratically, splitting into a warren of side veins that frustrated attempts to maintain a steady bearing. We navigated the labyrinth blindly, guided by dwarven markings when we found them.

With each step, the soul-shattering roars drew subtly closer. When at last the worn trail ended abruptly at a sheer cliff face, despair seized my pounding heart.

Leigh gave an urgent hiss to draw my attention, and she pointed at something. Hidden in the rock, an iron-bound door was just visible.

Approaching the weathered portal, I grasped the icy handle and pulled with fading hope. Amazingly, the ancient door groaned reluctantly open.

Beyond lay a well-preserved chamber lined with ornate stonework and dusty shelves. We had found a dwarven storeroom somehow untouched by invading forces.

A quick search of the area revealed something of interest to me — a simple, dusty tome titled "Potions and Concoctions". At first glance, it seemed to contain recipes for alchemy.

I tucked the book into my pack for later study. Our goal lay deeper still. We pressed on.

Passing crumbling machinery and mine cart rails snaking into black depths, we delved toward the source of distant blows and rumbles — the abandoned ore mines and vaults. But here the prints of two sets of passing boots were visible in the dust. They were unmistakably not goblin or kobold boots.

"Clara and Branik," I muttered, and the others looked hopeful at the prints before we continued.

Though the ancient stairs turned treacherous with age and ill-repair, we moved onward.

# Chapter 22

The crumbling stairs descended into stygian darkness, our flashlights barely piercing the gloom.

Step by tentative step, we followed the dusty boot prints leading the way down into the mountain's hollowed roots. If Clara and Branik yet lived, they surely were somewhere ahead in the abandoned mines.

The farther we ventured from the surface, the heavier the dread seemed to weigh upon our minds. Each faint skitter of rubble underfoot or plink of distant water made us tense, gripping weapons tighter. The stale air was devoid of life's breath yet rife with menace.

When at last the stairs opened into a high-ceilinged cavern strewn with rusting mining equipment and broken cart rails, we halted warily. Across the expanse, two dark tunnels gaped like sightless eyes — one sloping gradually up, the likely exit back to the Dungeon's top levels, the other delving deeper down toward the vaults.

But more ominous than the stygian depths was the unnatural stillness. Not a whisper stirred the dead air. The entire cavern seemed to be holding its breath, waiting. The fine hairs on my neck prickled. We were not alone down here in the smothering dark.

Motioning for utmost silence, I swept the flashlight beam slowly over the expanse, seeking any sign of Clara's passing or the source of my growing unease. The feeble light revealed only silent machinery, tumbled rocks, and support beams charred as if by fiery breath.

When the light passed over the rubble directly before the descending tunnel, the debris suddenly shifted. I froze, pulse hammering against my ribs. Amidst the jumbled rocks, two baleful reptilian eyes glittered as they focused unblinkingly upon us.

"David!" Celeste yelped, jumping forward as the other girls readied their weapons. The larroling gave a threatening snarl.

Then I saw it too. The dragon!

I stretched out my arm, holding my girls and Karjela back as the dragon reared itself. It had been lying in wait, its mottled scales and spines perfectly camouflaging it amidst the rubble!

But since it didn't attack at once, I realized at once there had to be something it wanted.

Now the great serpentine head rose from the ground, a guttural rumble emanating from its cavernous maw. The creature was easily twenty feet in length, its muscular body coiling and uncoiling lazily as it studied us.

Though dread coursed icy through my veins, I stood resolute before the beast's ancient gaze. If violence came, my companions and I would face it together.

But perhaps yet a bloodless path existed. This creature was no mindless brute but possessed cunning and intellect. I could see it in its eyes.

Keeping my tone level and gaze steady, I addressed the watchful dragon. "We are looking for our friends," I said. "If you give them up, we shall leave, and all will be well. No harm will be done!"

Around me, my companions remained frozen, awaiting the dread creature's response.

For endless heartbeats, the dragon only continued surveying us with those depthless serpentine eyes, smoke coiling from its dilated nostrils. When finally it spoke, its voice rumbled like boulders grinding, words shaped awkwardly around fangs.

"You trespass in my domain, little morsels, yet speak boldly of no harm when you bear weapons of war. Still, your words ring... intriguing." Its slitted pupils dilated further with interest. "Perhaps a conversation before dinner — or not — might offer some novelty to this dreary abode."

Suppressing a shudder at its casual mention of devouring us, I inclined my head slightly in acknowledgment of its willingness to parley. Much yet balanced upon a blade's edge, but thus far, bloodshed seemed forefended.

Choosing my next words with care, I explained our purpose in seeking out the abandoned dwarf hold. "We came seeking a lost expedition of adventurers that entered your domain some days past," I said.

"Indeed?" the dragon hummed. "How many were there? And why did they come? Pray tell..."

I could sense the slight mockery in its tone, and I gauged the beast for a moment. Yes, it was formidable, but it had relented its advantage of surprise over us by speaking and not attacking outright.

This meant it was either arrogant, believing it could take us in a straight fight, or scared that we might defeat it, hoping that some kind of deal could be struck.

As such, I decided to ignore its tone and continued in a businesslike voice. "A group of six, led by a woman named Clara. They sought treasure within this mountain. But it seems not all has gone well for them. Goblins ambushed and held captive one of their number until we arrived and enacted a rescue. Three others have fallen, so that leaves two: Clara, the leader, and Branik, a dwarf."

The dragon listened, head cocked, smoke wisping from its nostrils as it absorbed this information. It seemed to consider my words for a while before narrowing its reptilian eyes. "You say they came for my treasures... And what of you?"

I shrugged. "We came for *them*. I'm not interested in your treasures."

"So, you claim no desire for the treasures in my keeping," it rumbled. "Your scent carries no deceit. Perhaps you speak truthfully, though such selflessness seems... *unusual*, in my experience." Its tail tip thrashed pensively against the rubble.

The dragon's skepticism was understandable given the greed that had likely drawn many to their demise within its lair. Also, they were notoriously greedy themselves. It made sense that it saw everything from its own perspective.

"We seek only our friends' safe return," I reaffirmed earnestly. "Any riches this mountain holds are of no value beside a life."

The dragon remained silent for a long moment. "You offer a curious perspective for ones so small and short-lived," it mused at length. "But come no further. The one you call Clara met her end in the vaults below, seeking to steal what is now mine. Claw and fang made short work of her."

My heart sank even as anger kindled.

Around me, my companions tensed, eyes alight with fury at the loss. But provoking this dread beast to violence might not be the answer. I forced myself to relax and signaled the others to stillness.

Besides, doubt flared inside me. Call it instinct, but I found the dragon's account hard to believe. If it had defeated Clara, then where were her remains? And why had it asked details about the party of adventurers if it had defeated them all?

"If what you say is true, then at least grant us leave to recover her fallen body for proper burial," I said. I held the dragon's dispassionate gaze unflinchingly.

Silent communication seemed to pass between us in that frozen moment beneath the mountain. It narrowed its eyes and bared gleaming fangs, and I sensed that I had angered it. With a quick hand signal, I told my women to get ready.

"You are insolent, morsel," it warned; smoke pluming around its jagged fangs. "Press not your luck. Leave. And trouble me no further."

"You lie, dragon," I said.

At that, it bristled, eyes cracking open. "And what of it, *Goldblood*!? You will leave my lair this instant, or your bones shall be made into toothpicks! I care not one mite for your Bloodline! You morsels' blood tastes the same regardless of heritage!" Steam shot forth from its flaring nostrils. "Leave or become my next feast!"

With those words — mysterious as the allusion to my Bloodline was — I prepared myself in a combat stance. Having recovered mana during the rest after saving Clara, I summoned my guardian, and the dragon roared with fury at the hostile action.

It was time to kill us a dragon!

# Chapter 23

The dragon let loose an ear-splitting roar, baring its gleaming fangs as it reared up to its full imposing height. My guardian stepped forward without fear and braced itself, shield raised, as the creature's muscular bulk uncoiled with terrifying speed.

Flames erupted from the dragon's maw,

scorching the air as we dove desperately for cover. Searing heat buffeted my face even from behind the guardian's sheltering shield. The blaze illuminated the cavern in hellish light.

Even as I grimaced, I quickly popped a mana potion behind the guardian's shield. The concoction put me back to 11 out of 45 mana.

Not ideal numbers when fighting a dragon, but it would have to do.

As the flames subsided momentarily, I risked a glance toward my companions. Leigh and Karjela had taken shelter behind mining equipment while Celeste crouched behind a stalagmite, sword poised. Diane perched atop a precarious stone outcropping; crossbow trained on the dragon's flank.

Seizing the lull, I poured my will into summoning Aquana's shimmering avatar beside my guardian for another 10 mana. The watery being manifested just as another gout of dragonfire roared forth. My guardian braced against the blistering flames but dissolved under pressure, crumbling before fading back into its own plane of existence.

But the guardian had at least distracted the dragon. As I scrambled for cover, the avatar swept its fists toward the dragon's legs. The powerful watery blows connected solidly with the dragon's scaly limbs, staggering the beast momentarily.

It shrieked furiously, lashing its spiked tail and catching the avatar with stunning force, dispelling my ally.

My eyes widened at that — I had never seen Aquana's avatar defeated in battle — the dragon was a formidable foe!

"Aim for the wings and eyes!" I shouted over the din before tearing the cork out of another mana potion with my teeth and throwing it back.

We needed to ground this menace quickly. Diane and Leigh responded immediately, loosing bolts and bullets toward the leathery pinions as the dragon took flight with a rush of air. Most glanced off harmlessly, but one well-placed shot from Leigh punctured the thin membrane.

The dragon flapped its wings, just trying to take off, but the hole in its membrane made it flounder awkwardly amidst the rubble.

Sensing opportunity, Celeste darted forth, vaulting agilely forward and striking at the dragon. Her blade carved a long smoking gash down its scaly flank that left the dragon thrashing in agony.

Maddened with pain and fury, the dragon twisted and writhed violently, dislodging Celeste into a pile of mining debris. My gut clenched in fear at the sight, but she rolled swiftly to her feet, seemingly unharmed. Meanwhile, the larroling struck, clawing at the dragon, earning another shriek of pain from it.

Diane and Leigh circled warily, unleashing volley after volley at the dragon's eyes and snout as it flailed, trying desperately to bring its flames or talons to bear on its tormentors. Smoldering slits now marred its muzzle where steaming ichor flowed. Shrieks of frustration filled the cavern.

I used the moment to pop another potion, the taste making me nauseous after having consumed so many in such a short time. But I needed the mana if we were to come out on top.

The dragon beat its tattered wings fiercely,

managing to take flight once more. We scattered as a jet of flame scorched the ground where we had stood moments before. The ceiling trembled from the downdraft as the beast wheeled about for another strafing run.

Summoning a new guardian to shield us, I called forth my storm elemental as well. Lightning and bullets lashed the dragon's face as it swooped low over us, throwing off its aim of its next breath attack, so that the blistering fire only blackened the rocks at our feet before the creature was forced to retreat from the elemental's fury.

The dragon spat another fireball, but my guardian stepped in and took it on its shield. I could tell that with another strike like that, it would be gone, but it did its work stoically and without fear — a powerful ally indeed!

Enraged, the dragon curled its body sinuously as it hovered high above, glaring malevolently down with smoldering eyes. The shadow of its tattered wingspan eclipsed the cavern, emphasizing its daunting size.

We gripped weapons tighter, knowing the next

attack could come from any direction. But we were mobile, ready, and well-adjusted to each other's strengths from many combats before this one. Tracing it with my rifle, I squeezed off a few shots, but it was impossible to say if they struck home. If they did, they didn't deter the dragon.

When the dragon dive-bombed us moments later, we were ready. While my allies scattered, my storm elemental pressed the assault, mercilessly blasting the creature's hide with sizzling lightning, while the guardian stood ready for another of the dragon's fireballs.

But the dragon convulsed in midair under the shocking onslaught. It crashed heavily to the ground once more before it could launch a fiery attack.

Diane and Leigh immediately capitalized on its awkward landing, sinking crossbow bolts and rounds deep into the leathery wings to cripple the dragon's ability to take flight again. It thrashed and snapped feebly at the air, limbs uncoiling like massive serpents from its prone position.

"Curse you!" it shrieked, panic edging its voice.

"Curse you, Goldblood! Fiend of the ages!"

I couldn't suppress a grin as I sent a few rounds from my rifle into the beast, feeling profound satisfaction as the projectiles drove home with meaty thuds and the dragon howled in pain. Still, even in the midst of this fierce combat, I couldn't help but wonder at the moniker it gave me.

*Goldblood…* But there would be time to dwell on that later.

Seizing our hard-won advantage, Celeste darted forward, vaulting nimbly atop the writhing dragon's shoulders as I drank another mana potion.

Her blade carved smoking chunks from its neck in a blur while it struggled to dislodge this tenacious attacker. Dark blood spurted from the deep gashes as it shrieked and thrashed, its reptilian eyes now wide with fear of death.

Mustering my remaining mana reserves, I summoned a final guardian to protect Celeste and the larroling. And just in time, too! In its deathly fury, the dragon threw Celeste from its shoulders and spewed fire at her.

My guardians just managed to shield her. Both crumbled under the force of that fire, but Celeste was unharmed.

A moment later, bolts, bullets, lightning, the larroling's claws, and Celeste's sword — she had hopped to her feet with a doggedness I admired — inflicted lethal wounds on the thrashing dragon again.

Under combined siege, the mortally wounded dragon slowly collapsed onto its ravaged side, heaving shuddering breaths. Ichor pooled beneath it, mingling with the dust. The unbridled fury in its baleful eyes darkened into dull hatred as death crept steadily nearer.

Yet still, the stubborn beast clung fiercely to life, gathering itself for one final act of vengeance. Its eyes, wide with fear of death, fixed on me.

"Goldblood!" it shrieked. "I have called Father! He will come for you, Goldblood! He will eat your heart and grow powerful."

Then, jaws gaping, the dragon spewed a last, desperate gout of flame towards me. But I was in the zone, quick and agile, and I managed to roll away even as the fire slammed into the rock where I had stood but a moment ago.

Rising to my feet, I fired bullets into the crumpled dragon's body until the magazine ran dry. It thrashed weakly beneath the barrage and the attacks of my companions and summon, clawing furrows in the bloody earth as its strength rapidly ebbed away.

Above the din, Diane called for us to cease fire and save our remaining ammunition — the dragon was finished. She was right — its movements had slowed to feeble twitches.

The hoarse rasp of each of the dragon's final breaths sounded wet with fluid. Its scaly hide was rent nearly to the bone in places from our ruthless assault.

Yet still, defiant hatred smoldered in the dragon's dimming eyes as it surveyed us towering above its broken body. It seemed determined to fight for every wretched breath, refusing to fully concede defeat even at death's door.

Stepping forward grimly, blade poised for a coupe de grace, Celeste met the baleful reptilian gaze unflinchingly. Realizing her intent, the dragon loosed a final rattling growl that reverberated through the cavern like crumbling stone.

"A pox on you all," it rasped. "Father will eat you. Your bones shall be his throne, your blood his wine!"

Celeste's sword descended swiftly, plunging deep into the scaly hide just behind the jawline. The light in those ancient eyes extinguished in an instant. With a bone-deep shudder, the dragon's massive body went limp at last amidst the bloodied rubble.

For long moments afterward, the cavern rang only with our own ragged breaths as we gazed down at the vanquished terror that had plagued Hrothgar's Hope. Scarcely able to believe our hard-fought victory was real, I clasped each woman's shoulder in wordless congratulations. We had survived against impossible odds.

When the adrenaline finally receded, weariness crashed over us like a wave. Every inch of our bodies ached, our mana and ammunition utterly spent.

But notifications flashed in the corner of my vision, showing me how truly unusual this victory had been. I blinked, doing a double take to make sure I had seen right.

But I had. I had advanced not one, but two levels from this victory and was now level 8!

# Chapter 24

Exhaustion overtook us as the thrill of victory receded. Limbs leaden, we sank down amidst the carnage to catch our breath and tend to minor wounds from the fierce battle.

Though sore and depleted, we were triumphant, the dragon's shattered bulk a testament to our skills and courage. For now, it was enough to simply exist in this moment, resting our battered bodies and minds.

As my breathing and heart rate normalized, I made my way over to where Celeste sat silently gazing at the blood coating her hands, seemingly lost in thought. She had just downed a healing potion.

Gently, I rested a hand on her slender shoulder. She started slightly before meeting my eyes.

"Are you hurt?" I asked softly, seeing the haunted look lingering there.

Wordlessly, she shook her head, stifling a bone-deep shudder as she glanced toward the dragon's severed neck.

I gave her shoulder a comforting squeeze. "You did what was needed," I assured her.

Nearby, Karjela tended to a nasty bruise mottling Leigh's side. Though the blonde winced at the foxkin's gentle prodding, a fierce grin remained plastered across her face. "That was some real fun!" she declared.

Karjela just shook her head indulgently and

chuckled.

Meanwhile, Diane meticulously collected salvageable bolts from the carnage, nose wrinkled delicately all the while. I smiled, seeing her unflappable poise even now.

Catching my eye, she returned a subtle but satisfied smile. We had fought as one and emerged victorious, and the deserved pride of that achievement was plain to read on her face.

"You girls level up, too?" I asked.

"Hm-hm," Leigh purred. "Level 5, baby! I never would've thought I'd get that high!"

"Me, too," Diane agreed.

"Yes," Celeste said, still a little absent. "I am level 3 now."

It was the first she had ever revealed about her stats. She was a formidable warrior and had done much good work even at level 2 during our previous battles.

"Even *I* advanced," Karjela muttered, "although all I did was cower."

"You did more than cower," I said. "You braved this Dungeon with Clara and the others. And staying out of combat when you're wounded is just wise."

When we had recovered some strength, I announced it was time we pressed onward — Clara and Branik yet needed finding if they still lived. We would level later once everyone was safe or their fates known.

We gathered our scattered equipment and moved toward the tunnel mouth gaping darkly beyond the dragon's corpse. Celeste averted her eyes from its shattered cadaver as we passed.

The worn stairs descending into the depths were slick with moisture and slime, forcing us to proceed with caution lest a fall bring our quest to an abrupt end after coming so far. The stale air tasted of decay and minerals — the scent of the bones of the earth itself.

Our boots scuffed deafeningly loud off stone worn smooth by the steps of generations now dust. No other sound stirred.

Eventually, the claustrophobic stairwell opened into a high-ceilinged chamber shrouded in darkness. Sweeping my flashlight beam over the crumbling grandeur, I glimpsed rough-hewn columns and arched ceilings that spoke of dwarven craft. Intricate geometric designs had been carved into the walls, though much was lost to the years.

Spreading out, we began searching for any sign of Clara or Branik having passed this way. A fresh trail would stand out noticeably in the undisturbed dust coating the chamber floor. Each scuff of our boots across the debris prickled my senses. These ancient vaults seemed to be holding their breath.

"Here!" Diane called sharply, breaking the oppressive silence.

I hurried over to where she was crouched beside a sturdy wooden door banded with tarnished brass. Celeste moved up beside me and cut the padlock with her blade as she had done with Karjela's cage earlier.

Grasping the handle, I hauled it open with some effort. A gust of stale, mineral-scented air sighed up from the darkness within.

Stifling trepidation, I shone the flashlight beam down the worn stone steps revealed just inside the doorway, holding my breath. About halfway to the shadowy bottom, two crumpled forms were visible — dwarven armor glinting faintly beside torn leather and a shred of chainmail. My heart clenched.

Descending swiftly, I crouched to check the bodies for any flicker of life. Though filthy and battered, they were miraculously both still breathing.

And they were Clara and Branik without question!

The others swiftly joined me, relief palpable. By some grace, we had found them in time. Karjela hugged Clara fiercely, tears in her eyes.

Branik's brows knitted at the disturbance before he forced his one good eye blearily open. "By my beard..." he rasped in stunned disbelief. "You... Someone came." Recognition sparked faintly in his gaze as it moved over us.

"Lie still. You're safe now," I told him gently as Leigh and Celeste began tending to their injuries. Clara stirred weakly at the commotion, reaching blindly for Karjela's hand.

Though serious, their wounds seemed largely

superficial — painful and sapping vitality but not mortally threatening for now. We would be able to move them out of the Dungeon. Fortune truly had smiled upon us all.

While Leigh and Karjela cared for the two battered warriors, I quickly searched the rest of the vault by flashlight.

Piles of coins, gems, and other dwarven treasures glinted in the bobbing beam, and I quickly worked to secure what we could carry up on this first run. Of course, the wounded had priority — lives were at stake. We needed to evacuate our people from the mountain's depths with all haste.

By the time I returned, Leigh had succeeded in getting water down the two survivors' parched throats. Branik seemed to gain lucidity by the second as the life-giving liquid revived him. Clara sat slumped against Karjela, blinking slowly like one pulled from a dream or a nightmare.

Though they were far from restored, Clara and Branik both stoutly insisted on trying to walk with assistance rather than being carried up the long, arduous stairwell. Gripping my shoulder, Branik hauled himself resolutely to his feet, swaying slightly.

The stout dwarf would not be deterred from departing the scene of battle upright. Clara, too, struggled up with stubborn pride, leaning heavily on Karjela's sturdy frame.

With Leigh and I supporting Branik and Celeste aiding Clara, we began the torturous ascent back up the silent stairs toward daylight, one halting step at a time. The survivors panted harshly with effort, bodies quaking from exertion and blood loss. But we persisted, upward through the mountain's frigid bowels.

# Chapter 25

Exhausted and battered, we emerged at last from the lightless depths of Hrothgar's Hope, supporting Clara and Branik between us.

Their ragged breaths frosted the chill air as we shuffled toward the remains of the original base camp under the open sky. Our bones ached from the arduous climb, but elation flooded through us at this moment of triumph.

With care, we eased the two survivors down to rest beside the burned-out fire pit. Their eyes squinted against the muted daylight, having known only deep darkness below for untold days.

Though filthy and haggard, life yet stirred in their battered frames. Fortune had returned them to us against all hope.

While the rest of us collapsed in weary heaps, Diane swiftly melted snow and brought the precious water to their parched lips. Clara gulped it desperately before Branik could wrest the skin away to guzzle the rest in greedy swallows. A fierce vitality burned behind their eyes despite their weakened states. Warriors to the core.

As we caught our breath, I turned my attention to Clara as she leaned wearily against Karjela. Her torn leather armor bore the marks of fierce combat, and her graying hair was a wild, matted tangle. But determination set her sharp features as she surveyed our ragged company through reddened eyes.

"You have my boundless thanks for returning for us," she rasped at length, her voice still hoarse from smoke and thirst. "I confess, by the end there, I had begun to abandon hope." Her words were simple but heartfelt sincerity rang in each one.

I inclined my head in acknowledgment, too tired for unnecessary words. We all were. But though bone-weary, peace and contentment washed over me. Our long mission was fulfilled — we had brought them back alive from the very gates of death.

Beside me, Branik struggled to rise, new vigor kindling in his single good eye. "Ye have done a deed worthy of song this day," he declared stoutly, gripping my shoulder with a mailed hand.

Though battered nearly senseless, the sturdy dwarf's appreciation of our loyal service was unmistakable.

"I reckon there's a fair sight of treasure yet lyin' unclaimed down below," Leigh ventured casually, giving voice to my own thoughts regarding the abandoned vaults. Her eyes sparkled eagerly at the prospect despite weariness bowing her slender shoulders.

Branik grinned, his bushy mustache bristling. "Aye, the drake's hoard!" he growled. "That was the goal of our venture to begin with."

I raised my brows in surprise, curiosity piqued. Branik's vehemence hinted at unknown intricacies behind the ill-fated expedition.

Clara, too, shifted where she sat, unease crossing her drawn features at his words. Clearly, there was more to this tale.

"What do you mean?" I asked.

Clara and Branik exchanged a long look freighted with reluctant acceptance. At last, Branik nodded slowly, and Clara turned back to me with a sigh.

"You are owed an explanation, at least," she acquiesced wearily, "after coming to our aid like this."

She paused then to moisten cracked lips before continuing hoarsely. "Simply put, our mission was not just to delve into the Dungeon and grab what we could. Some wealth was promised to us, yes, but we came at the behest of another who claimed the treasure."

I listened intently as she elaborated on the patron who had asked them to undertake the delve.

"Lord Vartlebeck himself asked us," she said. "The hoard is made up of treasures of his clan, and he wanted them to be returned."

"Aye," Branik agreed. "And he *needs* the treasure, too. Drakelings have been a-gatherin' near Ironfast, and we need to up the hold's defenses. Mercenaries from the other holds, arming kinsmen, buildin' up the fortifications."

I nodded slowly. The dragon hoard in Hrothgar's Hope would've been nice to take home, of course, but if it was needed for the defense of a frontier settlement, then that was a nobler purpose.

Still, the reward for this mission would be good enough for us.

Clara's rueful stare bore into mine, divining the thoughts churning behind my eyes. "Had we known a dragon of this power laired below, we would certainly have refused. Or come better prepared for the beast, at least..."

Branik grunted agreement, glowering into the

distance.

"Now," Clara continued, "we lost Ergun, Talia, and Lander. Good souls, all three."

Sympathy welled up within me for their plight. "You fought as well as you could," I said gently. "Rest now; we will discuss the completion of your quest tomorrow once you've recovered your strength."

Relief flickered across Clara's haggard features. She nodded gratefully, not possessing the energy to converse further. Beside her, Branik's eyelids were already drooping with exhaustion. The dwarf looked near collapse.

While the others prepared a meal, I swiftly made the tents in order. Clara's expedition had left theirs, but wind and snow had had free play for a while, and so I made sure everything was ready for use. It was the least comfort we could provide after all Clara and Branik had suffered.

Once everything was ready, they sank gratefully into their bedrolls, succumbing to utter exhaustion almost instantly.

I touched Diane's slender shoulder as I looked at

the others. "You all should rest too," I said gently. "I'll keep first watch a while."

Diane smiled tiredly but gratefully squeezed my hand in return before moving off to join the others. Leigh blew me a kiss as she joined Diane in the tent. Karjela, too, was tired, and she slipped into her tent and slept.

But Celeste remained. She poked the fire, seemingly lost in thought. She had been in this mood ever since the battle with the dragon. And I was happy she didn't go to sleep just yet.

It was time she and I had a conversation.

# Chapter 26

As we settled by the fire, I studied Celeste's fair features in the flickering light. Though weary from the day's travails, unease still lingered in her luminous gaze.

"How are you holding up?" I asked gently.

Celeste glanced up, seeming to shake off her

pensive mood. "I am well," she replied with a faint smile. "Just... absorbing all that has transpired, I suppose."

I nodded. "You performed admirably in the battles we faced. But I feel like something is going on in your mind."

Celeste bit her lip, hesitating a moment. "I have told you before that I only took up the blade once before," she said softly. "To fight again... It stirs dark memories of that combat. I... I had promised myself I would not take up the blade again. But somehow... when you came into my life and spoke of adventure and companionship..."

She thought for a moment before shaking her head and continuing. "Well, I turned vain and desired these things that you spoke of. But now, wielding the blade once more, old injuries surface." She then looked at me with her blazing emerald eyes and scoffed at herself. "I am sorry... I should not bother you with this."

Surprise flickered through me. "You're not bothering me at all, Celeste," I said. "I *want* to know how you're doing. I *want* to know when anything's wrong, so I can try to help you."

I smiled to soften my words. "I love having you with us," I said. "You're an asset during these adventures, but I like who you are, too. If we want to work together more often, we need to let each other in."

Celeste ducked her head almost shyly before looking up at me, a smile appearing on her plump, kissable lips. "I know I must seem difficult," she murmured. "But you are right. Allow me to explain fully. But please... promise me what is said this night shall remain between the two of us."

I reached over and gently squeezed her hand in reassurance. "Of course," I said kindly. "I only wish to know if you are well. Anything you say will be confidential between the two of us."

Celeste gifted me with another tremulous smile. "Thank you," she said earnestly. "I want to share my truths with you, if you will hear them."

I nodded encouragingly. "You may tell me anything."

Taking a deep breath, she began. "As you may have surmised, my Class is not... an ordinary one.

I am a Stellar Maiden. Our gifts lie in the way of the blade."

I raised an eyebrow. "I believe I heard the legend of that Class," I said, remembering the tale of Storyteller at the Festival of Aquana. "Wasn't that the tale of Devaara, the wood elf, who ventured from Talamas-Adaa in wanderlust and took the heart of a dragon, blessed by the stars themselves?"

She smiled at that, her eyes softening as they roamed over me. "Indeed," she hummed. "You know our legends well! Devaara was the first Stellar Maiden. We are skilled in swordplay, imbued with the light of the stars. But our Class is more powerful than many others who focus on combat. And as it has always been, such things draw jealous ire from other Classes."

I nodded slowly. "Envy is a terrible thing."

"It is! Long have we remained hidden for our own protection," Celeste explained. "But when I left to live with my uncle, I was foolish and reckless with my gifts. And exposed."

Her luminous eyes took on a haunted cast. "A rival... with the Changeling Class attempted to steal my essence — to absorb my powers for his own use. He attacked me, and I defended myself, slaying him. But the Changeling's spell damaged me deeply, and I fell into a magically induced coma. Uncle Waelin saved me, but I lingered in that coma until you came along. Once I awakened — thanks to your assistance — I vowed I would not use my abilities again. But then you told of adventure and exploration, and I could not resist the call…"

Her eyes burned on me with a fierce intensity now, and I sensed desire hidden in that gaze — the desire I, too, shared. "And you *spoke* with me," she continued. "Like an equal. You did not treat me like others treat elves — either with disdain or distant admiration. You spoke, and you asked. You laughed, and you showed me your world." She reached out and placed a soft hand over mine. "And I wanted to be in that world. In *your* world."

I sat in silence, stunned by these revelations. The intensity of her feelings, the meaning of a few kind words and understanding from me had been profound. And now, she had revealed that a mysterious malady had been caused by an insidious attack.

"I'm glad to hear that, Celeste," I finally said. "But I'm sorry to hear what happened to you. It must have been a traumatic experience."

Still, I felt like there was something else going on, so I fell silent, leaving her the space to say whatever else she felt needed saying.

She nodded softly, then swallowed. "The Changeling," she finally continued. "It was my other uncle, my father's brother. We did not know he had a Changeling Class, and in his attempt to absorb my powers, he slew my mother, Waelin's sister."

"I'm so sorry, Celeste," I said.

She swallowed, fighting against tears that formed. "It has been years, but I have spent those in a coma, and the grief... It feels so fresh. To me, it *is* so fresh."

Gently clasping her hand again, I met Celeste's eyes earnestly. "You're right to mourn," I said. "An experience like that will shake anyone. You should take your time to process this, Celeste. I will gladly help, and I'm sure the girls would, too, if they knew."

Relief cascaded across Celeste's delicate features. Impulsively, she embraced me. I held her slender frame as she whispered her thanks, overwhelmed by the catharsis of finally sharing her long-kept secrets and pains.

When we separated, Celeste regarded me solemnly. "Forgive my reticence until now," she entreated. "I am unaccustomed to placing trust. But I vow I will not keep things from you."

I smiled warmly, letting her see the sincerity in my eyes. "You have my trust also," I said. "We walk this road together now."

"Together," Celeste echoed, some of the shadow lifting from her gaze. She gifted me with a radiant smile that warmed my heart before closing me in another hug.

I held Celeste for a while, reveling in the feeling of

having her pressed close against me.

Her tale was one of sorrow, and I knew my other women would accept her and sympathize if they knew Celeste's sad tale, but it was up to Celeste to share it. I would not intervene with that.

Finally, she pulled back, giving me a grateful look. "Thank you, David," she said. "For listening and being here for me."

"Anytime," I said. "I want to help, and I'm happy you decided to open up." I squeezed her hand. "I lost my parents, too, after the Upheaval. They were adventurers, and they never returned from the Wilds one day. I know what it's like to feel alone."

She gave me a thankful smile before her gaze turned pensive. "Your parents," she hummed. "The dragon spoke of your Bloodline, did it not?"

I nodded. "It did. It said it did not care about my Bloodline, as if it was something to be feared."

I had pondered the meaning of those words in the aftermath of our victory and on our way back to the base camp. So far, the meaning of it all still eluded me.

"It also called me Goldblood," I remarked. "Do you know what it could have meant?"

Celeste pursed her lips pensively. "Among elven lore, there are ancient legends of ones called Goldbloods," she said after a moment. "Supposedly, they were blessed with prowess in battle."

I leaned forward with interest, hoping she could illuminate this mysterious moniker. "What more do the legends say?" I asked.

"Little more that I know of, I fear," Celeste admitted regretfully. "Just that the Goldbloods became mighty champions. It has something to do with dragons, I believe, but I am unsure what. You would need someone schooled in the ancient lore to know more. I doubt even Uncle Waelin would know more."

I sat back, pondering her words as I watched the firelight dance. This scrap of elven myth aligned with the strange rapidity of my own advancement since coming to the frontier. Perhaps there was truth to the tales.

"Do you think that is the source of my luck in

advancement?" I mused.

Celeste gave an elegant half-shrug. "Your gifts do seem uncommon," she acknowledged. "And they seem to rub off on your companions, myself included. But I cannot say with certainty. Although..."

She hesitated, seeming reluctant to continue voicing her thoughts. I gestured encouragingly for her to go on.

"Well, the powers of a Bloodline are known to be... *strong,*" she said carefully. "The dragon detected them in some way, and it seemed to fear you."

I nodded. "I got that impression, too. It lay waiting in ambush. Instead of attacking, it decided to talk. At the moment, I considered that it was either arrogant or afraid."

"The latter," she hummed. "And substantially so. It must have had some Blood Mage talents to detect your might. It is known that dragons sometimes gain the abilities of those they consume. Perhaps it defeated a Blood Mage at some point. Either way, it knew, and it tried to avoid combat."

"But why wouldn't it just give up Clara and Branik if it wanted to avoid combat?"

"Simple," Celeste said. "To save face. It would've been shameful for the beast to submit to your demands. This pride runs so deep in dragon blood that they cannot even consider submitting to the will of others."

I nodded slowly. "So, it preferred to risk the fight over submitting."

"They are prideful beasts," she confirmed. "They prefer death over loss of face."

"And what of the Father it mentioned?"

Her face took on a dark look. "I... I do not know. But it bodes ill. Dragons gain power by age rather than experience like us who have Classes. This was a powerful dragon, but a juvenile one. Its father is likely to be ancient. If it called to it, then it will come to avenge its spawn. Dragons rarely get along with their siblings and oust them from the nest as swift as they can. But when their offspring are slain, pride and vengeance take control."

I pondered that for a moment. "So, a powerful dragon might be coming our way?"

"I fear so, yes."

I reached out for her hand, soft as velvet and pale as moonlight. "No need to fear," I said. "We will be ready. We will learn what we can of this dragon and of my Bloodline. And if this Father comes, we will fight it. And we will win."

She gave me a soft smile. "Your words comfort me, David," she said.

I decided to move our talk to lighter topics then, sensing we both needed respite from such weighty matters. There would be time enough to unravel mysteries of the past. Tonight was for peace, and I needed Celeste to be in a calm mindset before I would send her off to sleep.

We talked a while longer as the fire gradually dimmed. Though we both were bone-weary, it felt good simply to enjoy this moment of companionship beneath the emerging stars, sharing a laugh together.

When at last I could see Celeste struggling to stifle delicate yawns, I chuckled. "Get some rest," I urged gently. "Dawn comes early, and we'll leave this place tomorrow morning and make our way back to Gladdenfield."

Rising smoothly, Celeste inclined her head in graceful acquiescence. But she paused and met my eyes once more before turning toward the tent.

"David, I… thank you," she said simply yet with profound sincerity. And in that instant, the last of the barriers between us fell away. We understood one another perfectly.

With a smile lingering on my lips, I watched her go. Though darkness yet lurked beyond our sheltered camp, tonight my spirit felt at peace.

# Chapter 27

After my talk with Celeste, I sat alone by the dying fire, pondering all that had transpired this day. Though bone-weary, my mind raced with thoughts of mysterious Bloodlines and vengeful dragon fathers. But most of all, I dwelled on the breakthrough with Celeste. Now for the first time, I felt as if we were truly close.

Weary as I was, I decided to pace around a little, ignoring the biting wind and cold once I left the radius of the warm fire. I needed to ward off sleep. As I walked and kept a close watch on the camp's perimeter, my mind drifted to the advancement I had made.

Two levels after one battle!

Admittedly, we had fought goblins and kobolds as well, so I had probably been on the verge of hitting level 7 when we joined battle with the dragon. Still, considering how much effort it took to level, I supposed gaining two in a day was fairly rare!

When I was certain everything was calm, I focused my mind and brought up the status window. There, clear as day, were the twin notifications I had been awaiting. Two levels up. With a deep breath to steady my eagerness, I tapped the first notification.

For the first level up, a selection of three new spells appeared, from which I had to choose one. Then, there was the increase in 10 health and 5 mana I received on every level.

The spells I could choose from were Aura of Protection, a spell that protected those around me from harm. By the spell's description, I understood it to increase the difficulty to hit them. Combined with my guardians, it might be a useful spell!

The second spell was Call Familiar, which gave me the power to teleport any creature to me that I had bound with my Bind Familiar spell. The third spell was Air Bubble, which allowed me to envelop myself in a bubble of breathable air for some time, letting me move unharmed through dangerous fumes.

While Air Bubble had its applications, I found it too specific to merit selection. To me, it was a battle between Aura of Protection and Call Familiar.

And while Call Familiar was useful, it cost 6 mana, which was 1 more mana than it cost me to summon an entirely new domesticant. It would be economical to use for Mr. Drizzles, the storm elemental that patrolled the homestead, but the spell did not allow me to *return* the creature, so building up a stable of bound summons and calling and dismissing them from a central point was not possible. Yet.

In the end, I settled for Aura of Protection. It had a low cost – 4 mana — and it would strengthen me, my companions, and my summons.

After that, I leveled up to 8, receiving 10 more health and 5 more mana, as well as a selection from three more spells. First of these were Summon Gargoyle, which allowed me to conjure forth an immobile, three-headed statue that spat acid attacks at foes. According to the spell description, it did lots of damage, but its weakness was that it could not move.

The second spell was Banish, which allowed me to banish a summon or bound creature back to its realm of origin — a spell I would not like to be on the receiving end of. It had a small failing chance, but it would have been very useful in a place like Nimos Sedia, where we had faced several bound creatures.

The final spell was Imbue Weapon. This allowed me to channel my mana into a weapon, giving it magical properties like armor piercing or flame damage for a short time. It focused on damage output, but at the cost of 5 mana, I might as well spend a little more and just call forth another summon.

I settled for Banish. I liked the gargoyle, but I had Aquana's avatar and the storm elemental as main damage dealers in my deck of spells, while the guardian could tank. I was not eager to give up mobility, and I didn't want to increase damage output for myself since the summons did most of the work. The ability to remove summons or bound creatures from play, however, appealed to me.

In addition to gaining a new spell, level 8 also conferred an extra slot for a Bind Familiar spell. I already had two domesticants — Ghostie and Sir Boozles — and one storm elemental, Mr. Drizzles. Now, I could add another to the pack!

As the last notification faded, I took a moment to savor the rush of power thrumming through my veins. Already my senses felt honed, my reflexes quickened. Each level gained out here exponentially strengthened my attunement to this world.

Taking a moment, I reviewed my updated character sheet.

**Name: David Wilson**

**Class: Frontier Summoner**

**Level: 8**

**Health: 90/90**

**Mana: 45/45 (+10 from Hearth Treasures)**

Skills:

**Summon Minor Spirit — Level 17 (3 mana)**

**Summon Domesticant — Level 16 (5 mana)**

**Summon Guardian — Level 15 (7 mana)**

**Summon Aquana's Avatar — Level 11 (10 mana)**

**Summon Storm Elemental — Level 9 (10 mana)**

**Bind Familiar — Level 3 (15 mana)**

**Aura of Protection — Level 1 (4 mana)**

**Banish — Level 1 (6 mana)**

**Identify Plants — Level 14 (1 mana)**

**Foraging — Level 15 (1 mana)**

**Trapping — Level 16 (1 mana)**

**Alchemy — Level 17 (1 mana)**

**Farming — Level 6 (1 mana)**

**Ranching — Level 1 (1 mana)**

Studying my sheet, I discovered that my Summon Domesticant and Summon Guardian spells had advanced beyond level 15, lowering their mana cost by 1. I saw that two of my other skills — Foraging and Trapping — had also advanced beyond level 15, but that had not brought down their mana cost. Apparently, 1 mana was the minimum.

Still, I was thoroughly satisfied with my progress. And if the strange words of the dragon held any truth, then perhaps there were even greater heights yet to be attained. Glancing down at my hands, I wondered what gifts might yet lie dormant in my blood, waiting to be awakened.

The creak of a tent flap shook me from my thoughts. I glanced up to see Diane emerge, her delicate features etched with concern.

"Is all well?" she asked. "I haven't heard you pacing for a while." Always perceptive, Diane had picked up on me sitting down to level up. Apparently, she was really on edge.

I smiled reassuringly. "All's fine. I just leveled up."

She came over to listen as I described my new abilities. "Incredible," she remarked when I had finished. "You grow stronger every day. Whatever this Bloodline is, it's clear you have a gift." Her tone held a note of pride that warmed me.

"We all have gifts," I replied modestly. "Have you leveled up yet?"

She nodded. "Just before I went to bed. I learned a new empowered shot to deal more damage. I think the battle with that dragon would've been a lot shorter if I had that ability going in."

I chuckled. "See?" I said. "We all have our skills. I'm not much of a damage dealer."

Diane gifted me with one of her subtle, knowing smiles. "You have a good heart, David," she said fondly. "I'm thankful for that, most of all."

With that said, she leaned in and kissed me tenderly beneath the softly twinkling stars.

All my unanswered questions about power and destiny seemed to matter less in that serene moment. I drew Diane close, letting myself simply be present with her. For now, it was enough.

When we finally broke apart, weariness had

descended fully upon us both. The hour had grown late, and we needed what rest we could claim.

"Why don't you get some sleep?" she said. "I'll take over. Crawl in nice and warm with Leigh."

I nodded and yawned. "That sounds heavenly."

Before ducking into the tent to snatch a few hours' rest, I paused a moment more to glance up at the vast glittering sweep of the heavens arcing overhead. The stars seemed almost to pulse in time with the power thrumming through my blood. A strange fancy, perhaps, but it felt significant somehow.

Turning away from the jeweled infinity above, I slipped into the shelter of the tent. Nestling wearily beneath my blanket, comforted by the warmth of Leigh's slumbering body nearby, I let exhaustion claim me at last.

The last thing I heard before I drifted was Leigh's happy and sleepy hum as she felt my body connect with hers.

# Chapter 28

Morning sunlight filtered into the tent, rousing me from a deep sleep. For a moment, I lay there groggily trying to get my bearings.

Then memory came flooding back — the harrowing delve into Hrothgar's Hope and the miraculous rescue of Clara and Branik. It had been quite the adventure, but there was still work to do.

Rising quietly, I ducked outside into the bracing mountain air. Around the smoldering fire pit, some of my companions were already up and about, packing gear in preparation for the day's tasks ahead.

I spotted Celeste seated with Clara, speaking too softly for me to overhear. But I was certain they were speaking of the Dungeon's hardships.

When Clara noticed me, she rose gingerly to her feet with Celeste's aid. Limping over, she extended her hand.

"Once again, you have my deepest thanks," she said solemnly as we clasped wrists warrior-style. "What you accomplished is worthy of legend."

I nodded and smiled. "We did it together. My only regret is we couldn't get there sooner."

She gave an appreciative nod. "You did more than most," she said.

After a quick breakfast, our whole party prepared to return to the depths once more — this time to retrieve the expedition's rightful treasure from the vault below. Though still stiff and battered, Clara and Branik stubbornly insisted on accompanying us rather than waiting above.

The return trip through the gloomy tunnels was uneventful. All threats had been decisively neutralized by our previous efforts. Still, we remained vigilant and traveled tightly together. Before long, we stood once more in the dragon's lair, the dusty air heavy with anticipation.

Shining my flashlight beam inside, the heaped dwarven coins and artifacts glinted back. This hoard could sustain Branik's people through the coming clash and beyond. The riches now carried a deeper purpose. The only difficulty would be in transporting it all.

Before we got to work, we carefully took stock of the hoard. Eventually, we came to the conclusion that we should be able to bear it. It was a lot, but if we took it easy, we would bring it all back to the surface. The saving grace was the larroling and the domesticant I could bind to myself for extra aid.

"Our original party of six would have hardly been able to bring out the entire haul," Clara commented. "Another reason I'm happy you're here."

I summoned another domestican and bound it to me. I would dismiss it when its bearing services were no longer needed, but I had found that — of all my summons — the domesticans were best at hauling things.

Working swiftly, we loaded chests and stashed items of particular value into our packs. It would take us several trips, and I projected we would spend most of the morning working to get it all to the surface.

We hauled all morning, and the treasure hoard of the dragon saw light again for the first time in years. It was an impressive hoard, and Clara and her party had luckily brought enough packs with them to be able to stash it all. We could hang several of those packs on the larroling — although it growled annoyedly at being used as a pack animal — and the domestican carried a lot despite its small frame.

Our hauling task completed, we reemerged into the upper caverns. One more duty remained this day — laying our fallen comrades properly to rest.

Leading us back through the echoing tunnels, Diane and I navigated unerringly to the small cave where we had found Lander's body. Together, we carefully bore his remains out into the open mountain air. After that, we found Ergun's remains where we had left them.

Talia's remains were hardest to locate as we had to navigate by Karjela's disjointed account. Eventually, we found her, and there was little to recognize that she had once been an elven Sorceress. We brought her up, too, and then prepared the fallen by wrapping them in linen salvaged from the Dungeon and cleaned in a fresh and pure mountain stream.

In a sheltered valley nearby, we dug a grave using tools brought from the base camp. The simple ceremony was brief but deeply solemn.

Clara murmured words of loss over the quiet mounds, and I, too, remembered the vibrant — if somewhat belligerent — young man Ergun had been. Though we had intervened too late to save them, we could at least accord their bodies this final dignity.

Throughout this necessary task, Branik murmured prayers in his native dwarvish tongue. The survivors carried a burden of guilt that we could now help alleviate by ensuring their friends' spirits could move on.

As dusk's shadows descended over the makeshift burial ground, a sense of peace settled on our hearts. We had done right by the fallen. Their rest would be undisturbed on this scenic mountain slope until the end of days.

The final task was packing everything up and getting things ready for our departure. By now, it was getting late, and I did not want to brave the mountain flanks at night.

Instead, we would proceed in the morning, and we would have everything ready for then. As such, we packed up everything we didn't need that night.

Weary but satisfied, we finished up as a golden glow suffused the evening sky. It was still cold, but the sunlight was not as pale and hostile as it had been when we first climbed Hrothgar's Hope.

That night we sat around the crackling flames,

recounting the harrowing adventure and the deeds of the fallen. Though dangers still lurked beyond our base camp, for now, we relaxed.

Jokes soon mingled with solemn remembrances of the fallen. Diane broke into lively song, rousing Branik to stomp the gritty earth and sing of ancestry proud.

Gradually the lively conversations faded, one by one, as weary heads began to nod. A sense of fulfillment replaced the nervous energy fueling our initial revelry. This night, we had earned rest beneath the glittering sea of stars watching over us.

As the embers burned low and stillness descended, the others went to their tents, and I kept a silent watch. Several hours later, Diane relieved me, and I joined Leigh in our tent. Nestling in the soft sleeping bag, I closed my eyes and enjoyed some well-earned rest.

# Chapter 29

Pale morning light roused me from slumber. Careful not to disturb Leigh, still curled up beside me, I extricated myself from the sleeping bag and slipped outside to begin preparing for our departure.

A fresh layer of powdery snow blanketed the

campsite, but the sky overhead was clear and cloudless; ideal conditions for the long trek out of the peaks. We were lucky with that. Shivering in the icy air, I swiftly rekindled the fire before moving to wake the others.

Soon, we were all gathered around the crackling flames, bleary-eyed but eager to quit this place. We had bid the fallen farewell, and the dragon's hoard was packed up and ready for transport.

While we ate a hasty breakfast, I explained the plan to reach lower altitudes before nightfall. Clara, Karjela, and Branik still needed time to recover, so we would move at an easy pace.

"Once we're out of the mountains, we make for Ironfast first," I said. "We will return the hoard to Lord Vartlebeck. After that, Diane, Leigh, Celeste, and I will return to Gladdenfield Outpost. Any of you wishing to join us will be most welcome!"

Once fed, we swiftly broke camp and buried the remains of our fire beneath the snow before forming up for the march down.

Diane and I took the lead, forging a path through the fresh drifts, while Leigh and Celeste aided

Clara, Karjela, and Branik behind us. The larroling and the bound domesticant brought up the rear, plowing aside any deeper accumulations, laden in packs. The packs full of the dragon's hoard were heavy, but we bore them with stoic tenacity.

We moved with lighter spirits now that the way ahead promised warmth and safety. The vistas opened up grandly around us as we descended from that dread Dungeon's heights. It felt cleansing to leave those twisting tunnels behind.

Before long, the white drifts clinging to the rocks became patchy, then surrendered once more to bare stone and scree. The air marginally warmed. Two hawks swooped and called to one another high above, the only other living things stirring in these remote reaches.

Around mid-morning, we paused briefly to rest and drink from the icy stream tumbling down from the heights. The cold water reinvigorated our tired bodies for the march ahead, and we would need our strength considering the serious packs we bore with us.

Branik grunted appreciatively as he guzzled the

last drop before we prepared to move on. There was even some light chatter and joking among the remains of Clara's party as they regained some of their vigor.

The compass on my heart pulled steadily southward as we wound lower down the convoluted mountain paths. The way ahead seemed clearer and more certain with each step now that we had accomplished our mission here. But we remained ever watchful of our surroundings.

By early afternoon, the terrain leveled out into a series of plateaus and ravines still choked with patchy snow and ice. A cutting wind sliced through our cloaks and leathers if we lingered exposed atop the flat shelves of stone for long.

On one such exposed plateau around midday, the larroling suddenly halted, ears flicking as it lifted its blocky head to sniff the frigid gusts. I tensed, hand drifting toward my rifle.

But after a moment, the beast merely grunted and continued lumbering onward. Just the scent of mountain goats on the wind.

Still, my heart hammered for a minute even after the false alarm. The peaks kept you wired for trouble, and there were still plenty of goblins and kobolds around...

Relief washed over me when at last we descended into the shelter of the treeline as dusk gathered. Snow still blanketed the ground, but the oppressive chill eased once out of the wind. I smiled, feeling Diane squeeze my shoulder happily at the relative comfort of our upcoming campsite.

While there was still light, Diane swiftly shot a plump rabbit with her crossbow. After dressing it, she handed the carcass off to Leigh, who had volunteered to prepare a stew using some tubers and edible lichen.

The rest of us set about establishing camp as our meager daylight rapidly faded. Soon we had a merry fire crackling, tents pitched, and weapons within easy reach. The smell of rabbit stew filled the little glen, rousing hungry appetites.

Huddled beneath the fragrant pines, we shared the hearty stew Leigh prepared, along with crusty bread and dried fruit from our provisions. The simple travel fare satisfied our gnawing hunger after the grueling day's march. Clara and Branik ate ravenously, their strength returning.

While we lingered over second helpings, I decided the peaceful mood provided an opportunity to review my character progress from our battles in the Dungeon. The others listened with interest as I detailed the new abilities gained.

"Soon you'll be strong enough to take on that dragon's angry papa singlehanded!" Leigh joked, elbowing me playfully.

But her words stirred uneasy thoughts of whatever new threat might lurk over the horizon. For now, I pushed those concerns aside, savoring this calm interlude with my companions.

Around the dwindling fire, our conversation turned to speculation about the future and what new adventures awaited us beyond the familiar confines of Gladdenfield. Personally, I looked forward to returning for a while to the tranquility of the homestead after this excitement. But I knew there was a new threat on the horizon, and we would have to prepare for that.

When the girls' delighted chatter gave way to yawns, I bid them get some rest while I took first watch. By then, Clara's party — except the stoic Branik — had already withdrawn to their tents. Safety in numbers allowed us to drop our guard somewhat, but we were still in the Wilds.

One by one, the girls retired to their tents until only Branik remained awake with me, puffing solemnly on his pipe by the fire. But soon even his gruff determination to wait up could not best bone-deep exhaustion, and he too retired.

My watch passed swiftly beneath the crystalline canopy of the night sky as I patrolled the tranquil perimeter of our secluded camp. My breath puffed out in faint mist, but I was grateful for the solitude amidst the hushed pine boughs to gather my scattered thoughts.

Before long, I roused Leigh for her turn on watch and crawled gratefully into the shared warmth of the tent.

Predawn's chill roused me what seemed a mere moment later. But with movements swift from routine, we broke camp after a hasty meal and prepared to cover the remainder of the descent before dusk.

We shouldered the heavy packs filled to the brim with the dragon's hoard, and Diane took a moment to get her bearings and consulted for a while with Branik — a native of Ironfast — before we set off in the direction of Lord Vartlebeck's hold.

We set off on a brisk pace through the pines, making steady progress down the wooded mountain slopes. Though a chill still lingered in the shady glens, the worst of the biting cold had passed. Songbirds flitted from branch to branch, sending cheerful trills cascading through the quiet cathedral of the woods.

We hiked throughout the morning, our packs laden with the dragon's treasure won through such hardship. Though the gold still weighed heavy, our steps felt lighter now that we had accomplished our quest. It helped that the floor was even here and that we no longer had to struggle down the slope.

As we walked, Diane's clear voice rang out, leading us in a rousing marching song that helped eat up the miles. To my great amusement, Celeste at some point fell back to walk beside her, holding her pack steady with both hands and began humming along.

Soon enough, the two beauties were singing a marching song that mixed the jaunty and folksy qualities of foxkin song with the more solemn and artistic beauty of elven song.

[Diane]

"Oh the open road, it rolls on ever long,

Past the hills and trees, we're marching with our song!

No matter what may come, we'll see it through,

Together we will go, our fellowship so true!"

[Celeste]

"Though the path be dark, our hearts will shine the way,

Evil shall not dim, the light we hold today.

With voices raised as one, we'll banish threads of fear,

And from each soul a flame, of hope and joy appear!"

[Together]

*"So march on, sisters, brothers too!*

*The road ahead is laid for you.*

*Have courage, clan, we're here for all,*

*No matter what may come, we'll not let each other fall!"*

 *[Diane]*

*"When the rain comes down, we'll weather through the storm,*

*Though thunder crash and lightning flash, we'll keep the others warm!*

*The clouds can't block the sun forever in the sky,*

*So chin up, friends, embrace — soon we'll see dawn nigh!"*

 *[Celeste]*

*"The miles may weary, but songs will lift our feet,*

*Our voices entwined, make burdens light and sweet.*

*Take comfort, kindred, we walk as one this day,*

*The fellowship of heart and song will light our way!"*

 *[Together]*

*"Yes, march on ever more, O fellowship unending!*

*Through rain or sun, we'll see this journey through.*

*Have faith and fortitude, cling to those you're befriending,*

*Together we shall thrive, this stalwart, valiant crew!"*

As the last harmonious notes faded into the crisp mountain air, we broke into enthusiastic applause and cheers.

"That was mighty fine!" Leigh exclaimed, grinning from ear to ear. "You two songbirds have the voices of angels."

I let out an impressed whistle. "You both blended your styles beautifully together," I remarked. "The folks back in Gladdenfield would pay good coin to hear a duet like that at the tavern."

Celeste flushed delicately at the praise, looking quietly pleased by the reception. Though normally reserved, I could tell our positive reaction to her impromptu singing meant a lot.

Meanwhile, Diane waved off the compliments with characteristic modesty. "Oh, it just came to us spur of the moment," she demurred. "Celeste has a real gift. I mostly just kept up."

"Are you kidding?" Leigh scoffed. "The two of you were made to sing together. It was like listening to the Muses themselves!"

Even Branik rumbled his approval in his gravelly

brogue. "Aye, lasses, ye have voices fine as any Rune Singer of Ironfast hold," the dwarf declared. "Why, I'd wager the very trees were list'nin' to yer song just now!"

Celeste and Diane exchanged pleased looks at the hearty praise. Though diverse in culture and temperament, their shared musical passions had helped unite them.

I smiled seeing the warmth and camaraderie kindling between two women who had once eyed each other warily. Music transcended differences.

"We should sing together more often," Diane suggested amiably to Celeste as we resumed our trek.

Celeste's answering smile lit up her delicate features. "I would like that very much," she replied sincerely. The elven beauty then reached over and gave Diane's hand an appreciative squeeze.

My own heart swelled happily at this sign of true friendship blossoming between them. A simple, spontaneous song had done much to strengthen their bond.

Many good things came of this quest, and I was

optimistic for even more.

# Chapter 30

Around mid-morning, we reached a sun-blessed glade, and I called the first halt of the day. We gratefully shrugged off our packs and stretched our weary shoulders. While we rested, Diane circled the perimeter, ever alert for signs of danger. But all remained tranquil.

Passing waterskins, I checked with each companion in turn. Though still bearing bruises, Clara gave me a firm nod. Beside her, Karjela smiled wearily but made no complaint. Branik merely grunted when I asked if he required aid, bushy brows knit with stoic determination.

When we were sufficiently rested, we reclaimed our burdens and continued southward. The terrain gradually smoothed, and sparrows twittered cheerfully in the leafy boughs. My boots scuffed softly over moss and pine needles, at peace with the wild woodlands.

Around noon, Leigh spotted a winding stream tumbling merrily over smooth stones near our path. Gratefully, we refilled our canteens in the crystalline current, savoring the chill meltwater.

While we lingered, I managed to spear a few fat trout with my hunting knife, accepting Celeste's aid to clean and carry them. The elven maiden had learned much of survival during our time in the Wilds.

We walked on through the pleasantly warm afternoon, enjoying the gentle birdsong all around.

Though we remained wary, keeping weapons close, no threats emerged from the tranquil forest. Step by step, we drew steadily nearer to civilization once more.

When the shadows began to lengthen, we sought out a sheltered dell to make camp for the night. A small brook provided fresh water, and I gathered an armful of dry kindling. Before long, Diane had a cheery blaze crackling against the creeping chill.

While the trout cooked, I helped Celeste and Leigh pitch tents as Branik stumped off to find more firewood. Before long, our cozy camp was fully established for the night ahead.

We would take turns keeping watch, but all seemed calm. For now, we simply savored this peaceful respite from the peaks' perils.

Gathered around the dancing flames, we dined on deliciously smoked trout followed by crusty bread and dried fruit. Laughter and banter flowed freely as we relaxed around the campfire swapping tales of past exploits. The starry sky winked between swaying boughs as we lingered late into the night simply enjoying each other's company.

When yawns finally came too frequently to ignore, we reluctantly dampened the fire and turned in for the night. I sat smoking my pipe for the first watch, rifle across my knees. All remained still but for the muted rush of the brook and occasional hoot of an owl. Before long I woke Branik to relieve me. He accepted the duty with a gruff nod.

I crept into the tent I shared with Leigh and nestled into the warmth of our bedrolls. She murmured happily and cuddled against me in her sleep. Lulled by the gentle sounds of the forest night, I soon drifted off.

Morning came all too swiftly, but we rose with the light, knowing many miles yet lay before us. A quick breakfast of bread and dried meat fortified us for the day's trek. Soon we had tents broken down and packs secured. With Diane scouting ahead as always, we set off briskly into the sylvan morning.

The piney woods gradually thinned as we traveled throughout the sunny morning. By midday, rolling grassland rippled away on either side of the narrow trail. Wildflowers nodded cheerily in the gentle breeze. Though we slackened pace somewhat to accommodate Clara and the other injured party members, our progress remained steady.

When the sun climbed high overhead, heat shimmered off the waving grass, and we sought refuge beneath a lonely oak. This grand, spreading specimen offered ample shade, and we settled gratefully in its dappled shade to rest awhile. The fresh breeze felt blissful after miles with the sun blazing upon our shoulders.

As we caught our breath, I turned to Branik, who had lived his days beneath these very mountains now rising ahead. "How much farther to your homeland?" I asked. The stout dwarf tugged thoughtfully at his beard as he pondered the question.

"At this pace, we should glimpse Ironfast's walls by evenin'," he opined at length in his gravelly brogue. "Just follow the river road yonder, through the foothills, 'til the gates open up afore us."

His shrewd eyes glinted with subdued pride for

his clanhold as he gestured toward a ribbon of silver flashing in the distance — the Ironflow River.

Heartened by this news, we lingered only a short while longer in the oak's generous shade before resuming our journey over the sun-warmed plains. The river road provided a clear route through undulating hills patched with stands of aspen and pine. Herds of elk and deer grazed placidly, bolting off as soon as we passed too close.

Diane's ears pricked frequently as she ran ahead to scout the winding road, but she returned each time with all-clear. The wildlife seemed utterly untroubled, and there were no threats.

Still, we remained alert. Beneath the tranquil backdrop, one never knew what hazards the frontier might yet reveal. Such was the life we had chosen beyond civilization's walls.

By mid-afternoon, we reached a point where the river bent west but our path continued south. Bidding the roaring waters farewell, we struck off across gentler foothills blanketed in pines. Distant peaks still clawed at the sky, but the air warmed noticeably.

The sun was dipping toward the serrated western peaks when Diane halted abruptly atop a rise. "There!" she cried, pointing. Craning our necks, we beheld Ironfast for the first time, still miles distant but unmistakable. Excited murmurs rose from our weary party at the sight.

Perched upon a granite prominence, the mountain stronghold stood vigil over the surrounding vales. Even from this far vantage, the peak's fortified terraces and mighty stone bastions radiated formidable strength. Pennants fluttered defiance to the winter winds.

Branik's breath caught at the long-missed sight of hearth and home, love and longing writ plainly across his craggy features. "By my father's axe, what a glory it is!" he proclaimed thickly.

We afforded the dwarf a moment of solemn remembrance as he took in the sight of his home.

Though too distant to perceive the bustle of life, there could be no doubt that Ironfast's stout inhabitants yet kept their staunch watch. The lonely peak was an unbowed bastion in the Wilds. Our task would ensure its security.

When Branik had drunk his fill of the view, we continued down the winding forest path toward the valley floor, moving at an eager clip. Our weariness sloughed away knowing each step brought us nearer to food, fire, and comforts too long missed.

# Chapter 31

The sun was just starting to dip behind the snowy peaks by the time our weary party passed beneath the towering gates of Ironfast.

Dwarven guards in gleaming mail nodded respectfully as we entered the bustling town, allowing Branik to lead us unchallenged up the steep, twisting streets toward the hall of his lord.

All around us, stout dwarves paused in their labors to cheer Branik's return, clapping the weary warrior heartily on the back. He returned their enthusiastic greetings with gruff appreciation, clearly moved by his people's joy at seeing their kinsman safely home. Thankfully, he didn't stop to chat.

"I'll bring us straight to Lord Vartlebeck," he said. "He ought to be the first to hear of our return and his treasures bein' restored to him!"

The sights and smells of the thriving settlement were a balm to our travel-worn senses. Sturdy stone buildings lined the curving streets, candles and cook fires already winking cheerily in every window as dusk gathered. The scent of roasting meat set my stomach growling hungrily.

Branik set a brisk pace despite his lingering injuries, evidently eager for the coming reunion with his lord. We climbed higher, toward the peak's summit, where Vartlebeck's hall commanded an unrivaled vista of the surrounding valleys blanketed in shadow as night fell.

At last, we ascended the final stair and emerged into a broad courtyard before the soaring timber hall. Fiery braziers flanked the stout oaken doors, further warding off the mountain chill. Torches flared atop sturdy watchtowers, and mail-clad guards stood vigilant sentry along the crenellated walls.

Branik stepped forward and pounded loudly upon the entrada with a mailed fist. "Tis I, Branik Storsson, returned from the delve into Hrothgar's Hope!" he bellowed. "And I come with urgent tidings for Lord Vartlebeck!"

For several tense heartbeats, only echoing silence answered his hail. Then, with an ominous groan of iron hinges, one of the towering doors slowly swung inward.

Golden firelight spilled across the threshold, backlighting a broad, armored silhouette with a swaying beard.

"Branik?" the bulky warrior rumbled in disbelief, eyes widening beneath a prominent brow as he took in the tattered, dirty state of the new arrivals. Then a fierce grin split his beard. "Branik, you old goat! We feared ye dead! Come in, come in, all o' ya!"

The hearty dwarf warrior, who introduced himself as Garn, quickly ushered us into the cavernous hall with its soaring timber beams festooned with banners and weaponry from ages long past. Much of the dwarven heritage seemed intact, and I wondered if they had suffered less under the Upheaval than the elves.

Great fires roared in multiple hearths as shadows flickered over the revelry and song already underway at the rows of trestle tables.

A few curious gazes turned our way, but most of Vartlebeck's warriors and hearthmen remained fixated on overflowing platters of meat, bread, and ale. Mouth watering at the tempting spread, I hoped we might soon sample the dwarven bounty ourselves.

First, however, the lord waited.

Clearing a path through the crowd with booming voice and sheer bulk, Garn led us toward the dais where Lord Vartlebeck sat surveying the festivities from an ornate oaken throne studded with gilt and silver. A great bearskin was draped across his lap. Though past his prime, power still clung to the aged dwarf like a mantle.

At Garn's hail, Vartlebeck looked up, eyes narrowing. Then his shaggy, grizzled brows shot upward in stunned disbelief, and he half-rose from his carved chair.

"Branik?" he exclaimed. "You old bear! Ha! Ye're not dead after all!" He then thought for a moment before adding, "S'pose that means I still owe ye ten golden coins, then."

Mirthful laughter rippled around us at his words. Dwarves came up to pat Branik on the back, and many of the sturdy warrior folk took my forearm in the warrior's grip and thanked me for returning their kinsman.

When the ruckus died down, Branik stepped forward with a respectful bow. "Apologies for our late comin', m'lord. We ran afoul of evils in Hrothgar's Hope, but fortune delivered us." He gestured toward my own grimy, fatigued group. "These brave souls pulled us living from the depths when all seemed lost."

At this, Vartlebeck turned his scrutiny fully upon the rest of us.

I met the dwarf lord's piercing gaze squarely, chin lifted with quiet pride in our shared accomplishments. Power and wisdom both simmered in the dwarf's blunt-featured face.

"It seems formal introductions are in order," Lord Vartlebeck rumbled at length. "I know well yer name and yer weapon skill, David Wilson of Gladdenfield Outpost! Well do I remember yer daring victory at my tournament. But I know not your companions. Speak your names, adventurers, and how it is you came to play Branik's salvation." Though commanding, I detected naught but intrigued courtesy in his tone.

I stepped forward to make humble introduction of our band: Diane, Leigh, Celeste, and the larroling and domesticant that helped bear the treasure. He already knew Karjela and Clara, having charged them with returning the treasure.

"Well met!" he rumbled. "Now, if ye would be so kind to give me an account of the events."

We were tired and hungry, but I understood the

dwarven lord's wish to hear our tales first, and so I took the lead and spoke, delivering the details of our deeds since setting out from Gladdenfield, charged by the mayor of Gladdenfield Outpost to find Clara.

The aged dwarf lord listened intently, bushy brows drawing together as he absorbed the strange tale of lost comrades avenged and vanquished perils within Hrothgar's Hope. When I told of the dragon, his eyes widened and he looked to his kinsman Branik as if for confirmation, and Branik gave a solemn nod.

"A dragon!" Lord Vartlebeck rumbled. "Defiling Hrothgar's Hope! And ye did away with it, ye say?" He shook his head as if he could scarce believe it.

"Aye, my lord!" Branik confirmed. "They slew the beast, they did!"

"Such a deed has not been done in years," Lord Vartlebeck continued before turning his eyes to me. "Dragon-Slayer, I name ye, David Wilson of Gladdenfield, and know that to bear such a name is a great honor among dwarves. Ye'll not find a gate closed to ye in the lands friendly to the Silverheart clan!"

I inclined my head respectfully in gratitude as the dwarves in Lord Vartlebeck's hall stomped their sturdy feet and roared approval. Then, when they were silent once more, I continued my tale, of which little remained, recounting how we found Clara and Branik and how we brought up the hoard and paid a last respect to the fallen.

When all had been recounted, Lord Vartlebeck slowly stood before striding down from the dais to stand directly before me. Though he barely reached my shoulders, power radiated from him in palpable waves as he met my eyes.

"You have all demonstrated courage and valor worthy of the highest honor here." Vartlebeck's resonant voice carried to the hall's farthest corners. "In returning Branik and the lost hoard to our halls, you have won my deepest gratitude." He reached up to clasp my shoulder with a gnarled yet steely hand.

I inclined my head graciously. "The honor is ours, Lord Vartlebeck. Branik spoke highly of your people and mentioned the threat on your borders. We could not leave Clara's quest unfinished." Modesty felt appropriate before this proud dwarven lord who valued deeds over boasting words.

Vartlebeck squinted up at me, as if trying to peer into my very spirit. "Aye, humble you may be, but uncommon valor I sense in you, lad," he mused cryptically. "We shall speak more anon." He then raised his voice again to carry throughout the hall. "But come! Eat, drink, and rejoice with my hearthmen this night!"

A rousing cheer went up at his words. Before we even fully understood what was happening, our travel-stained party found itself swept up in the boisterous press of dwarves all shepherding us eagerly toward the trestle tables. My stomach gave an eager growl as platters were shoved before us, piled high with succulent meat, bread, and cheese.

Ale flowed freely in wooden tankards, and soon even the shy Celeste was laughing and chanting along with a bawdy dwarven drinking song. Weary to our very bones, it felt heavenly to finally relax among the warmth and revelry of Vartlebeck's hall, our long trial behind us, and only friends to surround us.

I found myself seated across from Clara as we ate. The aging adventuress gave me a weary but satisfied smile over her tankard.

"Even with all the struggles, I'm glad we undertook this venture," she remarked before taking a deep drink. "The payoff was worth it in the end, thanks to your aid, my friend."

Returning her smile, I lifted my own drink in a short salute. Our task was complete, and we had won the dwarves' hoard back from the dragon's clutches through solidarity and courage.

Tonight, warm firelight and cheer were our dues.

# Chapter 32

The hearty dwarven fare and fine ale filled our bellies after days of trail rations, fish, and foraged fare. I sank my teeth into juicy slabs of roast boar, washing it down with crisp, dark beer. Around me, my companions ate with equal enthusiasm.

Leigh tore into a leg of mutton, juices running

down her chin. "Mmm... Ain't nothin' better than fresh meat after travelin' for nearly a week!" she declared happily.

Celeste sampled new dishes with delicate curiosity, savoring the rich stews and game.

Laughter and singing filled Lord Vartlebeck's great hall. Though weary from the road, cheer and good company lifted our spirits.

Branik regaled his kinsmen with the harrowing tale of the delve into Hrothgar's Hope. They listened, enraptured, to the account of the dragon's defeat and the dramatic events that led up to it.

As we feasted, a young dwarf with a lyre moved among the tables, plucking out lively melodies. Celeste's emerald eyes followed the musician with keen interest as her slender fingers absently stroked the lip of her tankard.

When the song concluded, I leaned toward Celeste and murmured, "Why not return the gift of music? I know Lord Vartlebeck would be honored to hear an elven ballad."

Celeste nodded, her eyes kindling eagerly at my prompting. Rising gracefully, she glided up to walk over to the dwarven lord in his carved oaken throne and made her request. He nodded approval, bellowing for silence from his hearthmen.

As the lively halls stilled, Celeste lifted her voice in a haunting lament to ancient kingdoms lost beyond recall. The soaring melodies held dwarves spellbound, and more than a few eyes grew misty at the sorrowful beauty of her elven heritage.

*"O'er misty mountains lost to sight,*
*Beyond the forest dim,*
*There lies a land once green and bright,*
*Where elven voices hymned."*

*"In woodland deep where elm trees sleep,*
*And stars shine overhead,*
*The elven folk would laughter reap,*
*When daylight's gold had fled."*

*"Within the grove on mossy stones,*
*They danced with voices fair.*
*Their joyful mirth in song entwined,*
*Echoed on the air."*

*"But lo! the shadow fell on them!*
*Their hearts were darkened, dimmed.*
*And from that realm they now must roam.*

*Exiled, realms no more theirs."*

*"Of ancient woods and rivers fair,*
*Naught left but mem'ry pale.*
*Yet still their hearts will ever bear,*
*Love for each leaf and dale."*

*"So though their homeland now has passed,*
*Beyond the misty veil,*
*In elven hearts it still will last,*
*Immortal and unfailing."*

When the last plaintive note finally faded, awed silence reigned for a breath. Then thunderous applause echoed to the peak's rafters.

Lord Vartlebeck raised his tankard, toasting the raven-haired songstress with gruff appreciation.

"It's not often we hear fair elven song in these halls!" he roared, "but a pleasant song it is!" He sloshed his tankard, spilling ale. "To good memories of Tannoris: a thing we dwarves share with the elves!"

At that, the hall roared approval and drank deeply from cups. Before long, all dwarves spoke of their days in Tannoris, reminiscing and reflecting on what they lost.

Flushed with pleasure, Celeste returned to my side.

"Your voice could stir life in the very stone itself," I told her sincerely.

She gifted me with a smile that warmed my heart before we returned to the sumptuous feast. Platters were kept well-heaped, and spirits ran high in Lord Vartlebeck's hall.

Full night had descended outside, but within the torchlit halls, revelry carried on undimmed. My ears soon rang from the lively dwarven reels and boisterous tales swapped over brimming tankards. But weariness soured the strong ale's sweetness for me.

As the night wore on, I slipped outside to savor a breath of fresh air after so long surrounded by stone.

Here, the sky arched endless and glittering above the fortress peak. Torches flared gold along the battlements, keeping the encroaching dark at bay. Their light glinted on the helmets of armored guards, and I saw that we were now in the proper Wilds, for there was much danger outside these walls.

Lost in quiet contemplation, I barely noticed soft footfalls until Celeste appeared beside me. Wordlessly, she leaned against the parapet, following my gaze up to the field of winking stars strewn from horizon to horizon.

"Few nights have I felt such peace," Celeste mused softly, as if to herself.

The starlight limned her elegant profile with silver, and the night's beauty stole my very breath away. She looked at me, her eyes luminous pools of starlight. "It is since I have met you."

I took her hand. "I'm happy to hear that, Celeste."

Turning toward me, Celeste searched my eyes questioningly before whispering, "There is something between us, is there not?"

My heart skipped a beat at that; her sudden directness taking me by surprise. Perhaps another element of elven culture I did not yet understand.

But in human culture, there was only one answer to that question.

Ever so gently, I drew Celeste into my arms.

She came willingly, lips parted and eyes softly shuttered. Beneath the crystal dome of the heavens, I kissed her deeply at last, pouring all the unspoken longing of our journey and our time together into it.

When we finally parted, Celeste's cheeks were endearingly flushed. She made no move to leave the circle of my embrace.

I smiled, content simply to exist in this perfect moment with her. "I've hoped for this," I confessed. "You captured my heart, Celeste."

"And you, mine," the elf maiden murmured. "I hoped but dared not believe your heart could want me in return." Her vibrant eyes were luminous with joy. "But... pray, we must not rush these things... Uncle Waelin has not approved, and there is much that has to be done."

I didn't understand what she meant, but I expected there was something to elven courtship involving her family and other preparations that needed to be made. I nodded and offered her a smile, not pressing on the matter. I resolved to find out more soon enough.

"I am in no hurry," I simply said. "For now, it is enough to know that we feel the same way."

With those words, I drew her in. Together, we watched the night sky unfold and blanket the dwarven hold of Ironfast.

We lingered a while longer beneath the stars, words hushed between lingering kisses. But eventually, even the beauty of the moonlit peaks could not overpower my bone-deep weariness.

"We should rest," I murmured reluctantly against Celeste's amber hair. "Tomorrow brings a new day full of promise."

She sighed lightly but nodded agreement. Hand in hand, we made our way back inside the torchlit halls.

Most of the feasting dwarves had dispersed or passed out atop the trestle tables which now resembled the aftermath of a battlefield. Lord Vartlebeck was nowhere in sight. Branik directed us toward vacant guest chambers where we might all finally rest in comfort.

"Yer wives, the blonde lass and the foxkin are already sleepin'," he said. "Best join 'em! There be a separate room for the elven lass."

Before parting for the night, I drew Celeste near once more, desiring nothing more than the sweetness of her lips in a goodnight kiss. When we separated, her cheeks were endearingly flushed once more, eyes luminous, and a soft smile on her lips.

Feeling her soft body against mine left me wanting more, but I knew not to press the matter. With these things, I needed to be patient.

Too drained for anything but collapsing into waiting blankets, I entered the assigned chamber where Leigh and Diane were already breathing heavily, passed out like I was. The straw-stuffed mattress felt like bliss incarnate after the hard earth these past nights.

Tomorrow, Vartlebeck's folk would take stock of the recovered treasure, and there were still troubling matters to be discussed — the vengeful father dragon foremost among them.

As I drifted toward sleep's waiting embrace, my thoughts lingered on Celeste's joy beneath the glittering night sky in the wake of our first tender kiss.

# Chapter 33

I awakened in the early morning, the gray light of dawn touching the wall opposite the window, and I became immediately aware of the most delicious feeling.

Under the covers, soft and warm tongues and lips were teasing my shaft, which had grown rock-hard.

Diane and Leigh had a special wake-up in store for me, it seemed.

The sensation was exquisite, the gentle lapping and suckling made my body shiver with delight. I felt the warmth of their breath on my skin, sending jolts of pleasure up my spine.

I could see the bobbing of two heads beneath the covers, their silken hair brushing against my thighs. Their playful giggles vibrated against my skin, enhancing the pleasure of their ministrations.

My mind was reeling from the pleasure, my breath hitching in my throat. My blood pounded in my veins, and my heart raced as they continued their tantalizing torment.

With a groan of delight, I relaxed fully on the mattress, reveling in the wetness of their tongues and the softness of their lips. The sensation was intoxicating, their teasing making me gasp for breath.

The sheets ruffled softly, and the bed creaked as the girls sucked and slurped on my hard rod. The room was filled with the scent of sex, the musky aroma mingling with the delicious scents of my girls.

I craned my neck to see the outlines of their bodies beneath the covers, their curves highlighted by the dim light of dawn. Their movements were fluid, their bodies undulating with a rhythm that matched the beating of my heart.

I took in air with a hiss as a long, wet tongue ran along my shaft. Soft breasts pushed against me as Diane giggled; their softness pressed against my hardness. Their bodies were hot, their skin soft as velvet as they continued their teasing, and my cock was yearning to erupt.

Every nerve ending was on fire as they continued their expert teasing, licking, sucking, and slurping. The sensation was overwhelming, the pleasure building until I could barely breathe.

The pressure was building up; the pleasure mounting. My body was on the brink of ecstasy, the sensation so intense that I could barely contain myself.

Suddenly, I could resist no longer.

I pulled away the blanket, revealing them naked

on their knees, pretty asses up as they sucked my cock. Their eyes were wide with surprise, their cheeks flushed with arousal. At that moment, Leigh had her plump lips wrapped around my cock, the shaft halfway into her mouth. Diane held it at the base, her soft fingers playing with my balls.

Diane giggled, and Leigh continued sucking me off, keeping her eyes on me. They were beautiful on their knees like this, their skin glowing in the dim light.

Leigh's voluptuous curves were breathtaking, with ample, full, and round breasts. Her nipples were hard, standing at attention as she kept her blue eyes locked on mine.

Diane's body was just as enticing, her athletic build fit and curvy in all the right places. Her fox ears twitched as she watched her harem sister suck my dick, her bushy tail swishing behind her as if anxious until it would be her turn. Her breasts were smaller, but just as enticing. Her nipples were erect, her sapphire eyes sparkling with mischief.

They continued their ministrations, their hands

and mouths never leaving my body. Their bodies jiggled deliciously as they giggled and moved, their movements fluid and graceful.

I groaned as tongues swirled around my shaft and played with my balls, Diane's teeth gently grazing the skin of my thighs. The sensation was incredible, their teasing driving me to the brink of madness.

They moved faster, their lips and tongues exploring my balls. Their touch was gentle as they drove me on, their teasing making me groan with pleasure.

My muscles clenched with the effort to hold back. But the pleasure was too much, the sensation too overwhelming. I was getting closer, the pressure building to a fever pitch. My body was on the brink, my mind clouded with pleasure.

And when Leigh took me balls-deep into her mouth, gagging on my length and girth, I couldn't hold back any longer. With a loud groan, I came, my body shaking with the force of my orgasm.

The sensation was incredible, my body convulsing with pleasure. I could feel every pulse, every spasm, the pleasure rippling through me as I came hard between Leigh's soft and welcoming lips.

My seed spilled into Leigh's mouth, but she kept her lips wrapped tightly around my shaft, taking all I had to give her. The sight was almost as pleasurable as the sensation, her eyes never leaving mine.

When I was finally spent, Leigh pulled away, a satisfied smile on her face, her cheeks puffed out from my load — she hadn't swallowed it. She looked down at Diane, her eyes sparkling with mischief.

As if she knew exactly what her harem sister was planning, Diane lay down, her body spread out on the bed. Leigh hovered over her, her body casting a shadow over Diane's. I watched enraptured, my cock still twitching from my intense orgasm.

Leigh opened her mouth, letting my seed drip into Diane's. The sight of my seed trickling down into Diane's open mouth was incredibly hot. Some of it spilled down Leigh's big tits or onto Diane's curvy torso, and the sparkle of mischief in the girls' eyes was too hot.

At the sight of that little show the girls put on, my cock was growing hard again. And by the smoky bedroom eyes they were throwing me, I knew they were ready to go as well.

My lust rose, and my mind swam as I surveyed Leigh and Diane's glistening naked bodies. I needed to possess them.

I went over to Leigh, who watched me come with blazing blue eyes, ready to be claimed. I was drawn to the sight of her voluptuous curves, her breasts rosy and full, her hips wide and tantalizing.

"Well, aren't you two naughty this morning?" I growled as I flipped her around and pressed her onto the bed, her round ass up for my pleasure.

Her laughter rang out, sweet and coy, as I admired the way her ass jiggled slightly from the motion.

"Hmm," she hummed, her southern accent

sending a shudder through me. "And what do you plan to do with your naughty girls?"

I slapped my cock against her round ass, making her gasp. "I'm gonna fuck you till you can't think straight anymore," I replied, my voice low and husky with desire. "How's that for punishment?"

She purred her agreement, a sound that vibrated through me, fueling my arousal even more, as she wiggled her ass for me, my cock slipping between her delicious, jiggling buns.

Turning my attention to Diane, I could see the anticipation on her slightly blushing face. Her sapphire eyes watched me with curiosity, her fox ears twitching slightly. Inviting her over, she complied, crawling over to join Leigh and me.

She yelped as I grabbed her and flipped her over, stacking her on top of Leigh, tummy to back, as I wanted to fuck them both.

They giggled and laughed as I stacked them like that, creating a delectable sight of their bodies intertwined. Their wet pussies were on vivid display for me, a sight that made my cock twitch with anticipation.

"Oh David," Diane moaned, still giggling.

"You gonna do us both, baby?" Leigh purred.

"Hm-hm," I growled, my mind completely taken over by the sight of those stacked beauties.

Their moans filled the room as I ran the tip of my cock over their slick entrances, teasing them. The scent of their arousal was heady, intoxicating me, making me want to take them both right then and there.

Unable to wait any longer, I pushed into Leigh first.

"Ahn," she moaned. "That's it, baby!"

Her tight walls gripped me, drawing a low groan from my lips. Her body writhed beneath me, her moans encouraging me to push as deep as she could take me.

Thrusting into her, I watched as her ass bounced with each movement, my hands greedily kneading the flesh. Her cries of pleasure were music to my ears, spurring me on. And as I fucked her, Diane jiggled her ass for me, inviting me to claim her as well.

After a few more deep thrusts into Leigh, I

pulled out, leaving her gasping. My cock glistened with her arousal, a sight that made Diane's breath hitch as she looked at me over her slender shoulder.

I then plunged into Diane, her tight warmth engulfing me. Her fox ears twitched, her body arching as she took me in. Her pussy clenched around me, drawing a hiss of pleasure from my lips.

"Hmm," she moaned. "It feels so good."

"Yeah, baby," Leigh hummed. "Fuck that little vixen!"

I fucked them both, alternating between the two. Each thrust into their welcoming bodies was met with a cry of pleasure, their bodies shaking with each push I gave them.

The sight of their asses bouncing, the feel of their slick walls around me, and their moans of pleasure were driving me to the edge. My thrusts became more frantic, more desperate.

Leigh was the first to come, her body convulsing beneath me. I could feel her pussy clenching around me, milking my cock. Her moans grew louder, her body writhing as she rode out her orgasm.

She cried my name as she came, and Diane moaned along with her, close to her own orgasm. I plunged into Diane, leaving Leigh shuddering, and she gasped for air.

"David!" she cried out. "Oh! I'm cumming, David! Don't stop!"

With a few more thrusts, she fell over the edge. Her body tightened around me, her cries echoing around the room. Her fox tail twitched wildly, matching the rhythm of her climax.

The sight of them both, lost in the throes of their pleasure, was too much for me to handle. I could feel my own climax approaching, my balls tightening. And I wanted nothing more than to make a mess of their pretty asses.

Pulling out of Diane, I aimed my tip at their round butts, my cock throbbing with impending release. Their bodies were still trembling from their orgasms, their asses shaking enticingly.

With a final grunt, I came, my hot cum splattering across their jiggling asses. Their gasps filled the room as my cum coated their butts and dripping pussies.

"Fuck, David!" Leigh purred. "Cum on us! Oh! It's such a big load."

They giggled, a sound both innocent and utterly sinful. My cock twitched, the sight of my cum on their bodies something from heaven itself.

Still stacked, they chuckled softly as they continued jiggling their pretty asses for me, letting me enjoy the sight of how I painted their bodies. Leigh reached around, her fingers tracing lazy patterns through my cum, before she scooped some up and fed it to Diane, then took another scoop for herself.

Grinning, I sank back and gave Leigh a hard slap on her round ass that made her yelp and giggle. "You two are something," I said, voice still husky, before I collapsed on the rich bed, utterly spent, inviting them to come lie with me.

"Hmm," Leigh purred as she and Diane snuggled up against me, their naked bodies soft in the warm bed. "That was amazing."

I chuckled, my chest vibrating beneath their

heads. "I have to say, waking up to a blowjob from two gorgeous women has to be the best way to start a day."

Leigh's tinkling laugh echoed against the stone walls. She nuzzled into my chest, her soft blonde hair tickling my skin. Her freckled shoulders peeked out from under the drapes as I pulled them over us.

"Well, we might just have to keep that standard up, sugar," she purred.

I felt Diane's tail twitch against my leg, her sapphire eyes glinting with shy excitement. "I wouldn't mind that," she murmured, her midnight-black hair spread across my chest like a cascading waterfall.

Our bodies entwined in the comfortable intimacy of the large bed, the crisp sheets rustling with our movements. The morning was still young, the castle quiet as if respecting our stolen moments of blissful tranquility.

I ran my fingers through Leigh's hair, the strands feeling like spun gold in my hand. She sighed contentedly; her blue eyes fluttering shut as she leaned into my touch. Her full breasts pressed against my side, her heartbeat a comforting rhythm in the stillness of the morning.

My other hand traced the curve of Diane's waist, her athletic body fitting perfectly against mine. Her tail coiled around my leg, the soft fur a delightful contrast to the cool sheets.

Their combined warmth was intoxicating, their bodies a soft haven against the hardness of the world outside. Despite having just gone two rounds, they still stirred the primal urge within me, my manhood twitching in response.

"Hm," Leigh hummed, noticing. "Looks like someone's ready to go again." She bit her lip and threw me a smoky look. "Don't mind if I ride that…"

I chuckled. "You are insatiable," I said with a grin, feeling their bodies react to my arousal, their soft hands trailing my stomach and thighs, seeking to turn me on again.

Leigh giggled while Diane blushed, her tail brushing against me teasingly.

"And you love it, don't you?" Leigh whispered.

Her hand lazily traced circles on my chest.

"I sure do," I said with a grin.

Since we weren't on the road and not in a hurry to make the most of what daylight we had left, we were soon involved deeply in more play. After that, we let sleep overtake us once more, delighting in being a little lazy this morning.

After all, we'd had plenty of activity already...

# Chapter 34

Morning sunlight through the stone windows roused me from deep slumber. For a moment, I lay still, letting awareness return. All that was familiar was my girls' bodies against me.

But then, memories of the previous night flooded back — the feast, Celeste's song, our first tender kiss beneath the stars. It had been beautiful; a promise, I believed, of what was yet to come.

Beside me, Diane and Leigh still slept, blonde and raven hair tangled together on the pillow. I smiled, brushing a stray lock back from Leigh's face before rising to wash and dress. Vartlebeck would expect our company for breakfast, and there was much still to discuss.

When I returned, my movements had roused the girls. Yawning and stretching, they greeted me with sleepy smiles and morning kisses before readying themselves as well.

Soon we were proceeding down the torchlit corridors toward the grand hall where mouthwatering scents of cooking wafted to greet us. My stomach rumbled eagerly as we stepped inside.

Most of the dwarves still slumbered, worn out by the previous night's revelry. But Lord Vartlebeck sat awake at the high table, tucking into porridge and smoked meats. At his side sat Clara, Branik, Karjela, and Celeste already breaking their fasts.

Celeste's cheeks colored charmingly when our

eyes met, and we exchanged subtle smiles. Last night had awakened something powerful between us, but here was not the place to speak openly of it. For now, the comfort of her nearness was enough.

Spotting us enter, Vartlebeck waved us over. "Come, friends, eat!" he bellowed. "We've much to discuss after we've broken our fasts."

We joined them at the table where platters were swiftly heaped for us — eggs, sausage, fresh bread and honey. There was coffee and fresh milk, too.

Dwarves knew a good breakfast! I sat down and dug in.

As we ate, talk centered mostly on the recovered treasure and Vartlebeck's plans to bolster Ironfast's defenses. But a grim undercurrent lingered beneath the dutiful chatter. We all sensed more dire matters awaited discussion.

When the last platters were cleared, Lord Vartlebeck sat back and fixed me with his piercing gaze. "Now lad, before ye depart, there is the matter of this vengeful dragon Father to address." He tugged his beard pensively. "The beast threatens not just you, but likely all within my domain. And within the lands of Gladdenfield Outpost as well. If 'tis an elder dragon, we must all fear."

Celeste nodded, knowing a thing or two about dragons because of her elven lore. "The lord is right," she agreed. "The dragon we laid low at Hrothgar's Hope was young but a threat in its own right. Considering its age, its father is likely to be an elder dragon."

"Aye," Lord Vartlebeck said. "Such is my fear as well. All may suffer if it comes hither. Even the walled cities of the Coalition in these parts — New Springfield or perhaps even the Kansas City Enclave — might come under threat."

I nodded gravely. "You're right, Lord Vartlebeck. We should make efforts to locate and confront this new menace."

Branik and Karjela murmured agreement. Around me, Diane, Leigh and Celeste listened intently.

"Then we are of like mind," rumbled Vartlebeck. "I can provide men and arms to battle this threat. Together we can forge strategy to meet the drake afield and destroy it." His craggy features creased into a fierce grin. "My warriors are always spoiling for a fight."

Clara spoke up, idly fingering a dagger hilt. "I will stand against this beast," she declared, eyes sparking. "If Gladdenfield is under threat, I will defend it." Though still nursing injuries from Hrothgar's Hope, her desire to confront the threat was plain.

Moved by their stalwart courage, I inclined my head in appreciation. "With stout allies like you at my side, we cannot fail," I replied sincerely. "However, I'm not sure if it will come to a large confrontation where we get to field an army against the beast. Why would it risk that? And besides, if the dragon's promise of vengeance is true, Father should come after *me*, right?"

Celeste nodded agreement, and so did Diane and Leigh. "They are prideful beasts," Celeste said. "Its spawn communicated with it in its moment of death, and through such magical communication, it is likely the best knows the identity of David."

I nodded. "It will come after me."

"But it will lair first," Diane said. "Dragons do not enter a new domain without a lair. Likely, it will have minions to carry its belongings or whatever it would need."

Lord Vartlebeck thought for a moment. "So that means movement, aye?" he grunted. "Something we'll see. Creatures claiming a place for the dragon. Like in the Shimmering Peaks?"

"Very likely," Celeste agreed. "Dragons love the high places as they can reach them easily while others must struggle."

"Then we will keep an eye out," said Lord Vartlebeck. "Times are dire, and we must defend our holds with all the force we can muster, but I can spare a couple of scouts to keep their eyes on the peaks. I even have a few elves on retainer — Scouts, Foresters, Mountaineers — that I could spare." He gave a confident nod. "We'll know if a new dragon lairs here."

Plans were swiftly made. Vartlebeck would muster his scouts. Messengers would alert Gladdenfield, my homestead, and other settlements of the coming of the dragon so they could make their own preparations. Meanwhile, we would seek more knowledge of Father so that we could better prepare.

When the final details were agreed upon, we said temporary farewells. Clara, Karjela and Branik remained behind to rest and recover. Vartlebeck's grim nod spoke of dark tidings approaching, but also resolute courage against the coming storm.

Before I could depart Ironfast, Vartlebeck approached and drew me aside, his craggy features etched with concern.

"Lad, there is more we must discuss ere ye leave," he rumbled gravely, hand resting on my shoulder. "Matters of blood and birthright yet shrouded from ye, though they define the days ahead."

I nodded, pulse quickening. "You know more about this 'Goldblood' name the dragon bestowed on me?" I asked.

Around us, Celeste, Diane, and Leigh listened intently.

"Aye, some tales of old," Vartlebeck acknowledged, tugging his beard thoughtfully.

"And I believe I know one who may ken more." He met my gaze. "The dragon's words stir dark legends nearly forgotten by my kind. But if true, ye may play a pivotal role in the days ahead."

A chill ran through me. Whatever the dwarven lord's ominous intimations, this talk of my Bloodline and fate would not let my mind rest easy until I understood.

Seeing my agitation, Celeste moved nearer in quiet solidarity. Her luminous eyes searched mine for clues to my inner turmoil. But not even she could fully grasp the implications of this mystery yet.

Vartlebeck continued grimly. "I will send word to the Bloodmage Yeska of the Wildclaws and her to yer homestead. The lass is… unpredictable. But she will know more of this 'Goldblood' business and yer apparent gifts. She's the only Bloodmage I ken, but she's good at what she does and helped me lay bare the properties of my own Bloodline."

"Thank you, Lord Vartlebeck," I replied sincerely. "Any insight would be most welcome. This is a heavy burden to bear in ignorance."

Beside me, Celeste nodded agreement, clasping my hand in her delicate one.

"She'll ask for compensation," Lord Vartlebeck said, "but I'm certain you two will work somethin' out, aye."

I nodded. "Thank you, Lord Vartlebeck."

"Not a problem, lad!" he boomed. "Now, let's get you lot supplied and ready for the journey to Gladdenfield. By road, it should take ye no more than three days, but these are still the Wilds, and ye should prepare well!"

# Chapter 35

After the hearty breakfast and Lord Vartlebeck's counsel, our group gathered at Ironfast's gates to begin the journey back to Gladdenfield. Lord Vartlebeck's people had kindly resupplied our provisions for the road ahead and given us a reward of a few gemstones that would get us good coin in Gladdenfield.

Though eager to be off, part of me wanted to explore these stone halls some more. Perhaps there would be time to do so later.

Branik clasped my arm in a warrior's grip. "Safe journey, my friend," the gruff dwarf bid me solemnly. "And good luck unraveling this mystery of yer Bloodline. We'll be watching the peaks for a sign of this dragon called Father."

I thanked him sincerely before saying my goodbyes to Clara and Karjela, who were still recovering from their wounds. When all was said, I turned to join my companions.

Diane took the lead as we set off, picking up the road at an easy pace. Behind us, Ironfast's squared battlements and peaked towers dwindled, though sturdy sentries still stood their watch upon the heights.

Together with us, one of the scouting parties left the hall, although they quickly turned toward the Shimmering Peaks in roughly the direction of Hrothgar's Hope.

It felt good to be underway after feasting and

rest. My boots scuffed cheerfully over the gravel track as it led us onward through sweeping vales dotted with aspen groves and stands of pine. The forest air held a breath of coming autumn, but for now, the sun still shone pleasantly warm upon our backs.

We made good progress that first day, stopping only briefly to rest and take meals along the winding road. Talk was lively around mouthfuls of bread, cheese, and dried meat. Though we remained watchful, no threats emerged from the tranquil land all around us.

When evening shadows began reaching long across our path, we made camp in a sheltered hollow near a chuckling brook. Swiftly, Diane had a crackling fire sending sparks swirling up toward the darkening sky as the first bold stars kindled.

We lingered late around the dancing flames, bellies full and spirits relaxed after the arduous days behind us. As the larroling trailed behind her, Leigh enthusiastically recounted tales of past exploits and adventures on the frontier, blue eyes sparkling. Her irrepressible spirit never failed to lift my own mood.

Before turning in, I smiled to see Diane and Celeste move a small distance away from the fire, heads bent close in quiet conversation. A bond of true understanding now linked the elf and foxkin woman. Music had awakened friendship despite their differences, and they discussed their compositions and texts — sometimes with fervor.

When yawns could no longer be stifled, we dampened the cheery blaze and retreated to our tents. I took first watch, and after Diane relieved me, I settled gratefully into my bedroll, lulled by the muted symphony of the woods at night. Rest came swiftly.

At daybreak we swiftly broke camp and set off once more. The morning air was crisp under the canopy, but whenever we crossed into the open, the slanting sunshine felt pleasantly warm across our shoulders.

Our path grew steep and rocky as we traveled, switchbacking endlessly upward into craggy foothills still snow-capped in places. Rugged pines clung tenaciously to the stony slopes all around.

Here and there, a mountain stream tumbled down through sheer ravines, beckoning weary hikers to rest and drink of its chill waters.

When the trail leveled out somewhat by late morning, we paused in a sun-dappled glade to refresh ourselves and rest our legs. A plump rabbit caught by Diane soon sizzled merrily over the small fire as we prepared a humble camp.

Bellies full, we pressed on through the afternoon. Though the terrain remained hilly, the uplands were pleasantly green and dotted with wildflowers. Startled hares froze and stared from the brush until we passed.

Once, in the distance, a grizzled wolf turned to observe our progress before loping silently away into the trees. Its golden eyes held no malice, only quiet wildness.

Before we made camp, we came upon a stretch of road with signs of fighting. There was blood on the ground as well as spent cartridge cases and a few arrows. A wagon had been abandoned, pilfered of wares.

It was a grim reminder of the dangers of these

lands. A little farther down the road, we came upon two orcs, hoping to waylay unsuspecting travelers. They fled when they saw us, but we quickly dispatched them, making the road from Ironfast to Gladdenfield a little safer.

By evening, forested ridges and valleys opened up all around us. From atop a craggy prominence, I glimpsed Gladdenfield far in the distance, just visible in its valley amidst the forested hills.

Joy and anticipation kindled in my heart at the sight of the timber palisade walls, though we were still over a day's march off. Home lay ahead.

We made camp beneath rustling aspens as the clear sky darkened to velvet overhead. Bellies filled with rabbit stew, we lounged comfortably near the crackling fire exchanging stories and jokes. Leigh's clear laughter rang like music over the faint babble of a nearby stream.

When heavy eyelids could no longer be denied, we extinguished the cheery flames and turned in for the night. I drew first watch again, savoring the solitude and serenity beneath the sprawling star field. At times, a shooting star traced a fleeting incandescent arc overhead, and I reveled in the beauty of the starlight.

Morning's light came again soon enough, rousing me from a deep sleep curled beside Diane's slumbering warmth. Swiftly breaking camp after a hasty breakfast, we set off on the final leg toward Gladdenfield through rolling foothills awash in sunlight.

My boots scuffed eagerly along the winding trail as I reveled in the beauty of the living Wilds all around. Undulating grasslands shimmered beneath scattered oaks and stands of pine. Herds of elk raised graceful heads to mark our passing but showed no alarm. An eagle mewled faintly high above, describing lazy circles in the boundless blue vault overhead.

Around midday we paused to take our ease and refresh ourselves from a burbling stream before the last push onward. Despite the relatively tame lands here compared to the peaks, we remained on guard. The wilderness posed its own danger, and we would not drop our vigilance — not even this close to home.

Resuming the hike, our spirits were buoyed knowing each stride diminished the remaining distance. Before long, we would be back amidst crackling hearths, laughter, and song beneath Gladdenfield's sturdy roofs. There, we would turn in the quest and speak with the mayor.

The sun hovered low above the serrated western ridges when at last we crested a final rise. There below us, tucked amidst the foothills, lay the welcome timber walls and smoke of Gladdenfield. My heart swelled at the sight, made even sweeter by our days of arduous travel to reach them once more.

Eager anticipation quickened our steps as we crested the rise and saw the open gates of Gladdenfield awaiting our return. It was evening, and they would close soon, but we would make it in before that.

# Chapter 36

Eager smiles lit up our faces as we passed beneath Gladdenfield's open gates, the sun dipping low behind the palisade walls. Guards nodded in casual recognition, long accustomed to our comings and goings beyond the relative safety of the settlement.

Our boots scuffed eagerly down the main thoroughfare, drawing curious glances from townsfolk wrapping up evening commerce or conversations. Though travel-worn, our party moved with heads held high, taking pride in having successfully accomplished our quest.

We paused to secure the larroling in the livery stable, and Leigh greeted Colonel with a smile and a hug. The larroling woofed gratefully for a rub behind its shaggy ears before lumbering into an empty stall. Stable hands promised to see the beasts well-fed and watered for the night.

Having stabled the creatures, we moved on to the Wild Outrider. To turn in our quest, we would have to see the mayor, but we would do that tomorrow. It was too late for business, and we were tired.

Pushing through the swinging saloon doors together, we were greeted by familiar mingled scents of hearth smoke, ale, and roasted meat. Despite the late hour, the spacious common room remained lively, though not yet raucous. We garnered a few curious glances from dusty patrons as we moved toward the bar.

Spotting us enter, Darny looked up from wiping glasses and broke into a broad grin beneath his bushy mustache.

"Well, look who's back!" he bellowed in his usual jovial manner, setting down his rag. "Gladdenfield's very own fellowship of heroes returns victorious!"

Exchanging smiles, we clasped Darny's meaty hand over the scarred oaken counter as he came around to greet us properly. Though the barkeep tried to act nonchalant, I could glimpse the relief and gratitude kindling in his eyes at our safe return.

"It's good to see you too, Darny," I replied sincerely, giving his hand an extra firm squeeze.

The girls smiled warmly at the gregarious barman, and I was amused to see that Celeste, too, greeted him happily. She stayed at the Wild Outrider, and Darny had shown her kindness during her time here.

"Y'all found 'em?" he asked after the initial greetings, unable to contain his curiosity.

"We did," I said. "We found Clara, Karjela, and Branik. I'm afraid the others didn't make it."

Darny's expression clouded for a moment, but he then gave me a grateful nod. "Well, I'm happy to hear that Clara's alive and well. But come now, y'all take a seat. You still got the dust o' the road clingin' to your coats, and you look like you need some food and drink!"

Of course, he received no objections. While Darny readied a table, we turned to survey the familiar timber rafters, well-worn furniture, and lively patrons who had all become part of our story here.

Though humble, the Wild Outrider felt like home. Our spirits lifted simply breathing this air again.

Settling gratefully around the table Darny prepared, we let out collective sighs of contentment, the tension of the road melting away. My chair creaked familiarly as I leaned back, reveling in the simple comfort of stillness after so many days of arduous hiking.

Darny appeared a moment later, deftly bearing

four heaping tankards of ale along with menus scratched on slates. "Compliments of the house for our hometown heroes," he declared with a wink.

I gladly accepted the frothing drink, savoring that first deep pull. The girls followed suit, smiling over their mugs.

Perusing my menu, mouth already watering, I decided on the Outrider's hearty venison stew while we caught Darny up on our travels. His craggy face creased into a scowl hearing of the dragon and other dangers braved during the quest. But by the tale's end, a broad grin was back in place.

"Quite the daring deed, venturing into Hrothgar's Hope like that," Darny mused, stroking his beard once our account concluded. "Why, I'd wager Clara herself would blush to hear her rescue spun into legend!"

Before long, Darny returned, balancing four steaming bowls piled high with tender venison, potatoes, and carrots. The savory aroma roused our appetites honed by long days of plain travel rations. We dug in eagerly between swigs of ale as

Darny looked on approvingly.

Between mouthfuls, our conversation turned to speculation about the coming days. Leigh enthusiastically described ideas for expanding the store now that Randal oversaw daily operations. Celeste shyly mentioned hoping to return to her routine of performing at the Outrider again soon.

Diane suggested we would immediately purchase the supplies needed for the expansion of the homestead so we could take them with us in the Jeep. I nodded agreement, keen to get to work. But the mystery of my ancestry still lingered at the back of my mind, as did the looming threat of Father.

Over another round as the night deepened outside, Leigh launched into a spirited retelling of the battle in High Hrothgar against the dragon. The girl spared no colorful detail, and soon even Celeste was giggling at her dramatic embellishments. It felt good to laugh together, the concerns of the future held at bay for now.

When at last we grew weary, Darny shooed us upstairs to our familiar rooms. He offered it free since he saw we were tired, sparing us the walk back to Leigh's place and having to bring it in order. Ready-made beds sounded like heaven.

Weary but content, I sank into the straw mattress beside Diane and Leigh. My lips found Diane's in a tender goodnight kiss as I curled my arm around Leigh.

Soon enough, one thing led to another, and it took us an hour or so before we were finally and truly ready for bed.

# Chapter 37

We awoke to the aroma of sizzling eggs and sausage wafting up from the Wild Outrider's kitchen below. After washing and dressing, we eagerly descended the creaking stairs, where we met Celeste. Our bellies were rumbling for a good breakfast after three days on the road.

Darny stood humming behind the counter as we entered. "Mornin'!" he called cheerfully. "Figured y'all could use some fuel before meetin' with the mayor. My wife's cookin' up something for ya!"

He led us to a table, and we were greeted by the few patrons who had risen early as well — travelers and such looking to leave Gladdenfield early. Gratefully, we dug into the hearty fare as Darny served it up with fresh coffee, milk, and orange juice.

Over the steaming mugs of coffee, our conversation turned to the upcoming meeting. I admitted some curiosity at meeting Gladdenfield's leader for the first time, but the girls reassured me all would go smoothly.

"Just speak plain and honest," Diane advised sagely between bites.

Leigh grinned and added, "And don't forget to ask about that reward!" We chuckled at the cheeky but good-natured comment.

With full bellies and fresh resolve, we set out toward the mayor's home near town square. The cobbled avenue bustled around us beneath the rising sun. I straightened my coat and ran a hand through my hair, wanting to make a good first impression.

Mounting the steps of a well-kept dwelling, I rapped smartly on the oaken door. A gray-whiskered gentleman answered after a moment. Though of modest height, he carried himself with an unmistakable air of leadership.

"Welcome, welcome!" he exclaimed through his great gray mustache. "I am Mayor Wilhelm. And you must be David! And Leigh and Diane I already know, and Waelin spoke often of you, Celeste! Please come in! I've been told by Darny to expect you! A good man, but he can't keep anything to himself!"

The girls smiled warmly as we shook his hand in turn before following him inside.

The cozy parlor was decorated in handsome drapes and furnishings somewhat finer than the rustic norm here. As the mayor bid us take seats, a plump older woman brought in a tray bearing coffee and biscuits.

I gave polite greetings to the mayor's wife who

promptly bustled back to the kitchen. The mayor beamed in anticipation, clearly eager for the tale ahead.

Over the next hour I recounted our quest, occasionally pausing to let the others chime in with supplemental details. The mayor listened intently, bushy gray brows rising and falling as the account unfolded.

"By Jove!" he exclaimed when I described the dragon's size and ferocity.

Leigh happily provided colorful embellishment of that climactic battle, and Celeste gave more solemn details of the aftermath.

When at last I concluded the tale, the mayor sat back shaking his balding head in wonder. "Incredible, simply incredible!" he marveled. "Our fair town is in your debt. Clara is invaluable to us! And while I lament the loss of the others, we at least know their fates."

"We did what any would have," I replied modestly, exchanging smiles with the girls.

"Well said, son!" applauded the mayor. He then turned more solemn, clasping his hands on the table. "Still, you all showed such courage and skill out there. I wish more possessed it."

I nodded graciously, touched by his words. Around me, the girls politely demurred, but I could tell the mayor's sincere validation resonated deeply with them. And I was proud of them, too; it was praise well earned.

When our coffee mugs sat empty, the mayor's wife appeared once more, this time bearing heaping platters of eggs, ham, and fried potatoes. The savory aromas set our mouths watering anew. Even though we had just enjoyed breakfast, a brunch was more than welcome.

Over the sumptuous meal, the mayor shared colorful tales of his many years in Gladdenfield, reminiscing fondly of the settlement's earliest rugged days. Though humble, his knowledge of its workings was immense.

As the clock chimed noon, the mayor smiled at me. "As pleasant as this is, there remains still the matter of rewarding your courageous service," he said, reaching to pull a leather sack from his desk drawer. It jangled heavily as he passed it over.

"Every coin well earned!"

I took the pouch and gave a satisfied nod as I opened it, glimpsing a gleaming pile of gold and silver coins — it was far more wealth than I had ever held.

"A token of thanks from Gladdenfield's citizens," said the mayor sincerely. "I imagine that like most homesteaders, the coin is quite welcome!"

"You honor us, sir," I replied.

Beside me, the girls flushed, equally moved. This windfall would secure our homestead's expansion, making the place more comfortable for us all.

As we profusely thanked the mayor, I addressed the one final grim matter. "Sir, as we told you, we defeated the dragon at Hrothgar's Hope. However, with its dying words, it told us that it had called upon its father. We discussed this at length with Lord Vartlebeck in Ironfast, who has agreed to send out scouts and watch for the coming of a new dragon. However, Gladdenfield Outpost is in danger as well and should prepare itself."

The mayor's face creased with concern as I

explained the dire oath of vengeance sworn against me.

"Then we must ready ourselves," he said heavily once I had finished. "Gladdenfield has weathered many storms before. We have a fine elven guard, and I shall inform those known to brave the Wilds regularly that there may be a dragon about soon."

I nodded. "Good. The homesteaders should know, too."

"Ah, indeed they should," Mayor Wilhelm mused. He then shook his head. "I'm afraid there is little they could do to protect themselves from a dragon, however. Gladdenfield is not like Ironfast, where all industry and commerce are contained within the safety of stone walls of dwarven masonry. The homesteads can withstand lone beasts of the Wilds or perhaps a roving band of goblins. But a dragon?"

"I don't think they will be able to defend themselves against a threat like that either," I agreed. "Which is why our efforts should focus on making sure the dragon never reaches Gladdenfield."

The mayor nodded. "Indeed. We must strike once its location is known; before it gets its bearing."

"We will," I said, clasping his wrinkled hand to say farewell. "We will be in touch the coming weeks as events unfold."

After another round of hearty thanks, we donned our hats and coats. My companions smiled radiantly, our first official meeting now concluded in all aspects. Our homeward journey awaited, but we would acquire the necessary materials first.

After leaving the mayor's house, we headed straight to Leigh's shop to acquire materials for the planned homestead expansion. We needed a considerable amount of supplies in order to add a second floor and extend the existing cabin. Some of them we could get from Leigh's store, but most would come from the builders' market in Gladdenfield.

Entering the cozy store, the cheerful bell over the door announced our arrival. Randal looked up from stacking canned goods and greeted us warmly beneath his great gray mustache. Leigh gave him a quick hello and spoke with him for a few moments before leading us to the hardware aisle.

Selecting a sturdy lumber saw, wood chisels, a claw hammer, nails, screws, levels, sandpaper, and other essential carpentry tools, I gathered them carefully on the worn countertop. Good steel tools were vital for all the sawing, planing, and joinery work ahead.

Of course, Randal charged us no more than the store had paid for the hardware, and we quickly completed the transaction and loaded the supplies up in the jeep. There was still lots of coin left. After that, we bade Randal goodbye and headed toward the builders' market.

The builders' market was a bustle of mainly homesteaders like me procuring the needed supplies for their homes. Sturdy dwarves and humans from the frontier manned most of the stalls, and there was a commotion of haggling and shouting as the day's trades went on.

I first chose copper pipes, a new water pump, tubing, a sink basin, and the components needed to add a kitchen wash station and upstairs bathroom. Though still rustic, these additions would improve comfort.

In the next stall, I picked out more oil lamps and plenty of spare wicks so we could illuminate the expanded interior. Lantern oil, matches, candles, and lamp oil were added as well. Light would be crucial.

At the brick and stone display, I selected the hearth bricks, mortar, and chimney flues needed to add a second fireplace upstairs. With autumn on the way soon, we would need the place to be cozy and warm.

By the windows, Diane inspected glass panes and forged hardware to replace broken elements or expand existing ones. Leigh helped her choose sturdy hinges and latches for the new doors. The dwarf behind the stall provided tips on installation.

Moving to the wall paneling, I ran my hand over

the smoothly sanded planks until I located properly cured and sealed timber resistant to cracking. I could make those myself, but now that we had money to spare, I could focus my lumberjacking on firewood and purchase some higher quality wood. Several dozen eight-foot boards went into my pile. Wood treatment oils followed.

Nails, screws, bolts, brackets, ties, and other fasteners came next. I made ample selections, as attaching all the structural and decor elements required proper supports. Good joinery was vital.

Scooping up wood shavings, Diane strode over with jars of paints, brushes, rollers, and varnish for the indoor walls and outdoor facade when the additions were complete. The foxkin was drawn toward earthy, nature-inspired hues, and I agreed wholeheartedly on the selection.

Nearby, Celeste shyly considered the bolts of fabric for curtains, bedding, towels, and other soft homey touches. With Leigh's guidance, she selected floral calicos, checked ginghams, and dyed muslins in colors complementing our rustic style.

Moving on, I inspected the stacked lumber, choosing sturdy oak beams for the new load-bearing elements, floor joists, rafters, and logs for the exterior walls. These had to withstand the elements once assembled. Twisted grain or spots were rejected.

As I made my selection, I realized we would need to make two or three runs to move everything to the homestead, so I purchased some additional fuel for the Jeep. The money was practically flying out of the pouch Mayor Wilhelm had rewarded me with, but I knew it was for a good purpose.

Armloads of shingles, shakes, ridge caps, and flashing for the roof came next. I made sure to get extra to account for any breakage during projects above ground level.

Inside once more, I picked out a cast-iron stovepipe and joints for ventilation, then grabbed heavy welding gloves for working with hot materials. Eye and ear protection, dust masks, and work gloves covered safety needs.

By now, our piled selection was vast indeed — certainly two runs. But there were still finishing touches needed. Diane chose pots of antique glaze to refresh the clay daubing between the new log walls once they were erected.

Leigh helped me carry over mortar, stones, and bricks for the new chimney stack. Well-sealed masonry would prevent sparks escaping. This was vital with a wooden home, so we spared no expense there.

By the time we had gathered all the tools, hardware, fittings, accessories, and assorted needs for the major addition, the afternoon had worn on well, leaving us with too little time to return to the homestead.

The kindly merchants agreed to keep the supplies we had purchased ready for tomorrow, so we could come pick everything up at the warehouse. There was a fee to this, but considering the vast quantities we had purchased, the merchants agreed to waive it.

Our purchases made, the day's activities finally caught up with us. We retired to Leigh's house, with Celeste returning to her room at the Wild Outrider — we would bid her goodbye in the morning.

Tired like I'd rarely been before, we ate a satisfying meal before dozing off in front of the fireplace on a cozy pile of blankets and mattresses.

# Chapter 38

The next morning, we awoke and quickly readied ourselves before heading over to the Wild Outrider to bid Celeste farewell. She stood waiting outside the tavern as we approached through the dusty street, knowing that we would come.

She seemed a little wistful at the parting, and I

embraced her, holding her close for a while in silence.

"Safe travels, my sweet," she whispered when we finally parted.

I smiled at her warmly, taking her delicate hands in mine. "I will come back soon to check on you, and I would love to see you more often."

"I would like that also," she hummed, her emerald eyes fixed on mine.

Then, she leaned in and placed a gentle kiss on my lips. The way her body brushed against mine left me needing more, but I controlled myself and savored the moment.

After that, Diane and Leigh said goodbye as well. Having grown much closer to the enchanting elf during our adventure, they echoed similar wishes to see her soon, and Celeste graced us all with her vibrant smile.

"I shall miss our laughter around the fire each night," she said wistfully. "But the joy of reunion will only enhance time shared apart!"

With final embraces, we parted ways outside the Outrider. Celeste waved until we passed from sight down the bustling avenue.

Our first stop was the livery to ready Colonel and the larroling for the journey home. The beasts snuffled contentedly at Leigh's familiar scent as she secured saddles and bridles.

With the animals prepared, we led them from the stable yard toward the warehouse. I brought the Jeep around as well, happy to once again have the powerful vehicle under me.

At the warehouse, carts stood ready and waiting, piled high with our carefully chosen building supplies and hardware. The kindly proprietors helped us load everything we could fit into the spacious cargo hold of the Jeep.

We jammed in as much as could safely fit. Leigh would follow on horseback, and Colonel and the larroling carried some supplies as well. Still, we would need to make two more runs.

With the larroling lumbering along behind Leigh's horse, we rumbled down Gladdenfield's dusty main thoroughfare toward the open gates and the wilderness beyond. Guards waved in recognition as we passed into the verdant wilds under scattered clouds scudding rapidly across the vaulted sky overhead.

Despite the heavy load, Leigh guided Colonel ably along the winding dirt track through the gently rolling forest. She stayed to the side of the Jeep. Birds twittered in the rustling leaves, welcoming us homeward after days beyond the wilderness we called our own.

The journey passed swiftly. The verdant wilderness opened up around us as we gradually left behind the gentler land surrounding Gladdenfield. Here, the forest felt untamed — rife with bounty but also hidden hazards for the unwary.

Soon, we passed the cottonwood and took the turn toward the homestead. There, the trail became rougher and more densely wooded.

Through breaks in the swaying canopy, I glimpsed the Silverthread ribboning its way through the forest. Home lay on the banks of that glorious river.

Around mid-morning, familiar forest sights and scents surrounded us, drawing an audible gasp from Diane as she knew that home was around the next corner. Leigh broke into a broad grin, nudging Colonel into an eager trot toward the land we had claimed. The end of our journey was at hand.

Before long, the winding trail carried us fully out of the trees' embrace and to the banks of the Silverthread River. My heart swelled at the welcoming sight of the cabin's stone chimney. I already discerned Mr. Drizzles patrolling the grounds.

As we drove down the path to the homestead, Ghostie and Sir Boozles emerged to greet us with excited chirps, zipping eager circles around us like dogs excited that their masters had returned. Mr. Drizzles, the storm elemental, hovered nearby, making sure all was calm.

While Leigh saw to putting the beasts out to pasture, Diane and I entered the beloved cabin that, thanks to our efforts, would soon grow to match the scale of the dreams we nurtured here together.

Much work awaited, but it was good to be home.

By the time we had finished hauling all the supplies from Gladdenfield to the homestead, the last rays of the day's sun bathed the cabin in a warm golden glow.

I was tired to my bones but satisfied. I happily allowed the girls to pamper me, and so I just sat at the table as they bustled about in the kitchen.

Soon enough, Diane, Leigh, and I sat down to a simple but filling dinner. It felt good to be home again after so many days beyond these walls that sheltered us. Familiar surroundings grounded my mind and brought comfort.

Diane hummed a cheerful tune as she stirred a bubbling pot of venison stew, the aroma mingling with the crackling hearth fire. After hauling supplies all day, the promise of a hot meal revived weary bodies and spirits.

Around mouthfuls, we talked casually of small matters, taking comfort in the familiar surroundings. The wooden walls, exposed beams, and braided rugs were welcoming as old friends. Ghostie and Sir Boozles capered near our feet, making sure the place was clean and handing anything we might need.

Over crusty bread, our conversation meandered fondly through memories of past adventures shared beneath this roof — the first tentative nights learning wilderness skills, lazy mornings cooking breakfast together, quiet evenings reading by firelight. Each reminiscence was precious.

When the stew pot emptied, Leigh rose to fetch a bottle of honey mead she had picked up in Gladdenfield. Generous helpings filled our mugs as we moved to the hearth's warmth, letting food settle before bed, but I couldn't help but notice Diane drank none of it. A suspicion rose in my mind then — one that made me smile — but I decided not to speak up yet.

Leigh sank into the worn armchair with a happy sigh. "Never realized how fine it'd feel to sit in this ol' thing again," she remarked contentedly.

Diane and I nodded agreement from where we

lounged together on the braided rug. Simply being idle here together was bliss.

As flickering firelight danced over the exposed beams, talk turned to hopes for the future once our home was expanded. There were so many dreams to nurture here — a place of laughter, family, and belonging we three had forged through shared adversity.

Diane's gaze grew wistful as she envisioned tending lush gardens under the sun. Always she sought to cultivate and nourish.

Beside her, Leigh chuckled thinking of the larroling trying to fit through new doors. The thought of sundered frames made her snort with laughter, and we all agreed the larroling would stay outdoors.

My own thoughts lingered on Celeste's joyful smile, imagining her voice lifted in song within these very walls. Though parted now, the thought of her warmed me still. The bonds between us would only grow in time.

One day, we all might gather here as family.

As the hour grew late, a tranquility descended

over us all. No immediate duties or chores pressed upon the mind. For now, we simply savored the drink, fire, and camaraderie too often taken for granted when adventure called from beyond the valley.

My contented gaze roamed over the familiar surroundings — the roughly hewn furniture, shelves of supplies, and the tools in the mudroom. All spoke of a life carved wholly by our own hands.

Pride swelled in my heart for what we three had built together. And although we loved this cabin, I would soon remake it into something bigger and better.

Diane nestled against me, and I stroked her velvet-black hair. Leigh joined us, humming a tune to herself as the three of us gazed at the fire. Their presence brought me happiness untold.

When at last the hour grew too late to ignore, we banked the hearth fire and saw to securing doors and shutters. No threats lurked for now, and we had Mr. Drizzles to patrol the property, but wilderness living instilled habits of care.

Once everything was ready, we once again piled up the blankets and mattresses to make a little cozy nest. It would be one of the final times, because I planned on making us a new bedroom soon.

Diane and Leigh wasted no time preparing for bed, weary muscles eager for rest. Their movements spoke of the bone-deep comfort two people share in intimate domestic rituals. My own limbs felt leaden, longing for blankets.

Donning a threadbare nightshirt, I sank gratefully atop the mattress between my two loves. Their slow breaths steadied my own racing mind, lulling my scattered thoughts toward sleep.

Rolling over, I drew Diane's slender frame gently against mine, nuzzling her raven hair. On my other side, Leigh mumbled contentedly and nestled closer. They were cherished bookends sheltering me from darkness, warding off the lonely night. No words were needed as we lay together and basked in our happiness.

The stresses and questions still lingering melted away beneath the simple bliss of this unremarkable moment. No looming threat could shake the quiet joy in my heart tonight as we relaxed under our humble roof.

As I drifted toward sleep's embrace, I caught the faint shimmer of Mr. Drizzles gliding by the window, keeping tireless watch over us all. His presence reinforced the sense of safety this home gave us.

Because it had become home. Here, in this place carved wholly by our own hands, surrounded by those I loved most, I was more at home than I had ever been anywhere else.

My last fleeting thoughts were of what the coming days might bring. But happen what may in this untamed land, we would face it together — three threads woven stronger for the sharing. This truth followed me into slumber.

Surrounded by the profound stillness of the frontier night, I let go of my thoughts and surrendered myself to untroubled sleep.

# Chapter 39

The next morning, I woke eager to begin work on expanding the cabin. After a hearty breakfast with Diane and Leigh, I went outside to start laying out the foundation for the new addition.

First, I summoned my woodland spirit and earth spirit to assist with preparing the ground.

Together, we cleared away brush and leveled the soil where the new logs would sit.

The spirits used their magic to till the earth and assist with removing rocks and roots that could destabilize the foundation. Ghostie and Sir Boozles lent their assistance as well, and I was pretty proud that my talents as a Frontier Summoner had made me a team of capable helpers. I summoned and bound a third domesticant for extra help. After all, I could dismiss it later.

By midday, we had a wide rectangular patch of bare, flattened earth ready for the first logs to be laid. I dismissed the woodland and earth spirits, thanking them for their help. Then I whistled for Ghostie and Sir Boozles to come lend their aid once more.

The two domesticants eagerly got to work helping me haul and position the heavy oak beams that would form the perimeter of the new addition. Though small, they proved incredibly strong for their size. Their cheerful chirps and antics kept my spirits high as we labored. Much of it was careful measuring, but I had a solid plan worked out.

With the foundation laid, I turned my attention to assembling the wooden wall panels that would enclose the addition. Taking measurements, I cut planks and beams to size using my new saws and planes. The domesticants fetched tools as needed.

After a long day of sawing and chiseling wooden joints, we had fashioned sturdy wall sections ready for assembly. Tired but satisfied with our progress, I enjoyed a hearty dinner with Diane and Leigh — who had taken over all chores around the homestead while I did construction work — before retiring early.

The next morning brought another full day of labor. This time, I summoned three earth spirits to help dig us a new cellar and foundation. The old one was getting cramped, and the new one would be an expansion of it. I also wanted it to be a little deeper, so we could stand straight.

The spirits got to work digging, and we shored up the hole with sturdy planks. These were simply planks, well treated against the cold and moisture, but certainly not very beautiful. The cellar didn't need to be pretty; it needed to be functional.

It took us all day to dig that cellar and lay the stone foundation while shoring up the cellar walls with planks. The domesticants helped with shoring it up, but it was still a lot of work.

My women checked on me regularly, and they expressed their admiration at the quick progress. While I worked, they tended to the crops, fished, made sure the snares were empty and reset, and I was proud to see these two frontier women do the work without complaint and with great skill.

The next day, the domesticants and I set about raising and joining the wall panels. I was happy it hadn't rained and that we could do this work while it was dry. As we hoisted up and connected the heavy wooden sections, the cabin expansion began taking shape as I had envisioned.

With the large, rectangular new building joined to the old cabin, we would get an L-shaped home, with the smaller section of the L being the old cabin. The larger, new part would have two stories.

I gave a satisfied nod at confirming that everything was going according to plan, and we continued our labor tirelessly. Making the wooden staircase and raising the walls took all day, but by sundown we had most of the exterior walls assembled and fitted into place atop the brick foundation.

By the light of lanterns — literally burning the midnight oil — we continued until late that night as we reinforced joints and applied weatherproofing oils to the fresh timber walls.

Over the next few days, I fell into a steady routine of summoning spirits in the morning to aid construction efforts, then working alongside my domesticants until dusk. Together, we built a chimney, framed windows, and assembled interior walls for the first floor.

Sawdust piled up steadily around the work site from my constant sawing and sanding. But gradually, the shell of an expanded cabin took shape before my eyes.

The domesticants were invaluable, fetching lumber and tools as we incorporated each new element. They were pretty handy themselves as well, so long as the work wasn't too intricate.

Halfway through the week, I took a break from

construction work to harvest more wood from the forest. Swift swings of my axe felled several slender trees. After delimbing them, I used the domesticants to help transport the logs back to the cabin.

With the new batch of raw lumber, I set to work building furniture and other interior elements like railings and cabinetry to furnish the expanded home. The domesticants passed me chisels and nails, learning carpentry skills alongside me. The woodland spirit was invaluable here as well, lending aid in shaping the wood.

By the week's end, the new addition was really taking shape. Sturdy walls and rafters framed out spacious new rooms and windows now gleamed brightly, letting sunshine pour in. The cabin had truly begun its transformation into a more permanent home.

The furnishings for our sleeping quarters were now finished, with a massive bed to fit five — I was optimistic for the future. Additionally, there were furnishings for three spare rooms for guests or if someone needed time for themselves.

Sawing the final bed legs to size, I smiled picturing nights no longer spent atop mattresses on the floor. Once the upstairs floor was in place, I could assemble the furniture there.

On Sunday, I declared a well-earned day of rest. We lazed by the creek for a picnic lunch before returning to the cabin where Leigh surprised me with a decadent blackberry pie she had baked that morning. Sweetness melting on my tongue, I grinned thinking of all we had accomplished together in the past days.

The next week would bring additional long days of labor completing the roof, adding a second fireplace, and finishing all the interior rooms. But great progress had been made, and the beginnings of our dreams for this home were taking form.

That night, I stood gazing out on the addition still only partially silhouetted in the gloaming. But in my mind's eye, I could already envision the finished structure — tall and proud but cozy, filled with laughter and memories we had yet to make.

As dusk settled over the valley, Leigh and Diane joined me, slipping their arms around my waist.

Together, we surveyed the week's work in contented silence. Much sweat and toil still lay ahead, but great rewards of comfort and belonging would come for all who called this place home.

Before turning in, Diane helped me tidy the tools and work site while Leigh stoked the fire. Another long day of labor awaited with the rising sun, but rest would prepare us. Together, we would see this project through.

Settling down by the crackling hearth, weariness crept over our limbs. But a profound satisfaction filled my heart as I gazed around at those whose company had made this home — and these grand plans — possible. Our dreams were slowly taking shape before us.

# Chapter 40

The next morning brought more hard but honest and fulfilling work. After breakfast with Diane and Leigh, I summoned my woodland and earth spirits to aid in the day's tasks.

Together we focused on completing the roof of the new addition. Ghostie and Sir Boozles hoisted up shingles and beams while I hammered them into place, with the woodland and earth spirits guiding and shaping the wood and the shingles to make sure they were fitted perfectly.

By midday, we had most of the roof framed and watertight. A few spots still needed patching, especially around where the chimney protruded from the roof, but it was really taking shape.

In the afternoon, our work moved inside. Using planks purchased from the builders' market, I measured and cut floorboards for the new second floor with help from the woodland spirit and domesticants.

The woodland spirit assisted in smoothing and joining each plank, and between the four of us, we laid a seamless floor that had me beaming with pride.

As we fitted the flooring into place, I made sure to hammer down any protruding nails to prevent snagged clothing or blankets and hurt feet later on. Safety was important with so much activity ongoing around the construction site.

By sunset, sturdy oak floors spanned the length

of the new upstairs. Tired but satisfied, I released the spirits and headed downstairs to enjoy a well-earned dinner with Diane and Leigh. Their smiles and conversation soothed my weary mind.

The next day brought more indoor work. With the spirits' magic, we swiftly installed the second-floor walls and paneled the interior walls on the first floor that divided up spaces as I had planned for the new kitchen, dining room, and workshop. When that was done, we paneled the walls on the second floor.

The old cabin, which would adjoin the dining room, would be converted entirely into a cozy living area with a view of the Silverthread and double doors opening to a greensward that led to the riverbank — a lovely little stretch of garden for us to relax in.

I left one room on the ground floor undivided for the time being. I planned to make it a studio where Diane and Celeste could work on their music. A creative space for us all.

We followed up by laying the piping, and this was hard work for me. It took more than a day to get in order. We connected the tap for the bathroom and the kitchen to the artesian well, then disconnected the one in the old kitchen. It required digging, and I got frustrated with the work more than once.

However, a summoned fire spirit helped with the welding, and sweet words and gentle massages from my women helped with the frustration. And when the work was done, it was done well and to my satisfaction.

We wouldn't get hot water from the tap, but we could heat it up and get warm baths in the autumn and winter, which meant we no longer had to rely on the Silverthread to wash in.

Downstairs, I directed the woodland spirit to create ornate railing spindles for the staircase while the domesticants helped sand them smooth. Simple embellishments would lend the rustic home gracious touches. I wanted the place to feel special.

By week's end, the new addition was really transformed. Walking through the once empty, open rooms, I could vividly picture our shared life here — laughter around the expanded kitchen, cozy dinners and fun evenings around the dinner table, and languid bathing in the new bathroom.

But empty spaces still remained, awaiting the personal touches only we three could provide to turn a house into a home. I planned to construct some more simple furnishings next. Nightstands, beds, chairs. Our hands would shape every personal item, and the woodland spirit and the domesticants would help move that work along with great speed.

After another day spent sawing and assembling sturdy furniture to place throughout the house, I decided another short break was needed before burnout set in. Pushing myself too hard could lead to sloppy work or injury.

On the day of rest, Leigh surprised me with a decadent honey cake for dessert after dinner. Her thoughtfulness touched me deeply, as did Diane's shoulder rubs as we relaxed by the fireplace together that night.

Revived by their care and a day of leisure, I tackled the final interior elements with renewed vigor when work resumed. Cleverly concealed cabinetry customized for our frontier home added personalized storage options without sacrificing aesthetics.

The woodland spirits helped me meticulously chisel out alcoves and nooks in existing walls for shelving and cupboards while the domesticants assembled each finished piece under my watchful eye.

When at last all the furniture stood assembled in each intended room, I walked through with Diane and Leigh to make sure everything met with their approval. Their delighted smiles upon seeing the furnishings I had crafted to suit their passions assured me I had succeeded.

Our home was really coming together! Only a few finishing touches remained. The domesticants helped me install iron stovepipes and do a final round of the exterior of the home, making sure everything — especially the roof — was sealed well.

While I worked, Diane and Leigh busied themselves decorating. Soon colorful rag rugs warmed the new wood floors, and embroidered curtains lent the windows cheer. Wildflowers picked from the valley adorned each dining table. Their special touches graced each room.

Our own hands made this dream a reality together. Every item bore the mark of the devotion we had poured into it — imperfect yet all the more meaningful because of its imperfections. This hand-hewn home now reflected our life and love shared within its walls.

The final necessity was stockpiling ample firewood for the coming colder seasons. I spent several long days felling trees deeper in the forest, chopping logs and hauling them back to the cabin.

The activity kept my body strong and my spirits high after so much carpentry work. The domesticants aided with the hauling, and my woodland spirits imbued the severed stumps so saplings would sprout with magical speed.

By week's end, cords of split firewood and kindling were neatly stacked within easy reach of each hearth. With both fireplaces raging, the whole cabin was warm and cheerful despite winter's chill creeping into the valley air. Our efforts had secured comfort.

At last, with no tasks remaining beyond the day-to-day upkeep intrinsic to any wilderness homestead, I declared the expansion project complete.

It was time to show it all off to the girls!

# Chapter 41

After two weeks of hard work, the cabin expansion was finally complete. I could hardly wait to show Leigh and Diane all the additions and upgrades. They had seen it in various stages of construction and had helped, so it was hardly a surprise to them.

But still, I wanted to walk through these new spaces with them for the first time in a conscious way. I wanted to give them a tour.

I found them both by the banks of the river. Diane had been fishing, and Leigh had joined her. The two of them were laughing and talking, but they both perked up and smiled when they saw me coming.

"Ladies, the wait is over," I announced as I approached, arms spread wide.

They clapped their hands excitedly as they exchanged looks. They already knew what it was about, of course, and they both ran up to me.

"Let me give you the grand tour!" I said, beckoning them to join me.

We started outside, where I showed off the new larger footprint and sturdy log walls. "The water spirits and I tested it a lot, but these walls are completely waterproof!" I declared proudly. "And they isolate well!"

Then, I pointed up. "And the roof is perfect too! We're lucky it hasn't been raining to mess with the work! But we're ready for rain — even snow —

now."

The girls nodded approval, running appreciative hands over the smooth timbers. "It looks really nice," Diane hummed. "Such a perfect match to the existing structure."

"Good," I said. "That was just what I intended. But come on, there is more to see!"

Moving indoors, we stepped into the front hallway off the new dining room. "See all these built-in cabinets and shelves? That storage area was something we really needed," I pointed out.

"Indeed," Diane agreed. "Oh... I can finally give everything its own place!"

From there, we proceeded into the expanded kitchen where Leigh's eyes lit up at the enlarged hearth and new iron stove beside the brick oven. "Now we can do some real cookin' in here!" she enthused, inspecting the additional prep space.

Next was the new bathroom upstairs, equipped with gleaming copper pipes and basins. "No more trekking down to the creek when it's freezing out!" Diane laughed, trailing her fingers down the paneled walls of the new bathroom.

Upstairs, I showed the girls the neat row of bedrooms that branched off the central landing. "Now everyone can have their own space," I said, leading them into each in turn. They nodded appreciatively at the simple but cozy look.

"I do hope we'll all be sleepin' together, though," Leigh hummed, throwing me a smoldering look with those smoky eyes of hers.

"Just you wait," I said, grinning.

Of course, the grand finale was the master bedroom suite Diane, Leigh, and I would share. Their eyes lit up seeing the spacious chamber with its large bed, washstand, and wingback chairs.

"Why, it's like a little slice of civilization out here!" Diane exclaimed, taking it all in. She and Leigh wasted no time claiming spots on the thick feather mattress, reclining regally.

I laughed as I watched their nubile and delicious bodies hop onto the bed and test its springiness.

I placed my hands on my hips and grinned as they oh'ed and ah'ed at how soft and big the mattress was. Finally, Leigh rolled onto her tummy and propped her hands under her cheeks as she looked up at me.

"Room for lots more in this bed, though, David," she purred. "Somethin' you ain't tellin' us?"

I laughed and waved it off. "Who knows?" I quipped, but both girls knew well enough what my ambitions with Celeste were. We would have to have a talk about that sometime soon.

Leigh grinned knowingly. "I can't believe how nice this place looks now," she mused. "You did an amazing job with it, David!"

Diane nodded her agreement. "It's incredible how you were able to take those empty rooms and turn them into such a beautiful living space."

I flushed, smiled and touched by their enthusiasm. "I couldn't have done it without help from the spirits and domesticants," I replied honestly. "And from you, of course! But I'm proud of how everything turned out."

Leigh stretched languidly across her side of the big bed. "You should be, baby... You've built us our very own slice of paradise out here," she declared contentedly. "I say this calls for a proper housewarming!"

Diane giggled, and the two exchanged a knowing look.

"Or should we say... bed warming," Leigh purred as she rose to her hands and knees and crawled over to the edge of the bed.

"Bed warming sounds about right..." Diane hummed, her eyes blazing as they rested on me.

"Why don't you come over here, David?" Leigh said. "And show us if this bed is sturdy enough for what goes on in the Wilson manor at night..."

# Chapter 42

I grinned and crossed my arms as I watched both girls on the bed. "Looks like you two are up to something," I said.

Leigh, her blonde hair cascading over her shoulders, turned her blue eyes toward me, her lips curling into a mischievous grin. "We just might have a lil' plan," she purred. "It's a special moment, ain't it?"

Diane, her athletic body stretched out on the large bed, looked up at me through her sapphire eyes, her fox ears twitching, her tail swishing back and forth. She was beautiful, her black hair fanned out around her, her skin glowing in the light.

Leigh's hand was gentle as she teasingly undid the buttons on Diane's dress for my pleasure. Diane bit her lip, keeping her sapphire eyes fixed on me even as Leigh undressed her.

Diane's dress slipped from her shoulders, revealing her firm breasts with their perky nipples. Her panties followed, leaving her completely naked on the bed, her pussy cute and inviting.

Leigh's eyes sparkled as they met mine, her fingers tracing a line down Diane's body. "David, why don't you come over here and join us?"

I moved over to the bed, my eyes never leaving the two beautiful women before me as I flashed them a broad grin. "What's this naughty plan of yours?"

Leigh's grin widened as she leaned in close to

me, her accent thick as honey as she whispered, "Diane here has a little secret she's been keepin'."

I raised an eyebrow, glancing at Diane. She blushed, her fox ears flattening against her head, her tail twitching.

"Really now?" I asked.

Leigh nodded, her hand resting on Diane's thigh. "She told me she liked watching us that time in the hot springs at the Inner Sanctum, David." She licked her rosy lips, wickedness flashing in her eyes. "She liked watching you fuck my ass."

Diane turned red, biting her lip hard, but her body betrayed her arousal at the memory and at Leigh's dirty talk.

I smirked at the blushing beauty. "Is that so?"

Diane nodded, her voice barely a whisper. "Yes... I... I want to know what it feels like. I want to share that with you, David."

I felt a jolt of excitement at her words. "I'd be happy to show you, Diane."

Leigh clapped her hands, her eyes filled with anticipation. "Perfect! But we need to make sure Diane is ready first." She reached for a small bottle of oil. "We'll give Diane a four-hand massage. That should help her relax."

Diane covered her mouth and giggled. "That... that *does* sound good!"

Leigh threw me a meaningful look. "Can't give a proper massage with all these clothes on, though," she hummed. "I think we need to be naked for this, David..."

I nodded, my hands already eager to touch Diane's body and play with my girls. "Sounds like a plan."

I watched as Leigh undressed herself, her voluptuous curves coming into view. I followed suit, my cock springing free, already hard at the idea of giving Diane a massage and what would follow after that.

Diane gave a happy purr at the sight of me and Leigh naked before rolling onto her stomach on the bed, revealing her toned back and perky ass to us. My cock twitched as I studied that cute ass with her fox tail swishing over it, knowing I would soon have my way with it.

It took a measure of self-control to massage her

first, and Leigh gave a knowing giggle, her breasts bouncing, when she saw how hard my cock was.

"Easy there, stud," she purred. "Your time will come."

She kept her eyes on me as she poured oil onto Diane's toned back, and the fox girl giggled when she felt the cool, sticky liquid on her skin.

We started with Diane's back and shoulders, our fingers kneading and massaging her skin. Diane's moans filled the room, her body relaxing under our touch. As we worked on Diane, Leigh leaned over and kissed me, her soft lips moving against mine and making my head spin.

Our hands continued to move over Diane, their movements synchronized, even as we exchanged that kiss. Leigh drew back, shooting me a wink, and gave my cock a teasing little tug with her oiled-up hand.

We moved lower, our hands exploring Diane's firm ass. Leigh's fingers spread the oil, their movements slow and deliberate. She moaned with delight, lifting her back up from the mattress, and I couldn't resist the sight of her glistening and ready pussy.

My hand slipped between Diane's thighs, my fingers brushing against her wetness. I heard Diane gasp, her body arching against my touch.

Leigh's voice was husky as she spoke, her words filled with excitement. "You like that, don't you, Diane?"

Diane nodded, her eyes closed, her lips parted. "Yes... it feels so good."

I moved my other hand to Diane's asshole, my oily fingers teasing the tight ring while oiling her up, making her ready for me. Her gasp turned into a moan, her body trembling.

Leigh's words were a whisper in my ear, her breath hot against my skin. "Keep going, David. It looks so beautiful."

I increased the pressure, my fingers moving faster, teasing her little clit and her tight little rose at the same time. Diane's moans grew louder, her body moving against my hand as she trembled.

"David," she moaned. "Oh gods... You're making me... Uhnn."

"Don't stop, baby," Leigh moaned, playing with

her own breasts as she watched me pleasure her harem sister. "Make her cum!"

I intensified my movements, my cock poking impatiently against Diane's soft skin, eager to claim the asshole I was now massaging. She hummed and squirmed as I moved faster and faster, until her fists gripped the sheets and she bit down on the pillow.

"C-cumming!" she moaned.

I watched Diane as she came, her body arching off the bed, her scream echoing off the walls. Her pussy clenched around my fingers, her juices coating my hand.

Leigh moaned with admiration. "So good! Oh, look at that little fox girl go! She's cumming so hard!"

Diane's chest was heaving, her body covered in a sheen of sweat and oil as she came down from her high. She looked at me over her shoulder, her eyes filled with satisfaction and anticipation.

The sight of Diane coming undone like this fired me up; to be in complete control of her orgasm like that had been extremely hot… and now…

Now, I wanted to give her what she was longing for.

I panted with lust as I watched Diane's oiled-up naked body. My cock was rock-hard, and Leigh gave a cute little sound of admiration as she watched it.

"You ready for a good time, baby?" Leigh asked, her voice dripping with teasing anticipation. Her hand, slick with oil, wrapped around my hard length, oiling me up.

"Oh, I am," I replied, my voice husky with desire. I looked at Diane, her sapphire eyes wide with anticipation as she looked at us.

The light from the window shimmered off her oiled-up skin, highlighting the curves of her hips, the toned muscles of her back, and her thick and juicy thighs.

"We need to show her how it's done first, David," Leigh urged.

My eyes turned to the voluptuous blonde, and the thought of fucking her ass again made my cock twitch with delight.

I watched as Leigh, with her curvy, voluptuous body, poured oil over her round ass. The liquid slid down the curves like rivulets of molten gold, pooling in the crevice of her ass.

As she made herself ready, her slender fingers rubbing the oil on her tight little rose, she glanced over her shoulder at me with a mischievous gleam in her blue eyes.

"Come on, baby," she hummed. "Let's show Diane how it's done."

Positioning myself behind Leigh, I eased the tip of my cock into her tight hole. She let out a sigh of pleasure as I gently pushed into her, the ridges of her inner walls clenching around me.

"Oh, David," she moaned. "That feels so good."

I gently eased deeper into her, letting her feel the length and girth of me and easing into it. She moaned with delight as I filled her ass up, and Diane watched with wide eyes, mewling with delight as I claimed her harem sister's ass.

"Ah," Leigh moaned. "I'm ready, David…"

With a grunt of pleasure, I thrust into her with more force. With each push, Leigh's ass rippled, the oiled skin glistening under the soft light of the room.

"Fuck, David," Leigh groaned. Her hand moved between her legs, her fingers disappearing into her wet heat. "More… I need more."

I watched as Leigh's hand moved in rhythm with my thrusts, her fingers buried deep within her. The sight of her pleasuring herself while I fucked her ass drove me wild, making me push into her harder and faster.

Diane watched us, her fox ears perked up as she moaned with delight. Her sapphire eyes were wide and filled with curiosity. She bit her lip, her hand trailing down her body to her own heat.

"David," Leigh moaned. "I'm… I'm gonna cum, baby… Ahnn… Go easy! Go slow!"

I slowed down, letting her feel every inch, one second at a time, as she rubbed her little clit. Her body tightened, sending ripples down her muscles, and I eased a little deeper until a shock went through her, making her ample ass ripple.

"Oh God, David," she cried out. Her body shook, her ass clenching around me as she came.

I groaned as her ass tightened around me, but I stayed where I was, deep inside her, fighting off the need to cum in her ass. I wanted to do Diane next, and I wanted her to have this load. But damn, it was hard to suppress my desire.

"Leigh," I groaned, feeling my own climax building. But I stopped moving, pulling out of her with a pop before I could reach my own peak.

Leigh let out a whimper, reaching back to smack her ass. "Oh, sugar," she purred. "That was something else. I came so hard."

Grinning, I slapped her ass before I turned to Diane, her fox ears twitching in anticipation.

"Your turn," I said, my voice husky with desire.

Diane's eyes widened, cheeks flushed, and she gave an enthusiastic nod, eager to experience this pleasure for herself. She gave me a last coy smile before turning around on her knees, back still straight.

Diane bit her lip, and I took a moment to admire how the light played on her oiled-up curves.

"Hmm," Leigh moaned beside us, still recovering from the assfucking I'd given her. "Do it, David. Let her feel it."

I positioned myself behind Diane, my cock aching for the tight warmth of her ass. I wrapped my arm around her slender waist, and she gasped as my fingers pressed against the soft skin of her belly.

My cock came to rest between her oiled-up cheeks, and she wriggled a little, sending a jolt of need down my spine.

"You ready, Diane?" I asked, running my thumb over her wet, quivering lips. Her sapphire eyes met mine, and she nodded, her body shivering with anticipation.

"Please help him put it in, Leigh," Diane requested, her voice barely above a whisper.

Leigh, her blonde hair cascading over her shoulders, reached down between Diane's legs, her fingers gliding over the soft skin of her harem sister before guiding the tip of my cock to Diane's awaiting asshole.

The moment the head of my cock breached her tight ring, I nearly lost it. The pleasure of her tight warmth enveloping me was a sensation that threatened to overwhelm me. And since I had been close to cumming when I was still fucking Leigh, it was barely possible to contain myself now.

"Slowly," Leigh instructed purred, and I complied, the slow movements allowing me to postpone my own orgasm as well.

"Ahnn, David," Diane groaned. "It's sooo nice… Gods, I've never felt so filled up."

I eased a little deeper, the muscles of Diane's ass clenching around me, the sensation sending shockwaves of pleasure coursing through my body. My whole world was those two glistening buns, and my oiled-up cock slipping deeper and deeper between them.

Diane moved her body forward slowly, placing

her hands on the sheets of our large bed. Her fox tail twitched as she arched her back, her ass rising to meet my thrusts.

I pushed deeper into her, my hand gripping her tail as a form of leverage. Her ass jiggled deliciously with each movement, her body squirming beneath me.

"So pretty," Leigh crooned, tickling the undersides of my stones with her soft fingers. "Look at how well she's taking it, baby."

I groaned agreement, pushing a little deeper still, my hands firm on those ass cheeks.

"Faster, David," Diane encouraged, her breathy moans filling the room.

I obliged, my hips pumping in rhythm with her desire, and her fuzzy tail began sweeping left and right as I pounded her butt.

With each thrust, her ass bounced, the sight of her body writhing beneath me fueling my arousal. Her scent, filled my nostrils, adding to the intoxicating atmosphere, and her tail brushes my chest until I grabbed and pulled it with a possessive groan, winning a delighted yowl from my fox girl.

"That's it, baby," Leigh hummed. "Grab her like that."

"Ahhhn... Yes... David! Gods!"

My hand tightened around her fox tail, pulling gently to adjust the angle of my thrusts. Diane let out a gasp, her fingers digging into the sheets.

"Oh yeah," Leigh encouraged, her voice sultry and filled with lust. She moved closer, her hands still tickling and teasing my balls, her fingers gently massaging them. "Are you gonna give her this big load, baby? Fill up her tight little ass."

My mind was about to explode. The dirty talk, that delicious, bouncing ass... It was more than any man could take.

I continued to pound into Diane, the wet sounds of our skin slapping together echoing through the room. Her tightness squeezed me with each thrust, the pleasure building within me.

Unable to resist, I tugged harder on her tail, eliciting a sharp cry from her. The pain mingled with pleasure reflected in her eyes as she looked at me over her shoulder was intoxicating.

Leigh's fingers on my balls and the sight of Diane's bouncing ass pushed me to the edge. I could feel my orgasm approaching, my cock throbbing within Diane's tight ass.

Diane's body started to tremble, her moans growing louder as her orgasm approached. I quickened my pace, my hips slamming against her ass, the slapping sound echoing in the room.

"Look at that!" Leigh moaned. "She's gonna cum, David!" She bit her lip. "Who would've thought she enjoyed a good assfuckin' that much!"

Her words urged me on, made me move faster. "Cum for me, Diane," I groaned, my voice hoarse with desire as I fought off my orgasm, wanting her to go over the edge first.

"David!" she moaned. "I'm... I'm cumming!"

Her body tensed, and then her pleasure washed over her, her ass clenching around my cock as a wave of ecstasy hit her and swept her away.

"Now, David," Leigh urged, her hand gently squeezing my balls. "Fill her ass with your cum."

I could no longer hold back. With a grunt, I released my load into Diane's ass, my cock pulsing with each spurt of cum I unloaded in her tight little rose.

And she felt it, twitching and moaning as her ass milked me, urging me on with her gasps and spasms.

I kept thrusting, riding out my orgasm, my cock still lodged deep within her. The sight of her trembling, the feel of her ass clenching around me was pure bliss, and I gave her every drop I had within me.

Diane's breaths came ragged, her body still shaking as my cock finally eased its rough pounding, my seed spent inside her. I gave one final thrust before pulling out with pop.

As I pulled out, a last little spurt of cum glazed her trembling ass. Diane let out a soft moan, her body still sensitive from our intense coupling, and she collapsed on the bed with a gasp.

I watched as my seed trickled down the oily curvature of her pretty butt. I had thoroughly claimed this woman now, and she had enjoyed it greatly — as had I.

Leigh moved closer to Diane, her fingers

reaching down to swipe a drop of my cum from her ass. She brought the finger to her lips, tasting it with a satisfied hum.

I let out a sigh of satisfaction, my body still humming with the aftershocks of my orgasm. I looked at Diane, her body glistening with sweat and my cum.

"That was amazing," Diane murmured, her voice filled with contentment. Her smoky sapphire eyes met mine, a smile playing on her lips, as she looked at me over her shoulder.

The sight of my seed dripping down Diane's curves as she sat on her hands and knees, still trembling from the shock of her orgasm, was a beautiful sight to behold.

I lowered myself in the bed, a broad smile on my lips, and pulled her and Leigh toward me. The three of us lay in the bed, naked, panting. We were a sweaty mess, and we would need to clean up in the new bathroom soon.

But not yet...

Diane, her fox tail twitching in post-coital happiness, was pressed against my right side, her fingers tracing lazy circles on my chest. Her sapphire eyes sparkled with a delight that brought an unconscious smile to my face.

"Did you enjoy it?" I asked her, my voice a low rumble in the quiet room.

She nodded, a shy smile on her lips, and snuggled closer against me. "I did," she murmured, her voice barely audible. She glanced up at me through her long lashes, her cheeks flushed a soft pink. "I'm glad we tried it."

On my left, Leigh stirred, her curvy body brushing against mine. Her blue eyes twinkled with mischief as she propped herself up on an elbow, her naked breasts swaying enticingly. "I think Diane will be doin' this more often with you, am I right, Diane?"

Diane grinned and bit her lip. "Maybeee."

"I reckon that cute lil' butt of your will never be safe again," Leigh joked, winking at Diane.

The fox girl laughed and waved it off. "Oh, you!" she purred teasingly.

We lay there for a moment in silence, basking in the afterglow. Our bodies tangled together; our breathing synced.

"I think we broke in the new bedroom pretty well," I finally mused aloud, glancing around at the rumpled sheets, the discarded clothes.

"Think we can do it again?" Leigh asked with a wicked grin on her face.

Diane chuckled, her eyes meeting mine. I knew then, without a doubt, that they were both ready for more.

And so was I...

# Chapter 43

I awoke before dawn, slipping quietly from our new bed so as not to disturb Leigh and Diane's peaceful slumber.

After washing and dressing in the new bathroom, I headed downstairs and outside, stepping into the bracing morning air. The valley was still hushed and tranquil this early before the stirring of life.

Strolling the grounds, I smiled, seeing dewdrops glistening like tiny jewels on each blade of grass. Pausing by the garden plot, I inspected how the crops were faring. The soil remained rich and moist from yesterday's rain. Fat tomatoes were ripening on the vine, and I made a mental note that they would soon be ready to harvest.

Continuing my leisurely inspection of the homestead, I felt a deep sense of satisfaction. The once modest property had been wholly transformed by our tireless work over the months. Memories suffused each familiar sight — the sturdy alchemy laboratory, the expanded fields for the new crops, the neat wood piles. Our hands shaped this.

As I circled back toward the house, I took a moment to admire it. The morning sunlight lent the freshly hewn logs and timbers a mellow glow, like honeyed amber.

I admired again the graceful lines and proportions, delighting in small details, and sometimes smiling as I remembered some joke we made while working on a detail.

Mounting the porch steps, I trailed my fingers over the sanded railing posts and paused to test the integrity of the sturdy balustrades. A smile touched my lips, imagining nights ahead spent out here gazing at the stars after a long day's work.

Circling behind the house, I paused to watch the gentle flow of the Silverthread. Dragonflies darted and hovered over the dark water. At the muddy edges, industrious frogs croaked and waited for their next meal.

By now, the sky had lightened subtly, casting the clearing in soft pearl light. I could just discern the misty mountaintops to the north — the Shimmering Peaks where we had had our adventure. The sigh of moving water lent the morning a serene ambiance. All seemed utterly at peace.

Turning back toward the house, movement at an upstairs window signaled Leigh and Diane beginning to stir. I hoped I hadn't disturbed them, but knew we were all conditioned to wake early out here. The wilderness kept its own rhythms.

Taking a last look around the tidy clearing, I again felt profound pride and gratitude for all we had accomplished together. Each small task drew us nearer to realizing the dreams kindled in our hearts. Though only a humble cabin, this place had become our haven.

Moving to the woodpile, I selected some prime logs and kindling to fuel the stove for breakfast. I headed back inside and arranged them carefully.

Soon, footsteps creaked overhead, signaling Diane and Leigh readying themselves for the day. I put a kettle on the stove to boil water for coffee. The sharp aroma of the grounds helped banish the last cobwebs of sleep from my mind.

As I calmly worked, I envisioned the day Celeste would join us here in the valley. She could share music and songs, her lovely voice gracing each evening.

I knew in my heart the elf maiden belonged with us. It was only a matter of time, I hoped, before she would see this also and join us here.

And perhaps, if the girls approved, there might

even be others…

As my imagination roamed ahead to coming seasons, I went through the easy motions of making breakfast for my women. When a bout of laughter or giggles from the girls drifted down, I smiled, counting my blessings each and every time.

Our work here was never done, but that was a good thing. The future was ripe with possibility, and we had made a solid foundation for ourselves. And even though a threat now loomed — the elder dragon Father would come sooner or later — we would safeguard this precious gift through all that lay ahead.

Of that, I had never been more certain.

**Finished and eager for early access to my next book? Check out my Patreon: patreon.com/jackbryce**

## THANK YOU FOR READING!

If you enjoyed this book, please check out my other work on Amazon.

Be sure to **leave me a review on Amazon** to let me know if you liked this book! Like most independent authors, I use the feedback from your review to improve my work and to decide what to focus on next, so your review can make a difference.

**If you want early access to my work, consider joining my Patreon (https://patreon.com/jackbryce)!**

If you want to stay up-to-date on my releases, you can join my newsletter by entering the following link into any web browser: https://fierce-thinker-305.ck.page/45f709af30. You can also join my Discord, where the madness never ends... Join by entering the following invite manually in your browser or Discord app: https://discord.gg/uqXaTMQQhr.

## Jack Bryce's Books

Below you'll find a list of my work, all available through Amazon.

### Frontier Summoner (ongoing series)

**Frontier Summoner 1**

**Frontier Summoner 2**

**Frontier Summoner 3**

**Frontier Summoner 4**

### Country Mage (completed series)

**Country Mage 1**

**Country Mage 2**

**Country Mage 3**

**Country Mage 4**

**Country Mage 5**

**Country Mage 6**

**Country Mage 7**

**Country Mage 8**

**Country Mage 9**

**Country Mage 10**

## Warped Earth (completed series)

Apocalypse Cultivator 1

Apocalypse Cultivator 2

Apocalypse Cultivator 3

Apocalypse Cultivator 4

Apocalypse Cultivator 5

## Aerda Online (completed series)

Phylomancer

Demon Tamer

Clanfather

## Highway Hero (ongoing series)

Highway Hero 1

Highway Hero 2

## A SPECIAL THANKS TO...

My patron in the Godlike tier: Lynderyn!
My patrons in the High Mage tier: Christian Smith, Eddie Fields, Michael Sroufe, and Christopher Eichman!

All of my other patrons at patreon.com/jackbryce!

Stoham Baginbott, Louis Wu, and Scott D. for beta reading. You guys are absolute kings.

If you're interested in beta reading for me, hit me up on discord (JauntyHavoc#8836) or send an e-mail to lordjackbryce@gmail.com. The list is currently full, but spots might open up in the future.

Made in the USA
Monee, IL
14 April 2024

56938693R00270